Writers For Relief, Volume 2

WRITERS FOR RELIEF VOL. 2

AN ANTHOLOGY TO BENEFIT
THE BAY AREA FOOD BANK

EDITED BY
DAVEY BEAUCHAMP

Dragon Moon Press

Copyright Information: (stories reprinted with the permission of their author(s))
"Tree" copyright © 2007 by Todd McCaffrey
"Running on Two Legs" copyright © 2004 by Eugie Foster. First published in *The
3rd Alternative*.
"Though Hell Should Bar the Way" copyright © 1997 by A.C. Crispin and Christie
Golden. First Published in *The Highwaymen: Robbers and Rouges*.
"Angel's Keep" copyright © 2007 by Glenda Finkelstein
"The Barrow Troll" copyright © 1977 by David Drake, first published in *Savage Heroes*.
"I Look Forward to Remembering You" copyright © 2006 by Mur Lafferty. First published
in *Escape Pod*.
"Isabelle's Prince" copyright © 2007 by Elizabeth Blue
"The Importance of Undergarments & Science Fiction Conventions" copyright © 2007
by Tony Ruggiero
"Disconnected" copyright © 2007 by Christiana Ellis
"The Cat's Pajamas" copyright © 2004 by James Marrow. First published in *The Cat's
Pajamas & Other Stories*.
"Blood Sacrifices" copyright © 2007 by Valerie Griswold-Ford
"The World Through Patrick" copyright © 2007 by Stuart Jaffe
"Triceratops Summer" copyright © 2005 by Michael Swanwick. First published in
Amazon Shorts.
"Last Respects" copyright © 2007 by D.K. Thompson. First published in *Pseudopod*.
"Mister Adventure and the Emerald Turtle" copyright © 2007 by Davey Beauchamp ∞

Dragon Moon Press is an Imprint of Hades Publications Inc.
www.dragonmoonpress.com

Printed in Canada/the United States.

Dragon Moon Press and Hades Publications, Inc. acknowledges the ongoing support
of the Canada Council for the Arts and the Alberta Foundation for the Arts for our
publishing programme.

  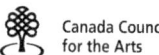

The Alberta Foundation for the Arts
COMMITTED TO THE DEVELOPMENT OF CULTURE AND THE ARTS

Alberta COMMUNITY DEVELOPMENT

Canada Council for the Arts   Conseil des Arts du Canada

This is for all those who survive natural disasters

†††

This is for all those that help the survivors of natural disasters

†††

Eugie without you this anthology would only be half of what it is, thank you once again for all the help

†††

Steve you also provided so much for this anthology, I can't thank you enough

†††

Thank you to all the incredible authors who were willing to donate the stores for this anthology

†††

Thank you Emily for all your help as well

†††

And finally my Mom

TABLE OF CONTENTS

Once More into the Breach, Dear Friends

An Introduction of Sorts

I can't believe I find myself here again, introducing a second *Writers for Relief anthology*. Although editing the first volume was a rewarding experience that resulted in a fantastic compilation of stories and poems, I had promised myself that I would never attempt such a project again.

How wrong I was. It wasn't the first time, and I highly doubt it will be the last. I know many of you out there may go into shock after seeing me say that - admitting I was wrong. But it has been known to happen, if only rarely. But I digress, as I am also known to do.

Let's go back to the beginnings of this second anthology, proceeds of which go to the Bay Area Food Bank, an organization that is still helping to feed the survivors of Hurricane Katrina.

It all began at MobiCon (2006), where I wound up meeting Jody Lyn Nye. Various people at the convention had already told me that Jody liked what I did and wanted to talk to me about it. I am not sure what was running through my head at the time.

I remember meeting her at the convention, although I don't recall exactly when or where. But I do remember what she asked me, because it kind of made me want to cry. She asked me if I would be putting out an extended volume of *Writers for Relief*, or if I would be doing a second volume, and told me that if I was, she would very much like to donate a story.

As I said, mentally, I almost wanted to cry. But I proceeded to answer her question in the only way I could. As they said in *Ghostbusters*, "When someone asks you if you are a god, you say yes." So when Jody Lyn Nye asked if I would do another volume so that she could donate a story, how could I say no? I couldn't. So I said yes. And *Writers for Relief, Volume 2* was born.

Now that a second anthology was in the works and I knew that Jody was interested in contributing, I figured I might be able to get a bigger publisher to produce the book. Time wasn't an issue, as it had been when I edited Volume 1, so I knew I'd have some time to work on finding a publisher and to find writers to donate stories. The one thing I did know before even considering who I was going to ask or beg for a story this time around, was that I wanted the proceeds to benefit a different charity from the first.

As it happened, that year's MobiCon had picked up a new charity to help with Katrina relief: the Bay Area Food Bank. Before the charity auction that would benefit the food bank, I heard one of the food bank's representatives speak about their cause. She was an incredible speaker, and sold me, almost before the anthology came into being, on where the proceeds from the anthology would go.

Next came the leg work. I figured that I should know who was willing to send me a story before I started looking for a publisher. So I began talking with authors I knew and authors I didn't know, once again asking for stories. An amazing thing happened this time around - I had many more authors offering to donate original stories, which really blew my mind. I think Todd McCaffrey, whom I had met at Dragon Con that year, gave me the biggest shock when he offered to donate a new story.

So I had authors and stories; now all I needed was a publisher. After putting out some feelers, I started talking with Gwen Gades of Dragon Moon Press. This was a publisher I was very familiar with because of my friendship with several of the authors she published. I had often been impressed by the high quality of work that she produces. So I was quite excited to hear back from her and as you can tell from this new anthology, things went very well during our ensuing conversations.

In the end, Jody unfortunately wasn't able to donate a story. Neither was Steven Euin Cobb, another major supporter of the *Writers for Relief* anthologies. However, there will be other causes and other anthologies, and trust me, I will be knocking at their doors again. As for this anthology, it contains works by many other talented authors, all of whom were more than willing to donate their work for such a good cause. But I know you didn't buy this anthology just to listen to me babble on. You came here first, to help and second, to read some incredible stories by some of the most generous authors in the industry. So let's get on with the show!

But before I go, I just want to make sure I thank you, the reader, for helping out a great cause.

Nov. 2007

Davey Beauchamp

TREE

Todd McCaffrey

Dad was the gardener, not me. At least, back then. Outside you could see his craft: he did not dominate the yard with his work; there was plenty of space to play—he liked to play—but where he worked, the places he planted, they would catch your eyes, hold you in a reverence.

Me? I was into stars and spaceships, chemistry and physics. The nearest I got to gardening was climbing trees. I never climbed my tree—it was too small.

He had planted my tree the day Mom found out she was pregnant. "This tree is my gift to Nature for its gift of my child," he had said, using words his father had used before him. "Let it grow to provide the air he breathes, let him grow to provide the care it needs."

It was a special tree, always carefully tended and fenced off from dogs. It was only after he died that I found out how special it really was.

I told him that he should not have used the pesticide, no matter what Mr. Jackson said. But Dad had done Mr. Jackson's gardens for years and I had wanted a telescope for my birthday. When Dad started coughing, Mom and I both told him to go to the doctor. He would not listen. He got some herb tea from downtown. By the time we took him to hospital it was too late to cure him.

The last thing Dad had said to me was to look after Mom. I did the best I could, but it is hard when you are only nine and you have to go to school every day.

The last of April, when I got home from school, Mom looked worse than ever. Her eyes were all red-rimmed and she'd been crying. She would not talk to me when I got home, making dinner in the microwave and leaving as soon as she could. I could tell that she had not written a word all day.

When we finally went to bed, I couldn't sleep.

"I promised I'll look after Mom and I will, but, please, can I have someone to look after *me?*" I begged the dark. Outside the wind shook the branches, rustled the flowers in the garden, blew the grass on the lawn. A cool gust blew through the curtains and whirled around the room like a giant's sigh.

———

My room was on the second floor, in the back corner of the house. I had two big windows, one on the side of the house facing east, the other in the back facing south. Unless I pulled the shades, I always woke with sunrise. I woke that morning to the sun and the sound of giggles. Both were coming in from the window to the east.

When I looked out the window, I saw a red-haired boy in the flowers just beyond my tree.

"Hey!" I called. He looked up and came forward. I flushed when I saw that he had no clothes on. "Where are your clothes?"

"Clothes?" His voice was piping, sort of like a piccolo. He cocked his head to one side and shaded his eyes with a hand. "What are those?"

I could not illustrate because, even though it was only May, it was already too hot to wear anything to bed at night. His skin was pale, whereas mine bore the color of my Japanese father. In fact, only in the freckles across my nose and shoulders, my fine hair, and the shape of my face did I resemble my Irish mother. This boy, red-haired, blue-eyed, fair-skinned, freckled lightly as though he rarely saw the sun, looked more like a child of my mother.

The boy gave up looking at me, shook his head and rushed back into the flower garden. "Get out of there!" I shrieked at him.

"Why?" he responded. There was no challenge in his voice, just pure curiosity. I heaved a sigh but it was no answer for him and he turned back.

My room, as I said, had two windows. The south one conveniently had a tree branch growing near it and I had long ago mastered the art of tree climbing. I pulled on some jeans, jumped up to the back window and dove out to the tree. I let go as soon as I caught the branch, diving up and forward to the waiting rope below. The rope and I swung around into the garden; I let go, landing on all fours.

The boy had watched the whole thing and was staring at me gape-jawed when I turned to him. "How did you do that?"

"Your Mom's going to kill you if she catches you out here without any clothes," I told him. "How old are you?"

"How old are you?" he retorted.

"I'm nine," I said. "Now how old are you?"

He didn't answer, turning to face my tree instead. "How old is the tree?"

I looked at it and noticed that the fence around it was knocked down. I went over to it, "Did you do this?"

"She didn't like it." The boy told me. "How old is the tree?"

"Dad planted her nine months before I was born."

"Then I am nine months older than you."

I didn't know what to make of that. "Your Mom's gonna kill you when she catches you."

He cocked his head at me, looked at my tree. "Why would she do that?"

I snorted and waved my hand at him. "You're not wearing any clothes!"

He frowned. "Clothes?" He looked to the tree. "What are clothes?"

I plucked at my jeans. "These," I told him. "Geez, don't you know what clothes are?"

He shook his head. I couldn't figure it out. "Are you homeless?" I asked him.

"Homeless?"

"Don't you have a home?" I pointed to my house. "Where do you sleep at night?"

He shrugged. "Here."

"C'mon." I grabbed an arm and tugged him after me. "If my mom catches you like this she'll freak."

Up in my room I threw some clothes at him: underwear, a shirt, some jeans. I got dressed properly myself, blushing uncomfortably as he scrutinized me. "What?"

"I was just watching how you put them on," the boy responded. Awkwardly he imitated me.

I made a face. "You've never worn clothes before?"

"Jimmy? Are you up?" my mother called from downstairs.

"Yeah, Mom!"

"I heard voices."

"I've got a friend." I told her, glancing shyly at the boy. He smiled back at me. The clothes hung awkwardly on him, like a cage around a tiger.

"Oh! What's his name?"

"What's your name?" I asked him for the first time.

He dug a toe in the carpet, looking nervous. Finally he pointed at a twisted shape growing in the garden. "What's that called?"

I looked. "It's a Joshua Tree."

He brightened. "My name's Joshua."

"He says his name is Joshua!" I yelled down the stairs. To him, I said: "Are you hungry?"

"So many questions," he muttered to himself. "I didn't think it was going to be so hard." I gave him a look. He explained, "My mother said that you were unhappy, she sent me to play with you." He pursed his lips, gestured at his clothes, adding, "I didn't think it was going to be so hard."

"Your mother?"

"Yeah." He pointed to my tree growing tall in the garden. "There."

"Jimmy! Josh! Breakfast!"

He gave me another look. "My name's Jimmy," I explained, adding when he still looked curious: "Josh - that's short for Joshua."

"Oh."

"Just like Jimmy is short for James." I continued. "My real name is James Takeshi Ki." He looked very confused, so I guessed: "Your real name is Joshua Tree, isn't it?"

Josh accepted that eagerly.

Mom's eyes were bright and full of questions when we got to the kitchen. She had made pancakes and bacon for breakfast. Josh watched me carefully before he picked up knife and fork to dig into the pancakes.

"Butter?" Mom offered him. He took it. I took a slice and rubbed it on my pancakes. Enlightened, Josh copied me.

Mom gave me a look. I shook my head, begging her not to ask. When we finished breakfast I ran up to get my bag, telling Josh he could wait downstairs. My mother followed me up.

"He's wearing your clothes," she said flatly.

"He didn't have any," I told her.

"None?" She was shocked. I told her how I found him, finishing, "He says that the tree is his mother and - she asked him to come play with me."

"Jimmy –" Mom began slowly. I held up a hand. "I'm not making it up, honest!" I told her about last night, about my wish and the wind's sigh.

A shriek from downstairs interrupted us. We both tore down the stairs to find Josh shivering in terror and pointing miserably at my school books.

"They're dead," he cried, staring at each of us in turn. "They're all dead!"

"What? What?"

He pointed at the pages. "The leaves! The trees, they're all dead!"

"It's paper, Josh —" My Mom began reassuringly.

"It's made from trees," I reminded her in hushed tones. She turned to stare at me, then back at Josh. Incredulity warred with belief but lost the battle against a mother's instincts. She cradled Josh into her arms, stroking his red hair, rocking back and forth, and crooning to him soothingly.

When he quieted, she looked at me. "Jimmy, grab your books." She made a decision, and said, "We're going to introduce ourselves to your mother, Josh." Josh brightened visibly.

Outside, in the bright sunlight and walking barefoot on the cool grass, Josh grew merry and scampered away from us towards my tree. I wanted to rush off after him but Mom's manner held me back to a docile walk.

"Here she is, here she is!" he cried gladly as he ran up to the tree. He extended a hand toward it, wrapped it around the trunk and *melded* it into the bark like a droplet of water. Then his whole body seemed to soak right into the tree and he was gone.

"Wow!" I said. "Oh, my God!" Mom said.

"See?" Josh said, emerging again from the tree. "I told my mother about the tree blood and she explained it but she's never heard about all the dead leaves and tree bone." His tone was questioning, one hand still rested *in* the tree.

My Mom pulled the schoolbook from my hand flicked open some pages. "We call them books, Josh," she explained. "We write things on the leaves – we call those pages – and also we put in pictures. See?" She pointed out a picture of a tall pine. Josh gasped in amazement and looked up at her with bright shiny eyes. "Books are things we cherish. We keep all our knowledge in them."

"My mother says that I should learn this knowledge." Josh told her in a puzzled tone.

I groaned, "All Moms say that!" My mother smiled and tussled my hair. Of Josh, she asked, "Why does she want you to learn?"

Josh turned to my tree to address the question. The answer disturbed him. "She says that I cannot tell you yet."

Now my mother, as I might have hinted, was Irish. Not of Irish descent – Irish. That she took all this so easily is due in part to the charm of the land she grew up in – it is far easier to believe in Dryads if the country of your youth looks a likely place for them to live. Also, I think it was easier for the two of us because it came at a time when we both desperately needed miracles. Joshua was my tree's response to that need.

So it did not surprise me when my mother said: "Well, if it's got to be a secret then let it be." She looked at Josh. "Tell your mother that I shall arrange for you to go to school with Jimmy."

I still do not know precisely how she did it but Josh was enrolled in my school and in my class that very day. I did overhear remarks about mildewed papers and "the Auld Country". In a class which had been just the day before pointing at me and sniggering because my Daddy was dead, I suddenly had not only a friend but a whole tribe of friends. Josh was immensely popular with everyone.

He slept up in my room and we shared clothes. Mom forced him into wearing shoes but he refused to wear socks and he always had his shoes off at recess. Mom and I taught him to read and, once he learned, he slurped books the way grass drinks water.

He was a regular boy in every way: he got dirty; figured out ways with me to avoid baths; loved to look at the stars; thought chemistry was neat; and always jumped out the window to the big tree. We built a tree house together after Josh asked his Mom if it was okay and I asked mine. We were incredibly happy.

But as May drew to an end, my mother got increasingly anxious. Josh noticed it first and we both tried everything we could to help her and make her happier. There was nothing we could do: it was grown up stuff and out of our control.

School was just about over for the summer when Josh and I came home one day to find Mom crying.

"What is it?" I asked her, standing beside her chair and rubbing her shoulder worriedly.

"We can't keep the house!"

"What? Why not?" I asked. Josh looked confused; I signaled him 'later' with a chopping gesture.

She glanced up at me bleary-eyed. "I can't make the payments." She shook her head. "There's just not enough money. We'll have to sell."

"Where will we live?" I cried.

She put an arm on my shoulder to comfort *me*. "We can rent a place somewhere."

"What about Josh?"

"I can't go without my mother!"

Josh got upset whenever he was too far from his mother. My Mom explained that a Dryad had to live near its tree. I was not so sure, so Josh and I had done some experiments: it seemed that he could go further away from my tree as time went on. Or as he became more human, for I had learned one part of the secret my tree had told Josh: that after a time he could become a real human just like me.

"We can take her with us!" I exclaimed, excited to have found a solution to at least one of our problems. Josh told his mother and she agreed to come with us: one night, on her orders, the three of us carefully dug her up out of the ground. Her roots were all curled tight in around her trunk, I don't know how she did it.

That settled my biggest worry. We found a new place to live in another state. Mom made so much money from the sale of our house that we could buy a brand new one in the other state.

Josh was faint and weak the whole time we transported my tree to our new house. The first thing we did when we got there was to plant my tree. I was careful to put in lots of peat and fertilizer but I had not ever paid much attention to gardening or soil. Josh got better almost immediately and was bouncing around while he hefted boxes into the new place.

It was a nice house. The whole development was new, perched at the top of a small hill and looked down into a valley. Sunny Hill, they called it. Behind us were taller mountains. The school was in the valley. There were some kids in houses already but a lot of the houses were still empty.

Josh and I played together a lot. I'd always wanted a big brother and Josh was perfect – he was willing, eager to listen to my ideas and work on my projects. He never tried to boss me around. We did everything together, even slept in the same bed. He absorbed my love of space and we would spend hours looking through the telescope. Together we explored the Moon and I told him how I would live there someday.

Summer passed. My tree grew taller, being the sole occupant of the lawn. Mom was happier. Josh grew taller and we worried about it because he did not fit my clothes any more, but Mom managed to sell another children's book and got us all clothes and a bed just for Josh.

We started school that fall in high spirits. Josh and I were not allowed to be together in class, the principal from our old school had said that we were "too boisterous" together. I did not like it, but we played together at recess and whenever we could.

We were doodle painting one day when Mrs. Horrocks, Josh's teacher, came rushing into our classroom, speaking hurriedly to Mr. Jackson. I knew something was wrong, I had felt it before the door opened. "Jimmy Ki?" Mr. Jackson called. I rushed up.

"Come with me, dear." Mrs. Horrocks said in the same sort of kindly voice my old teachers had used the day my father died. She took me to the nurse's office.

"Josh!" He was lying down, gasping and trembling like a leaf. I grabbed his arm and started chafing it. "Josh, what is it?"

"We've sent for your mother, Mrs. Tree wasn't at home," the nurse told me. The phone rang. The nurse answered it and passed it to me. It was my Mom.

"Is Josh all right?" she asked calmly.

"He's shaking!" I wailed.

"Don't worry, he'll be all right soon," she soothed me. "Tell him that his mother found the problem." She sighed. "The lawn's a mess."

"Lawn?"

"I'll come and get you two anyway," she answered and hung up.

"She's coming for us," I explained to the nurse. I went over to Josh and whispered: "It's all right: your mom found the problem." He unscrewed his eyes long enough to look at me. He was crying and he didn't like crying, especially with me. I guess it was because the first time he cried at school everyone teased him. I had tried to tell him that it was okay to cry but Josh could be stubborn that way.

Josh was better but still shaken when Mom got us. We were all silent on the way home until we turned into the driveway.

"Gosh!" I cried. Josh perked up and looked out: "Wow!"

The whole front of the lawn was torn up, like an earthquake had split it or a spider had crawled up from the ground or –

"She pulled her roots!" I cried. The car came to a stop and I bundled out. Josh followed a bit later.

Together we surveyed the mess. My tree was all right but the ground in the front lawn was all torn up where her roots had lashed to the surface. Josh trotted over to her and put a hand into her. It used to be that he could always talk to her but as time went on, he had to be *inside* to hear what she was saying.

"She says that something burned her," he explained to us. With a look at Mom, I turned to the garage. I returned with a shovel. Mom looked at me and went for a shovel herself.

We took turns digging: Mom, Josh and me. We got down ten feet before we found it: a discarded bag with a hole in one side where my tree had burrowed in. The bag was heavy and hard to haul up. I could barely read the label. It was a bag of pure lime.

"Must have been left over by the builders." Mom decided.

Josh was still upset by bedtime: we slept in my bed. Next morning he had recovered his spirits – he woke me up by tickling me!

———•———

September faded into October and we forgot about the bag of lime we had long ago thrown out. The leaves on my tree were falling off as it got ready for its rest through Fall. Josh was nervous about it: he had never spent a Winter away from his mother while she slept. But my mother and his both did not think there would be any problem.

It was recess, a group of us were playing soccer. I had just passed the ball on to Josh who was tearing up the field, barefoot as usual, grinning ear to ear as he zipped around frustrated defenders. Suddenly he stumbled, pitched to the ground.

"Josh!" We cried, angry that the other team got the ball. I started running back to the defense, then I noticed that Josh was still down.

"Josh?" I ran up to him. His face was blue and he was gasping for air. "Josh!" He turned to him, grabbing his throat. "*Teacher!*" I screamed at the top of my lungs. I knelt beside him.

He was gasping: "It's white, it's sticky! Mother can't breathe! She can't breathe!"

I grabbed him in my arms. "It's okay. Mom'll fix it, Josh. You'll be okay."

A faint smile crossed his face but he shook his head. There, in my arms, he faded out. Disappeared. Like smoke in a breeze.

"*Josh!*" I screamed. A teacher rushed up but it was too late. All the kids were clustered around me. I beat my way out of the crowd and ran back to the school, hoping to find Josh standing in a corner laughing at his joke.

When Mom brought me home I had already cried all my tears. I sat beside her in stony silence. We entered the driveway, she stopped the car and I jumped out. I rushed to my tree. It was dead.

Its branches drooped, were bare, leaves strewn all around on the ground.

"No." I pleaded. A wind swept by, picked the leaves up, swirled them away. "No!" A hand brushed my neck and I twirled around: it was my mother. "Mom!" I buried my head against her.

She had brought the shovels. We dug. When the sun set, Mom brought the car around and turned on the high beams. She tried to drag me to bed around four in the morning but I kicked and screamed at her. She left me, sobbing.

When the sun rose I was still digging feebly. My shovel bit deep and the white sticky stuff welled up from the ground. Paint. I got Mom.

"Oh, Jimmy!" She grabbed me when I showed it to her, hugged me tightly. "Get a sample, we have to find out why it killed Josh's mother."

It was lead paint. When Mom found out she got really upset. Then she got active. She met with all the parents in Sunny Hill, called the Environmental Protection Agency. The EPA took samples from all over the hill.

And we found out: Sunny Hill had been built over an old chemical company. There were wastes all over the hill. The lead would poison the water and, eventually, poison us. They made us move, bought every house in Sunny Hill. There was a huge legal battle and Mom got a big check from the government.

That's how I became a gardener. When we moved to our new house, I got a borer and dug up samples from fifty feet below the surface. I learned how to test soil acidity and discovered what were good fertilizers. I built the most beautiful garden in our county. Won awards.

It was when I was going through Dad's collection of seeds that I found it. It was a small seed envelope, folded over. Cryptically it was marked 'Jimmy's seeds'. But I knew the minute my hand touched it. There were six of them.

I had grown up by then: I did not need someone to look after me. But I took those seeds, only five of them, and carefully germinated them. I planted one by an orphanage, another in a forest, another by a hospital, one at an old folk's home and the fifth in a cemetery. I checked the ground for all of them down to a hundred feet and I made the soil myself, carefully planting them. I kept the last one.

After that I went to college, majoring in ecology. But I never forgot the Moon. And so I did not hesitate when they offered me the job as the first gardener for Luna City. I am married; Cherie's expecting. You can guess what I planted first.

The soil is great up here. I just wish I could tell Josh.

Running on Two Legs

Eugie Foster

My mother used to tell stories of how I talked to animals when I was a little girl. And then she'd laugh when she described how indignant I got because no one believed they talked back.

I don't remember much of that period of my life. There were a lot of hospitals—white rooms, other pale children next to me, all of us with clear IV tubes taped to our parchment paper skin—and doctors, smiling men with haunted eyes that they tried so hard to keep us from seeing. That's mostly what I remember.

And then came the miraculous words "in remission." I remember those, and the tears on my mother's face when the doctor said them, for once without the not-quite-hidden anguish in his eyes. Everything was better after that. After those words I remember summer days spent grubby and exhausted in the old abandoned shack behind our house. No longer did I keep company with hospital wraiths, but rather with neighborhood kids who had experienced no greater hurt than a scraped knee or a bruised shin; kids who'd never had to listen to their parents sob just outside their door, thinking you couldn't hear them; and kids who had no memory of being so sick that even the feel of a blanket was unbearable agony.

I think I stopped talking to animals then. Or maybe I just had better things to do than listen to the birds chattering at my window or the squirrels quarrelling in the tree outside.

But I heard them again today.

"Man chicks pelted my nest," I heard through the rolled-down window of our old Honda Civic as we pulled into the parking lot of the clinic.

"Did you say something?" I asked my husband.

Kevin shook his head. He needed a haircut. The waves in his hair were turning into frizzy curls in the Georgia heat. I mourned the Civic's air conditioner, its cooling breeze a memory of more prosperous days.

"Time to build again," I heard. And I recognized the voice—a shrill, helium babble, a tone I hadn't heard in over two decades. I looked up, and sure enough, I saw the muted berry-red breast of a she-robin hopping on a branch beside the tattered remains of a nest. Another bird, a brown one with white shoulders, cocked its head sympathetically.

That's when I knew. Even before I saw the doctor—a woman this time, but still with the same cheery smile that couldn't conceal the sorrow that was a requisite of her job—I knew.

Kevin held my hand in reception as we waited to be called. They didn't keep us stewing for long. Maybe when the results are bad, they try to cut you a break on the limbo time spent half bored, half terrified amongst the screaming children and the old issues of *People* and *National Geographic*.

Dr. Graykin didn't bother with small talk; she never did. "The results of your biopsy came back, Ginny. I'm afraid it's not good. The tests showed a malignancy."

I expected to feel horrified, or at the very least, afraid. But instead, all I could think of were the words of the robin. "Time to build again." How did birds mark time?

It was Kevin who reacted. "Cancer?" The word was a gasp, a choked whisper.

"I'm afraid so."

"What are our options?" he said.

Our options. Sometimes I got mad at Kevin when he inadvertently left my name off memberships he signed us up for—like the Paperback Book club, or the Music of the Month club. For that matter, the cable was still only in his name. But he remembered this time.

"I'd recommend a rigorous course of chemotherapy," Dr. Graykin said. "I'm afraid this is a fairly aggressive form of cancer. And because of the nature of the tumor, I believe a hysterectomy will be necessary. The last set of x-rays showed another mass already forming. Complete removal of the impacted organs will give us the best chance of beating this."

Now Dr. Graykin was included in my prognosis. Give *us* the best chance, she'd said.

"What are my odds?" With that one word: *my*, I let the illusion slip. It crumbled to dust like brittle flower husks in winter, exposing me to what the doctor and my husband had been trying to shield me from. But this was my fight and my sickness, mine and mine alone. In the end, it'd be me vomiting my insides out from the chemo, too weak to even raise a hand to brush the hair out of my eyes. No matter how supportive Kevin was, or how solicitous Dr. Graykin, they couldn't carry that for me.

"I'd say pretty good," Dr. Graykin said. "I think we've caught it early enough. Maybe seven out of ten women can expect to push it into remission, assuming you act decisively now."

Seven out of ten. My future was laid out, reduced to a number game of statistics and uncertainty.

I let Kevin make the follow-up appointments with the receptionist, scheduling when I would have the poisons pumped into my veins to kill the cells that had turned against me, setting the date for when they'd excise the organs that were killing me like Trojan horse invaders from the inside.

Back in the car, I sat listening to the birds.

"Wind's changing. Thunderstorm flying in on cloud wings," I heard.

I'd never learned what the birds indigenous to Georgia were, their feather patterns or migratory habits. But I knew what this one would look like from his voice. He'd be one of those little brownish-gray birds that dive at crows to scare them away from their nests. It always impressed me how fearless they were, attacking other birds that were two, sometimes three times larger.

Kevin stared into space behind the wheel. The keys dangled from his fingers, idle.

"Rain shoos worms out," the bird said.

"We'll get through this," Kevin finally said. "But no kids on top of everything else—"

His words dribbled away, and between us, silence dug its fingernails in.

No kids. After the hysterectomy I wouldn't be able to experience the wonder of growing a new life inside of me. I'd never feel a tiny person develop within me nor go through the process of expelling it forth in a gush of agony and hope. I wondered why I didn't grieve, why I didn't mourn for the children of my womb that I'd never have. But I felt distant, detached.

"Full gullet follows the rains," the bird chirped.

The Civic's motor revved as Kevin turned the key in the ignition, drowning out the bird's voice.

At home, Kevin fidgeted. I felt sorry for him. He didn't know what to do with himself. I wasn't reacting the way the tragedy-struck heroines on television did; I wasn't crying or shouting or throwing things. He was waiting to be my rock, my solace, and I just sat in the kitchen, staring out the window.

"You should go back to work," I said.

"I can't leave you alone at a time like this."

"We can't afford for you to lose your job." The words *and your health insurance* were left unspoken, but I knew both of us were thinking them. "I'll be fine."

I felt him at my shoulder, reaching out to comfort me. "You sure?"

I moved away, knew it when his hand fell back. "It's just cancer. I beat the odds once. I can do it again."

It was false bravado, but Kevin needed to hear it. It allowed him to gather up his briefcase and his keys and drive away from me.

And besides, I really wasn't alone. I waited until I could no longer hear our old car sputtering down the road before I went out to the host of voices I knew were in our backyard.

Our yard is large and fenced in. I think the previous owners had a dog. The fence is old and there are gaps in it large enough to admit cats, rabbits, squirrels, and once I saw a raccoon from the kitchen window. It's an unkempt area, our big backyard. Neither Kevin nor I enjoy yard work and the weeds had grown roughshod through the grass. Unidentifiable greenery sprouted tiny white flowers, like miniature daisies, cascading over a failing landscaped bush that sagged from the invader's weight. Thin, tall trees—fruit trees, evergreens, and shrubs—shaded the far corner; long-dead tree trunks intermingled with the quick. The evergreens spewed a profusion of pinecones year round, making mowing a risk-fraught undertaking; the flora itself endorsed our laissez-faire grounds keeping.

I sat on the old wooden bench; its white paint, slashed into streamers by time, revealed the dry, cracked wood beneath, and I listened.

"Got a seed? Got a seed?" trilled from the leaf-canopy overhead.

"Sky fly high."

"The sun. Lookit the sun!"

Then I heard a non-avian speaker. "Wanna bite," it said. It was a nasal voice; it reminded me of a young Jimmy Durante.

"No bite." That voice also had a nasal drone to it, but it was seasoned by maturity.

Out of the cover of a riotously blooming weed-shrub, a soft-furred black face pushed through, crowned with a cap of white. Small black ears and India-ink eyes swiveled to regard me. A round barrel body with two broad, white stripes down the back trundled out. Behind her, a miniature copy tagged at her heels. The ripe aroma of unwashed socks wafted over me.

They say that a skunk out during the day must be rabid, but I knew these two weren't. Rabid animals don't exude patient resignation, or, in the case of Junior, unbridled elation. Another urban wilderness myth debunked, I guess.

Mama Skunk trotted up to me, the size of a small housecat but with that sweeping tail no cat possessed. I breathed through my mouth and hoped that Junior wasn't trigger-happy. Mama didn't seem to notice my poised anxiety, or if she did, she didn't comment on it.

"Wanna bite," Junior said.

"No bite," Mama repeated. She sat down, not two steps from my bench; her hind legs sprawled out on either side of her.

I began to relax. The smell, though not agreeable, wasn't aggressively offensive, not much worse than a rain-drenched German Shepherd.

With great dignity, she scratched at a spot behind her ear—one hind leg a blur of movement. "Teeth on this one comin' in," she said. "Needs to set 'em in everything he sniffs."

To illustrate, Junior launched himself at Mama's hindquarters and sunk his gleaming white teeth into her haunches.

Mama gave a weary sigh. "Small ones." While Junior worried at her, she gazed up at me. "Third of the year, he is. First daughter and second and fourth sons crushed by four-wheels on the road."

"I'm sorry."

She swiped at Junior with a paw. It dislodged him momentarily. "My second breeding season. First was an only daughter. Owl took her. Takes a lot out, raising small ones and watching them die."

"I'm sorry," I repeated. I wasn't sure what else to say.

"One more season in me, I think. Then I'm done. No more egg crunch in my teeth or juicy caterpillar fur sticky on my tongue." She hissed at Junior as he dug his baby fangs into her leg. "No bite!"

"Wanna bite."

Mama snatched Junior up by the scruff of his neck and snapped her head sharply to the side. "No bite!"

"No bite," Junior squeaked, hanging from her mouth.

Mama released him and Junior sprang at her back, chewing at the thick fur there. She nodded to me, a single bob of her nose, and turned to go. Junior tumbled off in a sprawl of oversized paws and bushy tail, and scampered after her.

"If small ones could bite the moon, they would," she called over her shoulder. "But no one wants a chewed-up moon."

Bemused, I watched them flatten themselves under my fence, the flags of their tails disappearing beneath it. I made a mental note to put out a tray of snacks—leftovers from dinner, perhaps—for Mama and Junior tonight.

A flash of violet caught my eye as a blue jay fluttered onto one of our wild cherry trees. "Beware the wind!" he called.

"I'm watching. I'm watching," another voice replied.

I scanned the branches but couldn't see this newcomer. From the sharpness of the tone, I was betting it was a woodpecker, but wasn't sure.

"Won't rustle my nest," the maybe-woodpecker chirped. "Go fly."

The blue jay flitted away.

"Gotta build for a storm," the unseen bird said. "But sometimes blown down anyway. The sun's out now. Lookit! Lookit!"

Another voice joined in and a chorus of "Lookit"s ensued.

I listened to the birds discuss the weather until the labored engine of the Civic announced my husband's return.

Kevin tossed his briefcase into a chair and his keys onto the table as I started some rice boiling for dinner.

"I sat in the backyard this afternoon," I said. "I've decided I like the overgrown look. Some of the weeds are prettier than the landscaped flowers."

"I can get the mower out of the tool shed this weekend."

"No, I'm serious. I like it." I rinsed off a stalk of bok choy and began chopping it into chunks. The stem and the browning parts I deposited into a bowl. Mama and Junior Skunk would appreciate the tidbits.

"Ginny, did you call my folks with the news yet?"

I tossed a bundle of bean sprouts into the strainer and sent a cascade of water over them. "No. I don't really know what to say to them." I picked out several choice sprouts and set them in the same bowl as the bok choy stem.

"Want me to do it?"

I didn't look up from the carrots and parsnips on the cutting board. "Would you?" I made it a game, seeing how evenly I could chop them.

While Kevin dialed, I poured oil into the wok and dropped in some diced green onion and teriyaki sauce to simmer.

Outside, I saw wings flash in the treetops.

"Hi, Mom. Ginny and I got word back from her biopsy today—"

I concentrated on making dinner: mushrooms for us, mushrooms in the skunk bowl, eggplant for us, eggplant in the bowl.

Even across the room, with the headset against Kevin's ear, I could hear his mother sobbing. Part of it, most of it probably, was for me. But I was sure a little bit was for them too. From the moment we'd announced our engagement, his parents, especially his mother, had talked about grandchildren. I felt like I was shirking them by having Kevin break the bad news, but on the other hand, I knew the phone call would be good for him. His mother was reacting the way I should have, dissolving into tears and railing at fate. He spoke in soothing tones, the epitome of tender consolation. It gave him something to focus on, something to do.

The tang of cooking bell peppers suffused with curry and cinnamon drifted from the wok and permeated the kitchen. I dumped in the sprouts and turned down the heat.

"Dinner's just about ready," I said.

Kevin nodded and began the process of extracting himself from the phone. He was reluctant, but I heard him address his father. Undoubtedly my dad-in-law had taken over comforting Kevin's mother.

I poured us some iced tea out of the refrigerator as he replaced the headset onto the cradle.

Kevin watched me eat; I could feel his eyes, over the bottle of soy sauce, following me as I forked up mouthfuls of rice and vegetables.

"I spent today thinking," I said.

Kevin put down his fork, his food untouched. "About what?"

I'd forgotten to toss some peanuts into the stir-fry. Peanuts were one of Kevin's favorites. "The chemotherapy, the surgery," I said.

"I remember what chemo was like when I was a kid. I remember thinking that letting the leukemia have me would've been better."

The silence stretched. The sound of my own teeth crunching through celery and carrots was deafening.

"Did you ever think how unnatural it is, going through all that medical rigmarole to extend our lives?" I continued. "When wild animals get sick, they don't stress it, don't claw for those extra few weeks or months or years. They just accept it. Maybe it's better that way."

Kevin made a sound; I don't think it was a word. He stared at me, and I had to look away. I couldn't handle the confused hurt, stark on his face, that I'd glimpsed.

I stood up with my half-eaten plate of food and dumped it and the bowl of vegetable leavings onto a plate. The back door's un-oiled hinges creaked as I wrenched it open.

Kevin didn't follow me. I hadn't expected him to.

I'd just unlatched the screen door when I heard the scream.

"No! Not me! Aii!"

I rushed out and saw a calico tabby cat examining a tuft of gray fur between its paws. I recognized the cat as one of the strays that roamed the neighborhood from the jagged scar across its nose. As I watched, the cat opened the trap of its claws and the animal leapt free. It was tiny—a mouse, or a vole maybe.

"Run," the cat growled.

The terrified little creature scampered towards me. I didn't think it was seeking me out; it was just running away from the cat. It screamed, high pitched and inarticulate.

I took a step forward but the cat was faster. It pounced and the tiny animal's screams ended, cut off. I heard the snap of fragile bones shattering between sharp teeth.

My headlong rush petered out before the momentum could build beyond the first adrenalin jolt. It had all happened too quickly.

The tabby spat out the mouse-vole and prodded the now-limp body. His golden eyes gleamed in the twilight. "Fought well, small warm fur," he said. "Tried to bite me. Such small fangs. Mine are much finer." He shook his paws at the dead rodent and turned his back to it. "It's still now."

"Aren't you at least going to eat it?" I said.

The cat's tail flicked back and forth like a plump, furry serpent. "Not hungry."

"Then why'd you kill it if you aren't going to eat it?" Indignation made my voice harsh.

Yellow-slitted eyes met mine. "It was there."

Before I could reply, he bounded across my yard, scaled the fence in a single prodigious leap, and was gone.

I set the plate of food down, half surprised to still find it in my hands, and went over to the pathetic corpse in the overgrown grass. A trickle of blood spattered a soft-muzzled face, plastering the fur around its head and neck. It was still warm. I wondered if I ought to bury it.

Still undecided, I stood up. Movement from above caught my attention. Against the shading of the darkening lavender sky, I saw silhouettes flit and flutter. Voices drifted to me, excited and high-pitched.

"There!"

"Caught it."

"Mine."

"Listen."

Bats. Little brown ones out in the dusk, hunting insects. Such chaotic energy, a wild dance in the sky. And not once did a dancer misstep; they all seemed to know the exact cadence and meter of their frenetic waltz. I watched them dive and career above me until it grew too dark to see.

"Warm blood is sweeter, but tonight it is cold." The speaker's voice was precise, a softly calculating presence. An owl.

I wouldn't have to dig a grave for the tiny dead thing in my yard. I retreated, returning to the voice-free refuge of my kitchen.

It was deserted.

The door to Kevin's den was closed, but when I knocked on it, the knob turned and the door swung open as though he'd been waiting for me.

He hadn't changed out of his work clothes; his shirt was wrinkled and his tie loose and askew around his neck. I couldn't meet his eyes—familiar soft blue eyes that crinkled in laughter at our private jokes, ones that no one else would understand. Those eyes would hold anguish, I knew, pain I had caused. There might be tears in them if I looked up. I stared at his chin.

"I didn't write down when my appointments were," I said. "Do you still have the cards the receptionist gave you?"

I let myself peek after all. Yes, blue eyes the color of the evening sky, still pained, but also relieved. I'd given him back something to hope for.

———•———

I avoided the outdoors after that. I kept the windows closed and the radio or television, or both, turned up to drown out even the hint of wilderness voices. Trips to the hospital for the start of my chemotherapy were made with the car radio blaring and culminated in a hasty, unseeing, unhearing dash from parking lot to foyer.

The drugs made me tired and everything I ate became seasoned by flakes of rust. But the hint of nausea I felt when I watched the clear solution dripping into my arm during the first treatment didn't manifest beyond a suggestion of misery. I was thankful for that.

Days disappeared, unmarked and unremembered while the poisons did their work. Then came the one scribbled on my calendar by Kevin, like a birthday or anniversary.

He drove us to the hospital and hovered nearby as the nurses and interns took charge of me. In hospitals, nobody's clothing fits properly. Doctors flurried by, the wings of their white lab coats and smocks loose in their wakes. Fellow patients slouched or reclined under a stratum of blankets and hospital gowns. And my attendants' slate blue scrubs transformed them into anonymous, androgynous drones that buzzed and twittered about me. When they donned their facemasks, the illusion was complete—featureless, genderless eunuchs, all of them. In my baggy hospital garb, I joined their fellowship. But they could take off their uniforms and become people again. I, on the other hand, would be a true eunuch after today, hollowed out and sterile.

I watched as one of them tightened a tourniquet on my arm and slid a shining needle into the faintly pulsing vein in the crook of my elbow. I dutifully counted down from ten, and embraced the darkness that crowded the edges of the room when I hit four.

Three. Two. One.

Someone had erected a nest of cotton balls and gauze in my mouth and hastily dismantled it while I slept. I was left with the taste of desiccated foundation.

I opened my eyes and immediately closed them again. Surely the world was not supposed to be a dizzying slash of color and light?

"Ginny?" I recognized Kevin's voice. "I saw her open her eyes, doctor."

"She should be coming out of the anesthesia," Dr. Graykin said. "It can be disorienting."

I remembered now. I had been un-womaned in the limbo of three numbers, carved up and sewn back together again. "I'm awake," I said. Although it didn't sound right, more like "Mm, wwm." I tried again. "I'm here." I squinted my eyes open, relieved to discover that the room wasn't still canting sideways.

I felt Kevin's fingers against my hand, felt the brush of his lips on my forehead. "How're you feeling?"

"I wouldn't nominate today as one of my all-time favorites," I mumbled.

"You'll probably be sore for a while," Dr. Graykin said. "A week, at least. You'll need to take it very easy."

I had been blissfully oblivious of my body until I heard the word *sore*. Then I became aware of a deep ache running through me. Each breath pulled at low parts of me that were unhappy and eager to complain. My arm throbbed where the IV line punctured it, tethering me to a jellyfish-flaccid bag.

"The procedure went smoothly," Dr. Graykin continued. "We were able to visualize the tumor in its entirety."

"Oh. Good."

"You should rest now. Let the nurse on duty know if you need anything." Dr. Graykin patted my sheet-shrouded leg and was gone in a whirl of white before I could finish mouthing a thank you.

Kevin handed me a tastefully cheery, pink envelope. I produced the obligatory smile at the cuter-than-cute bunny on the cover of the card. The inside read "*Hopping* you get well soon!"

"Thanks, honey." The words sounded dismal, even to me.

Kevin leaned over and brushed his lips against my cheek.

I closed my eyes.

"Try to get some sleep. I'll see you tomorrow."

"Okay. Bye."

That night, alone in my hospital bed, I dreamed that I was Prometheus, chained to the bench in my yard while crows picked at me, tearing out my ovaries and uterus with their sharp beaks and crying "Lookit! Lookit!"

I didn't need a psychoanalyst to interpret it.

I woke with the curtains of my room just beginning to turn from a colorless gray to a pale dandelion-buff. Birds would be singing outside, announcing the dawn. I couldn't hear them, and suddenly I wanted to.

I swung my legs over the edge of my bed, careful not to tangle my IV line, and lurched the two steps to the window. My legs were uncooperative, intent upon tripping me up. The pain intensified and I staggered against the window casing. My eyes felt scalded, like a handful of salt had been tossed into them. I reached a hand up and discovered that my face was wet. Tears. Why was I crying? Weeping, standing, the window, it was too much for me to manage. My legs gave way and I crumpled, taking the metal tree that held my now-empty IV bag with me. Pain erupted through me and I couldn't stop myself from crying out.

The soft shushing of rubber-soled shoes on tile pattered to my door. The door opened; light enveloped me.

"Oh my goodness! Mrs. Broward, what are you doing?" It was the night nurse.

"The w—window," I sobbed. "I j—just wanted to open the window."

She righted the IV stand and half-lifted me to my feet. The tears wouldn't stop and each time I hiccupped, another spear of pain tore through my body. I no longer felt distressed at the closed window; I just felt ridiculous.

"There, there, Mrs. Broward." The nurse settled me back into bed, handed me a tissue, and checked my bandages.

My nose dripped disgustingly. Blowing it hurt. "I'm sorry. I don't know what came over me."

"It's the hormones and all the stress from the operation. It's perfectly normal." She tucked the blankets in around me. "Comfy?"

I nodded. My eyelids were heavy again, weighted by hot coins.

"Right then. Just hit the red button if you need me."

"Okay," I mumbled. The nurse's face grew hazy and the edges of the room softened around me.

She patted my hand. "Henry's coming 'round today. I'll make sure he swings by here first thing. He's good at getting a grin. Smiling is its own medicine."

I don't remember her leaving. When I opened my eyes again, the curtains were a radiant canary-yellow. A hollow rapping echoed from my door. It was that sound which had awakened me.

"Come in."

The door opened a crack and a man's face peered around the edge. It was an unobtrusive face; creases at the eyes and forehead spoke of time spent in the sun. He wasn't a doctor; there was too much buoyancy in his eyes.

"Did I wake you?" he said. "Judy, the nurse, told me I should come by."

Memories of a first light conversation filtered into my consciousness. I struggled to sit up. "Are you Henry?"

The man pushed the door wide. "Actually, my name's Dave. But Henry's with me."

I heard a soft clicking, like a strand of pearls being coiled together. A tawny yellow and black, indisputably canine muzzle, poked around my door. The head, level with Dave's thigh, was long and graceful atop a brindle-shaded neck. Bright brown eyes peered up at me while a wide mouth lolled open in a doggie smile. It was canine nails on hospital tile that had clacked and clattered so.

"This is Henry," Dave said.

"Oh." I had thought that Henry would be a therapist or a psychiatrist.

"You're not allergic or anything, are you?" Dave said.

"No. Not at all."

Henry's ears flipped forward. "Hi," he said. "Pleased to meetcha. Very happy to. Yup."

"Henry's a greyhound rescue from a track in Florida," Dave said. He didn't react to Henry's words, but then I hadn't expected him to. "We visit the hospital every Wednesday. Judy said you needed some company?"

"Come in."

Dave led Henry to the side of my bed. I noticed something. "Hey, you've only got three legs."

"I know. I know," Henry said. "My leg was sick. They cut it off."

"Bone cancer," Dave said. "We caught it in time, but that was pretty much the end of his racing days."

"Good as new. Better. Better," Henry said. "Doesn't hurt. Can't race as fast as I used to. Boy, I really could go when I was a pup, but I can still get the wind buzzing through my ears. I like running. I'd run with two legs if I had to. Sorry. No offense."

I smiled. The curve of my lips felt alien to me, like I hadn't smiled in a very long time. I reached out to stroke the dog's head. His short fur was warm, like thick velvet beneath my fingers.

"Pet my ears," he said. "My ears. Everyone likes my ears."

So I stroked the felt and sateen of his pale yellow ears.

"Y'know," he said. "Listen up here. Listen. It doesn't matter how many legs you got. The important thing is the running. That's what I always say."

It was soothing, just petting Henry. Some of the tension, a bit of the anxiety, leaked away as I ran my fingers through his coat.

Dave ruffled the dog's head. "Hey, I have to take Henry to the kid's ward now. He's got a date with a certain little boy who's very punctuality oriented. If you like, I can swing by afterwards. Maybe let you and Henry have some quality one-on-one time?"

"That's not necessary. My husband will be in soon to take me home. But I'm glad you both came by." I gave Henry a last pat. "Thank you, Henry."

"My pleasure. You're welcome. Any time."

"And you too, Dave."

"Hey, I'm just the transportation. I know who the real star of the show is." Dave grinned down at the dog. "Ready to go, fellah? Rickie's waiting for you."

"Yeah. Yeah. Gotta go see Rickie. Yup," Henry said. "Nice to metcha, lady. Glad to make your acquaintance. See you around."

Kevin arrived while the day nurse—a slender, pinch-faced woman with brusque manners but a soothing voice—was serving me a tray of red Jell-o, oatmeal, and toast.

I pushed the unappetizing meal away. "Hi."

"Hi back. How're you doing?"

"Not too bad," I said.

"Has Dr. Graykin been by yet?"

As though he'd conjured her, she appeared at his elbow. "Good morning, Ginny. Did you sleep okay?"

"More or less."

She performed a cursory check of my vitals—heartbeat, blood pressure, temperature—and oversaw the removal of the IV umbilicus before declaring me sound. It was such a relief feeling the plastic tube slide out of my arm. I had spent more time than anyone should have to endure, violated by a slender hose piping medicines and nutrients through my veins.

The pinched-faced nurse helped me dress into proper clothes before bundling me into a wheelchair for my exodus to the hospital's patient drive.

Kevin acted as though I was a sandcastle at high tide. He hovered over me, unhappy when I wouldn't let him bodily carry me from the car into the house. But he didn't press me either, as though he were afraid that I would melt away at a strong word.

"Do you need anything? Want me to make you a sandwich?"

"I'm not hungry."

"The doctor said you should eat something. I can heat up some soup. Maybe with some bread and butter?"

"No, really. They fed me at the hospital."

"You didn't eat it."

"Really, I'm fine. I just want to lie down."

"Of course. After we get you tucked in I can bring you something light to snack on. Maybe some fruit?"

My patience splintered. "Kevin, having my reproductive organs surgically extracted did not create a gaping hole that needs stuffing. And even if it did, I hardly think food would be an adequate substitute for what I've lost unless you were thinking of cramming that fruit into me from a different orifice than my mouth."

I pushed past him and stomped upstairs, trying not to flinch when the sudden movements caused my insides to twang and bite. I wanted to bang the bedroom door shut, but I managed to cling to the last threads of civility and merely shut it.

I barely had the strength to kick off my shoes before falling into the neatly made-up bed. The last thing I saw before my eyelids slammed shut was that the window overlooking our yard was open.

Crying woke me. At first, I thought it was Kevin, but it wasn't his throat that made those heartbroken, pitiful wails. It was dark outside, but it was only a little after noon, far too early for sunset. Somber gray clouds, heavy with rain and the promise of thunder, enveloped the horizon.

Peering out the window, I realized that the sounds were coming from the yard. Without bothering to slip my shoes on, I padded to the door. Nothing stirred inside the house as I made my way through it, blinking in the false twilight.

The grass was cool under my bare feet. Edges of crabgrass like crinkly knives slashed my ankles. I nearly tripped over a white plate, hidden by overgrown weeds. It was the licked-clean plate of food I had set out an uncountable number of days ago.

The noise was coming from the tool shed nestled in the furthest recesses of our yard where we kept the neglected lawn mower and other underutilized paraphernalia.

The door squealed as I pulled it open; the hinges were too rust-encumbered to perform smoothly. The stench of recently-fired skunk musk assailed me. No, it wasn't a *stench*; that word didn't do it justice. Fresh skunk is a transcendental state, an experience more profound than anything encompassed by as simple a sense as smell. My eyes streaked with tears and I struggled not to retch, knowing that to do so would require me to take another breath.

Through the blur of my tear-filled eyes, I saw a small black and white bundle of fury charging me. His tail stood up straight behind him, the long hairs bristling out like a Christmas tree. He was puffed up, standing on his toes to appear as large as possible. It was Junior.

"Go 'way!" he shrilled in his Jimmy Durante voice.

"Don't shoot," I whispered, half-choked. "I'm going away, see?"

At the sound of my voice, he stopped mid-charge. His tail drooped and he deflated. "Wait. Need help," he said.

I tried breathing through my mouth, but I could still smell the musk. When I inhaled, my tongue and the back of my throat became swathed with a foul, oily coating.

"What's the matter?" I gasped.

"Mama poofed someone. I run away. She won't wake up."

"She was attacked?"

"Just here. Lookie."

A still puddle of black and white lay in the shadows. It was Mama Skunk. She was dead, her neck snapped.

"Oh, Junior, I'm so sorry. Your mother's not waking up."

Junior butted and pawed at her, whining and snuffling forlornly.

"What happened?" No sane animal would tangle with a skunk. And obviously Mama had got in a shot. For her assailant to have managed to snap her neck after being hit, I couldn't fathom it.

"Cat," Junior said. "All scarred up. No sniffer."

And I remembered the calico cat, the one that had killed the mouse-vole.

Junior's liquid black eyes gazed up at me. "Lonesome," he whimpered. "Scared." He began to cry, small snuffling noises both like and unlike a weeping human child.

"I'm sorry," I said again. The words felt inadequate. "Are you hungry? You're probably hungry. Let me get you something to eat." I reminded myself of Kevin, an uncomfortable sensation.

"Leaving me? Come back?"

"I'll be right back. Stay here."

The air was fresher outside; I inhaled with relief. The first droplets of rain plunked on my arms and shoulders.

Kevin had made soup, after all. I found a large Tupperware bowl in the refrigerator filled with some cream-based concoction. It would have milk in it, and vegetables, maybe cheese. I ladled up a bowlful and debated whether I needed to microwave it for Junior. But no, I was still inundated by the residue of Mama Skunk's last stand. The less time I spent in the house, the less exhaustive the fumigation efforts would have to be. I hoped.

I was on my way out the door when I heard Junior's screams. They were high-pitched and shrill, inhuman. The bowl shattered on the kitchen linoleum as I ran out. Tendrils of sizzling pain oscillated from my nether regions up through my chest in a pulsating rhythm. I doubted whether Dr. Graykin would classify sprinting as "taking it very easy." I caught my breath, and instantly gagged. I'd thought that the stink couldn't possibly get any worse. A fresh infusion of skunk spray proved me wrong.

I tried to ignore the raindrops now hammering down from above, but they trickled into my eyes and made the grass slick. The throbbing turned into a persistent flare of pain as I slid and stumbled through our yard. Despite the toxic miasma that hovered around the tool shed, I rushed in.

The relief from the rain vied with a wave of nausea from the re-doubled aura of skunk. In the storm's gloom, the shed was pitch.

I pushed the door wide. A single strobe of lightning splashed whiteness and shadows in with the rain. In the moment of washed-out over brilliance, I saw Junior, huddled in the scant shelter of the mower where it leaned against the wall. The lightning framed the calico cat in mid-leap as it sprang.

Blinded again, but trusting in the afterimage memory, I dove.

"Don't shoot!" I shouted at Junior.

My hand closed over a screeching, furious ball of teeth and claws. The cat sank its fangs in but I didn't let go. Red-hot wires scored my wrist and I felt teeth grate against bone in my palm.

Another slash of lightning lit the shed. I wrestled the scratch-ing, biting demon to the dust-covered crate that housed mol-dering copies of Kevin's old comic books and magazines. I threw the cat in, slammed the lid shut, and latched it.

My hands and arms felt like I'd set them on fire. More worri-some, I felt wetness trickling down my side through the bandages. "Junior?" I panted. "Where are you?"

"Mama?" I felt a cold nose nudge my ankle. "Mama?"

I kneeled, doing my best not to breathe, and picked Junior up with my smarting arms. "You okay?"

He immediately nestled into me, snuffling at my face. It felt good, his warm, soft body snug against me.

"Oh my God!" Kevin exclaimed behind me. I turned and was blinded by a flashlight beam.

Junior squawked and tried to burrow under my arm.

Kevin repositioned the light so it no longer blazed into my eyes. I could imagine the picture I presented. I was drenched, barefoot, my hands and arms scored and bleeding, rank with musk, and cuddling a baby skunk. But Kevin surprised me. After only the shortest of explanations, he helped me and Junior back to the house, phoned animal control to collect the cat I had trapped in the shed, and took charge of Junior, setting him up with a bowl of soup and a blanket-lined box in the spare bathroom.

"We're adopting a skunk, huh?" He got out the peroxide and began dabbing at my bites and scratches. "Y'know, if you wanted a baby substitute, I would've thought a puppy or cat or something would've been less problematic than a skunk." He glanced up at me as he said it, his tone teasing and light. When I didn't rebuff him, he smiled shyly. "So, uh, you think we can get him de-scented?"

The rueful expression on his face made me giggle. When was the last time I had giggled? I couldn't remember. I took his fingers in mine and winced when they brushed against my wounds.

"Kevin, I'm sorry about how I've behaved," I said. "It's just, I'm so scared all the time, I don't—"

He pulled me close and rested his chin on top of my head. "I know, honey. It's okay. I'll always love you, no matter what. Kids or no kids, even if you decide you need to adopt stray skunks and get into fights with alley cats, I'll still love you."

I laughed and something rigid that I'd been holding tight inside me dissolved away. The laughter metamorphosed unexpectedly into tears, great gasping sobs that swelled until I was helpless to stop them. I felt my knees fold. I would have fallen, but Kevin caught me. He held me in his arms as I cried, stroked my hair as I wept, my body wracked with tremor after tremor. I clung to him, my rock after all.

———•———

People look at us funny when I tell them we have a skunk living with us.

Kevin drew the line at Junior sleeping in bed with us. But when he's at work, Junior usually curls up with me on the couch for long skunk naps. He follows me around as I tend the new vegetable garden in our backyard and gets underfoot as often as he can. When the chemotherapy made my hair fall out, his antics lured me away from fixating on the freakish apparition in my mirror. And when I feel too wrung out by the drugs to get out of bed, he drags all the covers off me, puffing and straining to haul the mass of blankets away. I laugh and find I *can* get up.

The backyard has acquired some strange attraction to four-legged and feathered types. It's especially the sick or the scared or the lonely that come to me. Cats thrown out of car windows, puppies dumped by the roadside, they find their way here and tell me their stories. Sometimes the only thing I can do is make sure they don't die cold and alone. And sometimes I have the joy of watching a newly healed bird fling itself back into the sky.

Kevin is building bat houses and birdfeeders and squirrel perches for me. And he's going to tear down the tool shed and build something better, sort of a triage sanctuary for outdoor beasties to take refuge in who can't or won't come into the house.

Dr. Graykin was displeased with me for pulling my stitches, but she thinks that between the chemo and the surgery we'll get all the cancer cells. God, I hope so. But there's never any certainty in life, no guarantees, no promises. The only thing I can do is take each day as I can and do the best by it. Or, as someone once told me: "It doesn't matter how many legs you got. The important thing is the running."

Though Hell Should Bar the Way

A.C. Crispin and Christie Golden

The Highwayman

PART ONE

I

The wind was a torrent of darkness among the gusty trees,
    The moon was a ghostly galleon tossed upon cloudy seas,
    The road was a ribbon of moonlight over the purple moor,
    And the highwayman came riding—
    Riding—riding—
The highwayman came riding, up to the old inn-door.

II

He'd a French cocked-hat on his forehead, a bunch of lace at his chin,
    A coat of the claret velvet, and breeches of brown doe-skin;
    They fitted with never a wrinkle: his boots were up to the
        thigh!
    And he rode with a jewelled twinkle,
    His pistol butts a-twinkle,
His rapier hilt a-twinkle, under the jewelled sky.

III

Over the cobbles he clattered and clashed in the dark inn-yard,
    And he tapped with his whip on the shutters, but all was
      locked and barred;
    He whistled a tune to the window, and who should be waiting there
    But the landlord's black-eyed daughter,
    Bess, the landlord's daughter,
Plaiting a dark red love-knot into her long black hair.

IV

And dark in the dark old inn-yard a stable-wicket creaked
    Where Tim the ostler listened; his face was white and peaked;
    His eyes were hollows of madness, his hair like mouldy hay,
    But he loved the landlord's daughter,
    The landlord's red-lipped daughter,
Dumb as a dog he listened, and he heard the robber say—

V

"One kiss, my bonny sweetheart, I'm after a prize to-night,
    But I shall be back with the yellow gold before the morning light;
    Yet, if they press me sharply, and harry me through the day,
    Then look for me by moonlight,
    Watch for me by moonlight,
I'll come to thee by moonlight, though hell should bar the way."

VI

He rose upright in the stirrups; he scarce could reach her hand,
But she loosened her hair i' the casement! His face burnt like a brand
As the black cascade of perfume came tumbling over his breast;
And he kissed its waves in the moonlight,
(Oh, sweet, black waves in the moonlight!)
Then he tugged at his rein in the moonliglt, and galloped away to
the West.

PART TWO

I

He did not come in the dawning; he did not come at noon;
And out o' the tawny sunset, before the rise o' the moon,
When the road was a gypsy's ribbon, looping the purple moor,
A red-coat troop came marching—
Marching—marching—
King George's men came matching, up to the old inn-door.

II

They said no word to the landlord, they drank his ale instead,
But they gagged his daughter and bound her to the foot of her
narrow bed;
Two of them knelt at her casement, with muskets at their side!
There was death at every window;
And hell at one dark window;
For Bess could see, through her casement, the road that *he* would ride.

III

They had tied her up to attention, with many a sniggering jest;
    They had bound a musket beside her, with the barrel beneath
      her breast!
    "Now, keep good watch!" and they kissed her.
    She heard the dead man say—
    Look for me by moonlight;
    Watch for me by moonlight;
I'll come to thee by moonlight, though hell should bar the way!

IV

She twisted her hands behind her; but all the knots held good!
    She writhed her hands till her fingers were wet with sweat or blood!
    She stretched and strained in the darkness, and the hours
      crawled by like years,
    Till, now, on the stroke of midnight,
    Cold, on the stroke of midnight,
The tip of one finger touched it! The trigger at least was hers!

V

The tip of one finger touched it; she strove no more for the rest!
    Up, she stood up to attention, with the barrel beneath her breast,
    She would not risk their hearing; she would not strive again;
    For the road lay bare in the moonlight;
    Blank and bare in the moonlight;
And the blood of her veins in the moonlight throbbed to her love's
    refrain .

VI

Tlot-tlot; tlot-tlot! Had they heard it? The horse-hoofs ringing clear;
  Tlot-tlot, tlot-tlot, in the distance? Were they deaf that they did
    not hear?
  Down the ribbon of moonlight, over the brow of the hill,
  The highwayman came riding,
    Riding, riding!
The red-coats looked to their priming! She stood up, straight and still!

VII

Tlot-tlot, in the frosty silence! *Tlot-tlot,* in the echoing night!
  Nearer he came and nearer! Her face was like a light!
  Her eyes grew wide for a moment; she drew one last deep
    breath,
  Then her finger moved in the moonlight,
  Her musket shattered the moonlight,
Shattered her breast in the moonlight and warned him—with
  her death.

VIII

He turned; he spurred to the West; he did not know who stood
  Bowed, with her head o'er the musket, drenched with her
    own red blood!
  Not till the dawn he heard it, his face grew grey to hear
  How Bess, the landlord's daughter,
  The landlord's black-eyed daughter,
Had watched for her love in the moonlight, and died in the dark-
  ness there.

IX

Back, he spurred like a madman, shrieking a curse to the sky,
  With the white road smoking behind him and his rapier bran-
    dished high!
  Blood-red were his spurs i' the golden noon; wine-red was his
    velvet coat,
  When they shot him down on the highway,
  Down like a dog on the highway,
And he lay in his blood on the highway, with the bunch of lace at
  his throat.

X

And still of a winter's night, they say, when the wind is in the trees,
  When the moon is a ghostly galleon tossed upon cloudy seas,
  When the road is a ribbon of moonlight over the purple moor,
  A highwayman comes riding—
  Riding—riding—
A highwayman comes riding, up to the old inn-door.

XI

Over the cobbles he clatters and clangs in the dark inn-yard;
  He taps with his whip on the shutters, but all is locked and barred;
  He whistles a tune to the window, and who should be waiting there
  But the landlord's black-eyed daughter,
  Bess, the landlord's daughter,
Plaiting a dark red love-knot into her long black hair.

Alfred Noyes, 1906

Mist...

Mist it was, insubstantial and barely seen. The mist rose above a mound of weedy, winter-blighted grass, hesitating beside the iron-barred fence. Inside lay the kirkyard proper, hallowed ground where headstones bore mute testimony that this one or that had once lived, once loved... once died...

Mist it was. Wispy-white in the light of the silver crescent Moon, incorporeal as smoke. Feeble, drifting Awareness awakened. The Awareness struggled to survive, to grow stronger, to Know.

What am I? How and why did I come here?

The mist moved, in response to a barely sensed need. It flowed onto a ribbon of moon-washed road, gaining strength, coherence, identity...

I am... I... was. Was. Dead now, but was... I must...

Must what?

Unknown. Despite the cold, brutal wind that assaulted it, the mist thickened, steadied. Now it had Substance.

It? No, not "it." *She* had substance.

Knowing her sex brought a moment of pride, and included a vision of herself. A woman, wearing a rust-colored dress, white apron. Long black hair, wound with a red ribbon... a ribbon tied in a love-knot as crimson as blood.

Memory supplied a face. Large, coal-dark eyes, strong jaw. There was beauty, yes, tempered and honed by strength, and by love...

The cold ribbon of road led her, drifting over frozen slush bearing the marks of hooves and wagon wheels, to a town. She knew, somehow, that she should know it. Here, a baker's shop, closed and still, about which the aroma of bread still clung. There, a tavern that serviced the garrison that topped the hill.

Baker. Tavern. I know these things. I. Know.

The building by the tavern drew her. No sign, only a candle gut-tering in a hanging globe of red glass. Memory supplied distaste for what transpired within, but she found herself at the window, experiencing a moment's distress as her fingers went through the solid pane. Peering inside, she found that, despite the whorls in the thick, greenish glass, she could see and hear clearly.

The sounds of laughter drifted out, interspersed with drunken singing, accompanied by off-key music from a fife and a penny-whistle. Women dressed in chemises and robes, their breasts spilling free from their bodices, their hair hanging lank, laughed shrilly as they sat in the laps of men who had discarded their uni-form jackets and weapons, and sometimes even their breeches.

Why? she wondered. *Why here?* Yet, disgusted as she was, she could not move.

Then she saw him. A man sat in the corner by the fire. Hate flowed into her, hot as the flames. She wasn't sure how, but she knew him. He had iron-colored hair, tied back with a ribbon, and pale, thin features. A flush of hectic color stained his cheekbones, and his eyes glittered feverishly. A woman clad only in a scanty chemise brought him a pewter mug, laughing as she handed it to him. Fear and loathing washed through the observer at the win-dow. *Why? Why him? What is he—or was he—to me?*

The blowsy woman giggled as the man guzzled. "Thirsty to-night, ain't we, Captain?" The man nodded and shivered, pulling his red coat with its shining buttons and fringed epaulets close. "Sure you wouldn't like a nip of something warmer?" she cooed, cupping her barely-covered breasts.

The officer guffawed, but the laugh turned into a wheeze. He coughed, burying his face in a handkerchief. The whore backed away from him, eyes wide. When he took the white linen away from his lips, it was spattered with red.

The watcher's full lips curved in a cruel smile. *If I could drink, brave Captain, I'd drink to your death. May it be long and painful and but a taste of the Hell you are bound for!*

She did not know why her curse was merited, but she had no doubt that it was, and richly so. Turning away from the tavern, she headed up the street, misty feet barely touching the cobblestones. A soldier on his way back to the garrison staggered into her, then through her, without ever seeing her, leaving her saddened, but not really surprised. She'd realized quite some time ago that she was a ghost.

Barely glancing at the surrounding buildings, she drifted on, drawn by her unknown goal. A large, half-timbered structure loomed before her in the moonlight. She slowed, stopped, and gazed up at the creaking sign.

The Black Mare. Beneath the words, a black horse pranced on the whitewashed wood. She blinked, confused. No, that was wrong, it wasn't The Black Mare, the name of the inn, was… was… it was…

The White Swan.

With a choked sob, she fell, crumpling into the snow without marring its virgin drifts, or feeling the cold. Sobbing, incorporeal tears pouring down transparent cheeks, she remembered… remembered the inn, remembered…

Names.

Father. Jamie. Bess.

She was Bess, the landlord's daughter, and she had stood at that window to watch her beloved Jamie come riding, riding up to the old inn door. He'd promised to come to her, the dashing highwayman, with his pistol butts gleaming in the liquid moonlight, though hell should bar the way.

Jamie. Bess.

And hell had come, in the form of King George's soldiers, and—and—

"Oh, merciful God," she wept, now remembering what had happened on that night, the iron hardness of a muzzle pressing the warm flesh of her breast. Now she knew why she not been allowed to rest in hallowed ground.

———•———

"Are you certain you can't go on?" Lieutenant Robert Larrimer asked his wife.

Anna, pale, rubbed her swollen belly and nodded, just as the carriage gave a particularly savage lurch. "I'm sorry, my love, but the jouncing…" she bit her lip, then, and gasped. "Oh! A cramp, Robert!"

"Birth pangs?" he demanded, frightened. Anna was more than a month from her time.

"I don't think so. But I must stop! Please, Robert!"

He nodded, and leaned out to shout to the coachman to head for the village that lay a few miles away. He had hoped to avoid the place. They had neither relatives nor friends in the vicinity, and that meant they must stop at a public lodging-place.

There was only one inn in that little northern town—and that place held only bitter memory for him. He gazed anxiously at Anna, who sat braced against the bumps, one hand pressed to her belly, the other grasping the locket with both their pictures that she wore strung on a crimson ribbon. Larrimer's heart swelled with love. They had been wed barely a year. He would rather be tormented by memories than see her suffer, or risk their child.

Anna knew nothing of the ... incident, in fact had wed him after his transfer to another unit had been granted. He didn't want her to find out. *Perhaps no one will recognize me...*

Larrimer licked lips suddenly gone dry, and shivered despite the cape he wore over his red coat with its bright buttons.

———•———

Dawn came, and cockcrow. Bess expected to vanish—wasn't that what happened to ghosts at sunrise? – but she remained.

Her memories had returned, but she still had no idea why she was here, what she must do. Her control over her movements and form was better, now, and she could see herself, even feel herself. She watched the inn, saw a slatternly girl come out to empty slops, and a brawny middle-aged cook bustling about. Tasks that she herself had done, when alive. But where was her father? Drifting, she entered the inn and glided through the rooms, familiar, yes, but strangely altered, and not for the better. Dust lay in the corners of the furniture, and dirt and cobwebs had invaded every corner. The floor appeared not to have been swept for a fortnight or more. Bess tried to pick up her old broom from its corner, but, of course, her misty hands could not grasp a solid object.

She drifted past the room where she had died, and, after a single hasty glance, averted her eyes. A dark stain still married the floorboards before the window.

In her father's room, a man slept in the bed. Not her father. Bess stared in horror at the white face, the closed eyes that mercifully hid the dark, mad gaze of Tim Alcott, the ostler.

Tim was master of the inn now? How could that be? Tim was half-mad and simple, as stupid and dull as a beast, and nigh as dumb as one. In all the times he'd trailed about after her in life, gazing at her with smoldering eyes, Bess had only heard Tim mutter a few garbled monosyllables.

As Bess watched, Tim stirred, rolled over, groaned, then sat up and scratched. "Damned bedbugs!" he snarled. "I'll beat that lazy slut silly for this! I TOLD her to change these sheets!" Bess gasped silently. *He can speak! Sweet Jesu, how can this be?* Whirling, she retreated down the hallway and raced out of the inn.

Determined to leave this place that brought only pain, she headed for the street. But she could not leave, she discovered. Some unseen force tethered her to the grounds of the inn. Bess flung herself forward, only to rebound, unable to take another step. She moaned, longing for the peace of her un-consecrated grave.

Back in the courtyard, Bess "sat" upon the mounting block, gazing at her surroundings, utterly bewildered. Why was she held here? Who had summoned her? What was she supposed to do?

Memories…memories filled her, though she tried to push them away. Jamie, her Jamie, had stood upon this mounting block. He had tethered his horse over there. Over there, in the shadow of the bayberry bush, he had kissed her, long and sweet. Tears filled her eyes.

Jamie. Oh, my love. I hope you made a clean escape. I hope it was worth it.

Perhaps that was why she was here. She was a suicide, albeit a suicide in a noble cause—to save the life of the man she loved. Perhaps she had to make atonement, or some such?

She wondered what day it was, what year it was, and then she realized, with a jolt, that it was already early afternoon. The light had changed, become robust and golden instead of thin and pale. Time had passed, for her, in the blink of an eye.

Rising from the mounting block, she drifted about the court-yard, then into the stable. As she moved past the horses, it became obvious that, if humans could not see her, the horses could. Their eyes rolled white-rimmed, and they backed away, snorting.

Bess came nearer, talking in low tones, but many animals panicked, rearing and kicking. Others simply stood, sweating and trembling.

"Good boy, good girl," she tried to soothe them, but to no avail. She stood wringing her spectral hands in distress.

"They do not understand. Stupid creatures."

Bess whirled. She found her gaze locked with the large, intelligent brown eyes of a shining black mare who might have been the inspiration for the inn's new name. *No, surely not…*

"Yes, it was." The mare nodded her head. The "voice" had echoed inside Bess's head, but it was clearly the mare that had "spoken."

Bess shrank back from something so unnatural. *A beast, talking?* "How…why…?"

"Oh, in your present state, we can all speak with you if we wished. But they are too afraid. As I said, they're stupid creatures. Dogs will snarl and whimper, and most cats, save witch familiars, will hiss. Ravens…they care not if one is spirit or flesh, they view everything without wings as beneath contempt."

Bess laughed, a strained, shocked sound. "Merciful Heaven," she breathed. "Are you a witch then, in the shape of a mare?"

The horse nickered, as if laughing itself. "I hardly think a self-respecting minion of Satan would permit herself to be locked up all day, fed poor hay, and be tended to by the loving kindness of Tim Alcott. No, I am what I seem—a mare. A living creature, one who pities you, Miss Bess."

"Tim," said Bess, slowly. "He was asleep in Father's bed. He can speak, now. He used to be dumb and simple. How can this be?" She rubbed her arms, feeling a chill not of body.

"Yes, he is now the innkeeper of The Black Mare. As to how he gained his new wit and wagging tongue, I remind you of what they say about those who wager with the Horned One. Great power may be granted—for the gamble of a soul."

"He wagered with the Evil One? For wits and speech?" Bess gasped, shocked. She'd never thought of Tim as a good man, had always known there was something *wrong* about him, but to risk one's immortal *soul*…

"For that…and for the opportunity to become master here at the inn. Wager he did, and he got what he bargained for—all except for one thing." The mare snorted, fixing eyes the color of peat upon her.

Bess ran her tongue across her lips, frightened. "And what was that?" She asked reluctantly, already knowing the answer.

"Your own sweet self, Bess. You cheated him out of what he wanted most."

Somehow she'd always known. Tim's lust for her had been something she'd tried to ignore, to avoid acknowledging. She'd been too wrapped up in Jamie, and between Jamie and Tim… well, the contrast between them was laughable. Bess drew a deep breath and asked the question that could be put off no longer— though she dreaded the answer.

"What happened…to my father?" *And to Jamie?* her mind added, but she could not force herself to ask that, yet. As long as she did not ask, she could hope that Jamie was safe.

The mare took a step toward Bess and attempted to nuzzle her comfortingly. The velvet muzzle passed right through Bess's misty form. "Your father died the same night you did," she said softly inside Bess's head. "Found dead with a knife in his throat. The soldiers always claimed that your highwayman did it, but…"

The mare tossed her mane in the equine equivalent of a shrug, and said no more.

Bess closed her eyes. *Hasn't there been enough pain and death and suffering?* she thought miserably. A memory floated back to her; Tim, listening intently to the captain, then hastening off on some task. *It was Tim all along, god rot him.*

A sudden bustle and clatter in the courtyard distracted her. Bess turned to listen, heard voices.

"Welcome to The Black Mare, young sir. And the missus, I take it." Tim's voice, and it fitted the rest of him. Even dead, Bess felt her skin crawl at the raspy, obsequious tones.

"Thank you," came a man's voice. Young. Earnest. *Familiar, though. I've heard him speak before. Who is he?*

"Here now," said Tim, "don't I be knowin' you, sir?"

Curious, Bess left her equine friend and floated to the entrance of the stables. In the center of the courtyard, a carriage had pulled up. The horses stood puffing steam from their nostrils, and the coachman flung a blanket's over their sweating bodies. A young soldier stepped out. He turned to extend his hand to a pretty young woman, probably his wife, whose belly was heavy with child.

"I know you," Bess whispered softly. "I remember you…"

"No," said the young redcoat, addressing Tim but seeming to avoid the ostler's gaze.

"We've not met."

"Liar," said Bess. "Oh, you liar, you were there, that evil day."

Tim's eyes widened, then he touched his forelock in exaggerated deference and gave the soldier a sly wink. "All you soldiers, I s'pose you look the same. Well, I'll give you m'best, for your lady to rest in, sir. Please to follow me."

"You? But I thought the landlord was —" The soldier stopped in mid-sentence, and his shoulders sagged. Bess's lips twisted in a silent snarl. Ah, but he was handsome, wasn't he, with his wide blue eyes and fair hair tied back with a red ribbon. She remembered his name: Lieutenant Robert Larrimer.

The innkeep and his guests walked away, and Bess returned to the mare. "That was Larrimer! He was one of them!"

"Balance," the mare replied, pawing with one black hoof. "The wheel turns. It has been one year since your death, Bess."

"And he has come, this day of days," said Bess. Her spectral hands closed into translucent fists.

"Now you know what drew you here," the mare's "voice" was intense, a hot needle piercing Bess's mind. "Larrimer is the reason you rose from your uneasy rest. He is one of those responsible for your death, and the death of your beloved. Revenge is yours to grasp, Bess."

"My beloved—merciful Heaven," Bess could scarcely speak. Breath was agony in her throat, and tears sprang to her eyes. "They killed Jamie, too?"

She had given her life so that Jamie might be warned of the ambush, might flee. And her sacrifice had been for naught! Sobs choked her.

The horse nodded, and her eyes were sad. "The next day, he returned. In broad daylight. He knew only that you were gone, and he couldn't live without you. They gunned him down, Miss Bess... shot him down like a rabid dog, on the highway. Larrimer was there when they did it. Your Jamie died in a pool of his own red blood, and they buried him at the crossroads, in an unmarked grave."

Bess buried her face in her hands, weeping wildly. "No! No!"

The mare was relentless as she finished, "And now, one of the men responsible is out there. It is your turn to kill."

Bess shook her head. "But Larrimer—he didn't—he tried to stop them."

The mare was inexorable. "He was one of them. Never forget that! And he is within your grasp. Heaven is merciful, Bess, for it's given you a chance to win your passage on to the afterlife. Kill the man who killed your love, and the balance is restored. An eye for an eye."

"But I can't…" Bess protested.

"Do as you will," the horse said, suddenly indifferent. She reached for a mouthful of hay, began chewing. "You can always stay here with me. I enjoy the conversation. You're much more lively to talk to than the other horses. All they talk about is eating and foaling."

Trapped here in the inn forever? Bess shuddered at the idea. *If I'm being given the chance to go on, to leave the earth for the afterlife, hadn't I better take it?*

"How do you know all this?" she whispered. "Who *are* you?"

"Just a mare. My name is Midnight, but Tim calls me 'Night,' Miss Bess. As to how I know…well, beasts know things, see things, that humans wot not of," the mare lipped up another wisp of hay and chewed. "Just as we can see you, where they cannot, we know things."

"I see," Bess whispered. It made sense. The stories always talked about animals being sensitive to Otherworldly forces, able to see spirits. She thought of Larrimer again. That handsome young man, alive, married, the father of a child, while her darling Jamie lay in unhallowed ground, trodden on by man and beast alike. "It's not fair!" she cried.

"No, it isn't," the mare agreed.

Bess nodded, her mind made up. It could not be mere coincidence. She, dead by her own hand, a ghost returning on the eve of her death, and he, one of the men who had killed her, returning as if by fate. *Larrimer, he's the key to the afterlife. Jamie's dead, but perhaps if I avenge him we can both rest.*

Tonight. Please God, she would have revenge tonight, hurt that handsome, sweet-faced youth as badly as he had hurt her, as badly as he'd hurt Jamie. The thought filled her with hot pleasure. Bess turned back to the horse and smiled, and the mare closed one eye in a conspiratorial wink.

———•———

Larrimer was appalled to realize that "the best room" was the one in which Bess had died. Anna, tired and drained, had been too distracted to notice her husband's reaction to their quarters. After the midwife had examined her, given her a potion, and prescribed a day's rest, Anna eased her bulk onto the bed, and was asleep in minutes.

Her husband sat in a chair near the window, his head buried in his hands. The memories haunted him at night, lurked on the edges of his consciousness by day. And here, in this room, where the worst of it had happened, they flooded his mind and would not be dismissed...

Is that all the ale you've got?" Captain Jennings bellowed, slamming his empty tankard down on the table in the taproom. The innkeeper, a tall, thin man, shook his head. "But, Captain, you've not paid —"

"Bring me more ale, damn you!" thundered Jennings, and the landlord scurried to obey.

Larrimer cleared his throat. "Captain, with due respect, we ought to pay the man for—"

"Larrimer, you irritate me," growled the older man. "He's been giving aid to a killer. Taking his ale is little enough punishment.

Ha, look how he sends his daughter to wait on us!" His voice dropped. "I've got other plans for her tonight."

Larrimer closed his mouth in miserable compliance. Bess, he believed the girl's name was. It was she who had been consorting with the highwayman James "Bonnie Jamie" MacLaren.

The girl wore a dress of dull red, and a white apron. Her feet were bare as she walked over the cold stone floor, and her breasts moved with quick, shallow breaths. Larrimer could see she was terrified.

"Miss," he said gently. She turned sloe-dark eyes upon him. "Our orders are to capture Bonnie Jamie, so he can be tried, but he's never harmed anyone. Likely the judge will spare his life."

She smiled then, red lips curving hesitantly, shyly. Sweet Jesu, but she was lovely.

"Ha! The Colonel said if he resists, he's a dead man!" Jennings snarled, and then showed crooked teeth in a cruel smile. "Miss Bess…I'm glad you're here. Lads, did you know that if you wish to catch the big fish, you need proper bait? I'd say this slut is proper bait indeed!"

As Bess backed away, furious but too frightened to defend herself, Jennings made a sudden, deadly lunge. Clamping a hand upon Bess's arm, he dragged her into his lap. She struggled, then froze, a drop of sweat trickling down her suddenly pale face, as Jennings placed the muzzle of his pistol to her throat.

Larrimer bolted to his feet. "Captain, this is outrageous! I will not—"

Then he, too, fell silent and still as a tiny sound—the almost unnoticeable click as the pistol was cocked—reached his ears. Smith, Jennings' second in command, had drawn his own pistol and now stared down the sight directly at Larrimer.

"We soldiers work hard," said Captain Jennings in a deceptively gentle voice. "We deserve a little … sport … now and then. The girl's a whore, Robbie, and we've got the authority to send her whole bloody family to a very nasty gaol cell if we so choose. All I'm asking is that she help us snare her elusive fox of a highwayman." Without removing the pistol, he tangled his fingers in her hair, tugged her face down to his, and kissed her wetly.

Larrimer looked away, sick. He'd accepted the offer of a commission in the King's army, thinking that the life of a soldier would be filled with travel and excitement. He'd had no idea that officers like Jennings even existed—men who enjoyed causing others pain. But Jennings was in command. What could he do?

He wished for a moment that he could leave on some pretext—leave and warn the highwayman not to come. That ugly scarecrow of an ostler, Tim, speaking in a voice that sounded rough and somehow unused had told Jennings that he'd overheard MacLaren promise to come to Bess "by moonlight, Cap'n. He said he'd come t'her by moonlight, though Hell should bar the way. His very words, Cap'n."

Larrimer cursed silently as he stared at Bess's terrified face. Bonnie Jamie MacLaren had robbed a good many travelers on the road, 'twas true, and had been a thorn in the side of the law for almost four years now. Capturing him would be quite a coup. But MacLaren's glittering pistols and rapier had always been for show. No one had ever been injured by the highwayman—save, perhaps, their pride.

He remembered something else that Tim had said. At the time he hadn't understood, but now he did, all too well. "Don't forget, Cap'n. When you're done wi' Miss Bess…"

"Yes, yes," Jennings had said. "You have my word. Now hurry along and attend to that other matter we discussed, Tim, that's a good lad."

The ostler had tugged his forelock, and melted into the shadows.

Now Larrimer knew what Tim had meant when he'd said, "when you're done…"

My God, Larrimer thought, in horror, *I can't let this go on! I must do something!*

But he hadn't, had he? Larrimer lifted his head from his hands, not at all surprised that his face was wet. "I should have done something, damn it," he said aloud to the dark stain on the floor.

His words had woken Anna. She stretched, and smiled sleepily at him. Larrimer's heart turned over. He went to her and kissed her softly, sweetly. The shadows had fallen outside as well as in his own heart, and he told her, "It's time for supper, love."

———•———

Bess hovered over them as they ate.

The serving wench commented on the strange chill that haunted that corner of the otherwise cosy, firelit taproom. Pale, pregnant Anna shivered and put on her shawl. Lieutenant Robbie Larrimer rubbed his cold hands and glanced reflexively behind him. Bess watched them, excitement flowing through her. *Soon… soon…*

The words of the black mare in the stable, Night, spurred Bess on, warmed her. Revenge would win her rest—revenge, and nothing else.

Before retiring, Larrimer and Anna sat beside the fire in the taproom for a while. As the minutes stretched by, Larrimer grew increasingly uncomfortable. Bess drank in his apprehension like wine. He was nervous, nervous about lying down to sleep with his warm wife and baby-to-be in a room where he'd watched an innocent seventeen year old girl die.

Be nervous, Robbie, Bess silently urged. *Be nervous while you still can…*

———

Surely it was his imagination that had him so rattled, Larrimer consoled himself. He didn't believe in ghosts, not in this rational Age of Enlightenment. He was haunted, true enough, but by memories and shame, not by specters.

Despite the diligent application of a bedwarmer, Larrimer was cold. His wife slept peacefully, her breast rising and falling, the swell of her stomach arching up beneath the covers.

Larrimer tossed and turned. It had been a year ago, tonight, in this room, and he had tried, but not hard enough…

They tossed the sobbing girl back and forth between them, each of them taking crueler and more vulgar liberties. The harder Bess sobbed, the louder they laughed, slobbering and pawing and pinching.

Larrimer stood by, feeling wretched. He could no more have stopped this than he could have stopped the moon from rising in a few hours. The Lieutenant glanced out the casement at the road that waited in the darkness like a serpent, and himself hoping that the highwayman would break his promise—that Bess would not have to watch Bonny Jamie Maclaren die in the ambush Jennings was planning.

"That's enough, lads," the Captain said, finally. Larrimer sighed with relief. They'd had their fun, they'd let her go, now, lock her in her little room in the attic, while they waited for her lover. Bess was rumpled and sore from pinches, but mostly unhurt, save for her dignity.

Larrimer turned back from the window and winced. They had torn her dress, using a bit of cloth as a crude gag.

Chuckling, Jennings took a dagger and slit the chemise that peeked through her torn bodice. The men laughed and slavered as the girl's breasts bobbed free, white and rose-tipped in the candlelight.

"Now, watch this," said Jennings. He took a musket and rubbed its muzzle over the girl's nipples, then made lewd sounds when they stiffened in response to the cold iron. The soldiers hooted.

"Good God, Jennings!" Larrimer protested. "Haven't you done enough?"

"You and I will have to have a talk when this is over, Lieutenant," replied the captain, his eyes never leaving the wide, frightened ones of the girl.

"Yes," said Larrimer, in a strong voice that shocked even him with its edge. "Before God, we will."

Surprised at Larrimer's tone, Jennings turned his head and regarded him. The younger man stood his ground, sticking out his chin. "You and Smith keep watch, then," he said. "See that the girl doesn't escape. And to make your task a bit easier—"

He bent and propped the musket up on its butt, wedging the barrel firmly beneath the girl's left breast. "Oh, good job!" said one of the men, who began to tie the weapon against Bess's body.

"Now, keep good watch!" laughed Jennings. He removed the gag and kissed her lips, then jerked back, his hand to his mouth. "You bitch!" he cried, staring at the blood on his hand. "The wench bit me!"

He cracked her across the face with his hand. Larrimer winced. Bess's eyes filled with tears and the imprint of Jennings' hand welled up red on her face, but there was no surrender in her expression.

Angrily, Jennings shoved the gag back in her mouth. "I had half a mind to keep you for myself, and not give you over to that madman of an ostler—but now, you get what you deserve."

The Captain straightened and glared at Larrimer. "Watch her." And then he was gone.

Silence fell. The minutes crawled by. Larrimer and Smith alternately stood by the window, and sprawled in chairs. Larrimer tried not to look directly at Bess, sparing her what small amount of humiliation he could, but once he caught her in the act of twisting her hands against the knots. When she saw him looking, she froze like a frightened deer. Trying to get the blood back into her hands, poor lass, Larrimer thought, and he looked away again, wishing he could loosen the knots. But Smith would never stand for it.

The minutes stretched into hours, and more than once Larrimer caught himself drowsing. The moon rose like a silver ship tossed on cloud-waves.

Tlot-tlot, tlot-tlot. Hoofbeats along the road.

"Bastard's on his way," said Smith softly. He began to prime his musket. "And it looks like we'll have a clear shot at 'im from here."

Larrimer realized that they weren't even going to allow Bonnie Jamie the opportunity to surrender. They were just going to kill him in cold blood. Sickened, he heard Bess take a breath, a deep, deep breath, and he turned toward her.

Afterward, he was never sure what he planned to do—free her, perhaps. But time suddenly seemed to slow as he faced her. He realized, too late, that she had managed to work a finger free— one finger, placed on the trigger of the musket, and she gave him a blazing look of triumph as she pressed down and —

"Bess, no!" Larrimer screamed, bolting awake.

"Oh, yes," came a soft, angry whisper. His heart slamming against his chest, Larrimer looked wildly around the room.

She stood beside the open casement, transparent as gauze, white as moonlight, floating a foot above the floor.

"Bess," he breathed. His skin erupted with gooseflesh and his blood was mountain water in his veins. "You've come back!"

She nodded, and floated nearer. "Yes, I've come back. For you."

He would have thought it impossible for his fear to deepen, but it did. He clutched the coverlet. Somehow, impossibly, Anna slept on.

"Bess, I tried to stop them—I tried—"

"But you didn't," she interrupted. She moved closer still, floating gracefully toward him like milkweed down. "You didn't stop them. You didn't save me. And you helped murder my Jamie!"

Out of the corner of his eye, Larrimer noticed that a pile of rope was slowly uncoiling. It undulated like a snake in the air. His pistol floated upward, too, as if borne by an unseen hand.

He opened his mouth to protest, but that was all she needed. Her body contorted into a slim thread and she dove down his throat.

She was there, inside him, and Larrimer felt the terror, the same terror she'd felt that night one year ago. The pain, the humiliation, the fear, the futile hope that her sacrifice would save her beloved...

And suddenly Bess saw what Robbie had seen, that night one year ago. Through his eyes, through his memories, she saw her own death. The gun exploded, shattering her breast. She convulsed, but she was already dead, had to be dead, with a hole in her chest and the red blood spattered, trickling down her pale features like red ribbons, like the love-knot in her black, black hair...

With her spirit animating him, Larrimer moved. He climbed out of the bed, and stood beside the open casement, against the bedpost while the rope snaked around him, binding the primed pistol into place, the muzzle pressing into his chest. His fingers writhed, seeking release from the tight bonds, stretching, stretching…but not to find release, only to touch the trigger.

Tlot-tlot, tlot-tlot. Hooves on the cobblestones. For a wild moment, both ghost and mortal thought the highwayman had returned, as he had vowed, for his black-eyed Bess. But a shadow moved across the courtyard, trotting over to the window; a black horse, riderless. And beside it, a man, a white-faced man with eyes the color of madness, and hair the color of moldy hay.

"Come," said a voice inside his (her) head. "Take your revenge, Bess, and let me bear you away to a better place."

And his mortal ears heard the ostler's rasping tones, "Kill him, Bess! He killed your Jamie!"

Blood oozed from his bound hands, staining the ropes as Larrimer's fingers strained to reach the trigger. *This is justice!* Bess's wild exultation reached Larrimer. *A life for a life—your life for Jamie's!*

Larrimer knew he had only seconds to live. Images from his life flashed through his mind—and Bess shared them. She saw Robbie, in civilian garb, approaching the highwayman at a tavern, delivering the sad news with a warning to come not near the inn. Larrimer had wept as he'd spoken to Jamie. And then, later, when Jamie lay dead, Larrimer had challenged his Captain, had dueled with him, rapiers flashing by torchlight—and he would have won, save for the Colonel's interference. Larrimer's report had ended any chance of Jennings achieving his longed-for promotion and reassignment. Instead the Captain had been permanently assigned here, to this backwater village, the site of his disgrace, to languish.

Pity flowed through Bess, as she lived Larrimer's torment, his grief, his guilt and shame. He'd suffered for a year, suffered as much as any prisoner locked in a gaol of his own making…

"No!" echoed words that Larrimer somehow understood came from the black horse. "No, do what you must, Bess! You must avenge your Jamie, for vengeance is sweet!"

More than one life, Bess thought, even as Larrimer's fingers, under her guidance, brushed the trigger. *More than one life lost and ruined… Jamie's, mine, Father's…* She turned her (his) head back over the shoulder, to see the sleeping woman on the bed. *Shall there be three more lives, ruined, then? Larrimer's and Anna's and the wee babe's shattered this time not by Jennings, but by ME?*

"No!" shrieked Bess, pulling herself abruptly out of Larrimer's body. The soldier sagged against his bonds, gasping. "I will not do this! I will not ruin more lives because mine was cut short!" She wept freely, and tried to touch Larrimer's face. Her fingers passed right through him. "Larrimer, Robbie, I forgive you. I forgive you with all my heart."

The soldier staggered as the rope fell as if it had been abruptly cut. He dropped to his knees.

Bess leaned out the casement and confronted the mare, who half reared, her eyes glaring wildly in the moonlight. "He had no part in it, Night! How will killing him send me on to eternal peace? It cannot be right, it cannot!"

Bess's gaze fastened on Tim, who was staring up at her in horror, horror, she realized, that had nothing to do with seeing a ghost. "Night," Bess said, slowly, in confusion, "Night, why is Tim with you?" She stared down at the ostler, frightened now. "Tim killed my father, he betrayed Jamie and me. He is no friend to either of us!"

Larrimer crawled over to the casement, beside Bess's spectral image, and looked out. The horse screamed, a harsh, unnatural sound, and then—Larrimer moaned with terror—it began to change.

The creature retained the outward seeming of a horse, but its pawing hooves left trails of fire. Its mane and tail erupted in sheets of black flame. Larrimer could feel infernal heat against his face. The black beast roared angrily, exposing sharp teeth—the teeth of a carnivore. Its eyes flashed red, and sulfurous smoke belched from its nostrils.

Beside Larrimer, Bess sank to her knees and he heard her gabbling something that sounded like a prayer.

The creature turned to Tim, who had fallen to his knees and was groveling in fear.

"We wagered for a soul, and you wagered that I'd have hers, Tim," it thundered in a terrible silent "voice" that filled the night. "She is proving … difficult."

"Take her! She vowed to kill him, and by doing so, damned herself," Tim urged.

"Take her, take her!"

"Take her I shall," the beast growled.

The beast suddenly grew long arms, black as pitch. They reached for the specter. Bess cried out and struggled, but unlike human hands, these were able to close upon her misty form. The hands clasped her arms. Bess shrieked, a lost, desolate sound.

"Leave her be!" cried Larrimer. He was determined to fight for Bess, as he had not fought before. His gaze darted desperately around the room, seeking something to serve as a cross.

Nothing … but wait! With a gasp, he dragged his rapier from its sheath, and, with one swift snap, he broke it across his knee, ignoring the blood that slicked his fingers. To make a cross, he needed something…rope, or ribbon…

The spectral arms pulled Bess up from her knees, until she was poised at the end of the casement. One good pull, and she would be through it.

"Fight, Bess! Fight it!" he shouted.

Larrimer's fingers fumbled at the nightstand, and then they closed on the ribbon Anna used to hold her locket. Feverishly, Larrimer bound the broken sword into a cross.

Larrimer thrust his makeshift weapon between Bess, who was half through the casement, and the Nightmare, brandishing the holy symbol in the face of the thing from Hell. It hissed violently, and drew back, but it did not release the ghost girl. "I am no simple demon, foolish mortal! Think you a simple cross can defeat me?"

Larrimer felt his conviction waver, but he looked at the locket, then at Bess. "Ah, but this is no simple cross!" he declared. "I have broken my sword, and will never wield it against man nor woman again. And I have bound it with a symbol of the deepest love of which man is capable—my vow to my wife. I challenge you in the name of a God that bade us show mercy and love—as Bess has shown mercy and love to a poor, unworthy soldier!"

The Nightmare cried out, a low, ululating sound, and fell back. "I wagered for a soul, and a soul I shall have!" it shrieked.

Tim was already up and running across the courtyard. The Nightmare was upon him in a single leap, her hooves clattering against the cobblestones, leaving ribbons of fire writhing in her wake.

"Nooooooo!" screamed Tim, as the beast, never pausing in her giant strides, swept him up, onto her back. He shrieked, but stayed on as if tied there.

A moment later, the Nightmare, bearing its damned burden, was gone. Bess fell back into the room in a heap. Larrimer's "cross" fell from nerveless fingers, and he clutched the casement sill to steady himself. He drew a deep breath, then another. Finally, he looked down at Bess.

She was not looking at him. Slowly, she gathered herself, then sat up. Her head was cocked, in a listening pose. Then Larrimer heard it too.

Tlot-tlot, tlot-tlot. Hoofbeats on the road.

Bess smiled, the secret smile that only women in love can know, and leaned over the casement, looking out. She began to loosen her hair.

Larrimer could see him now, coming along the ribbon of highway—a man on a horse, a smoky dappled beast that shone like mist in the moonlight.

There he was, the French-cocked hat, the thigh-high boots, the doeskin breeches. His spurs glistened and jingled. It was Bonnie Jamie MacLaren, come at last, as he had promised so long ago, for his Bess.

The highwayman paused beneath the window, to fondle a length of hair that had once been black, inhaling its sweetness. "My love," he said in the rumbling, warm burr that Larrimer had heard once before, when he'd broken the news of Bess's death. "My love, I've been waiting. But I could not come for thee until the stain of thy suicide was purged. Had thou killed yon soldier boy, I'd have never been allowed to see thee again."

"Jamie…" Bess whispered. "Oh, Jamie…"

The highwayman held out his arms, and Bess slipped over the casement sill. He clasped her close, and then bent his head to kiss the landlord's daughter—kissed her with a fierce tenderness that Larrimer understood, had shared with his Anna.

Neither of them looked back, as the ghostly figure spurred his spectral steed. Away they went, following the highway until, at last, they were gone.

The cock crowed. Larrimer slumped against the window sill, his eyes filled with tears of joy. Softly, he whispered a blessing upon both of them.

It was, finally, over. He need not carry his burden of guilt a step further. He was free to hold his head high, to love his wife and child, with no secrets between them. For the highwayman had come for his love by moonlight, as he had vowed, though Hell had barred the way.

Angel's Keep

Glenda Finkelstein

Karen Winslow was driving home from an out of town business meeting late on a Friday night. The roads were hazardous due to a torrential rainstorm that she drove right into about an hour ago, and there were no signs that the storm would be subsiding any time soon. In addition, she was achy and feverish suffering from the flu. The only lights besides the occasional lightning flash were those on her compact car. Just when things couldn't get any worse for Karen, the oil light on her car came on.

"Oh great, just what I need," Karen muttered. She knew she had been forgetting to do something, and now realized that she had been spacing taking her car in to be serviced. Her car was over ten years old, and when the idiot light comes on you better find a station. Unfortunately, nothing was open nor was she familiar with this stretch of lonely mountain highway. Dark takes on a whole new meaning in the mountains.

She thought she should telephone her husband to let him know that she may be delayed because she knew her car was about out of steam. She grabbed the cell phone and went to dial when she noticed that the battery had died and she left the car's cell phone charger on the dining room table at home.

"Could this day get any worse? I didn't clinch the deal, I'm sick, my car's oil light just came on, and my cell phone is dead," Karen expounded amid coughs to the little dog attached to her dashboard. Suddenly the car's engine just stopped.

"Oh crap," she said aloud as the car slowed to a stop. The rain was coming down even harder now, and there was no one else on the road. She turned her flashers on in hopes that someone would come by, but no one did.

She sat there for about an hour, but didn't notice a light shining amongst the trees until after a spell of coughing that racked her entire body. The light caught her eye. She wiped the accumulated moister from the window with the sleeve of her blouse to get a clearer view of what the light was attached to. After staring intently for a moment, she realized that the light was attached to a house. Thinking that someone might be able to help her, she got out of the car. By the time she made it to the covered porch she was soaked to the core. There were no lights on inside the house, nor did she see a car, but she knocked anyway.

"Hello," she called. "Is anyone home?" No one responded. She slid down the door to the floor. Too weak to move, she remained there. Every joint and muscle in her body was hurting, and she was shivering. She felt her forehead, the temperature of which you could fry egg on, just before she fell unconscious.

When she finally regained consciousness, she found herself lying on a long fluffy sofa in front of a blazing fire. There was a glass on a nearby table filled with water. When she went to feel her forehead there was a towel lying upon it. She took it in her hands and realized that someone must have found her and been taking care of her through the night. She sat up to get a better view of her surroundings. As she did her eyes caught the image of a man with long dark hair that hung straight down around his face. He was handsome, and was dressed in a white collared shirt and black pants. In his hands, he carried a tray of hot tea and toast.

"You're awake," he commented. "You had a hard night."

"Who are you?" Karen asked.

"My name is Leslie. What's yours?"

"Karen Winslow. Thank you for taking care of me."

"It's not every day a beautiful woman is dropped on one's doorstep. How are you feeling?" Leslie asked, setting the tray down on the coffee table.

"I feel weak, but I'm alive."

"That's a good start. Your fever broke sometime around 3:00 a.m. Try to drink some tea, and then if you're feeling up to it try the toast."

"Thanks," she said, taking the tea from his hands. She carefully took a sip. She waited a moment before taking another sip. Then she remembered that her husband must be worried sick. "Do you have a phone? I need to call my husband. He must be worried sick about me."

"Sorry, I don't have those sorts of things. I live too far out. I took a look at your car. You're out of oil."

"Yeah, I know."

"I might have some in the shed out back. Once you're strong enough, and out of danger from passing out, I think we can get you to a station where you can call your husband."

"You're very kind, Leslie."

All of a sudden there could be heard several male voices coming from outside. One of them sounded distinctly like that of her husband. She could discern that they were looking at her car.

"It looks like that the calvary has arrived," Leslie commented. He helped Karen off the sofa and walked her to the door.

"Ted?" Karen called.

Ted, Karen's husband, heard her voice and responded immediately motioning the officers to follow him.

"Karen?" he called back, and then saw her in the doorway of the old house. Ted ran toward her having been worried sick about her safety. Upon reaching her location he took her into his arms, hugged her, and kissed her all over her head.

"Boy am I glad to see you," Karen whispered into his ear.

"Baby, not half as glad as I am to see you. I thought I'd lost you."

"Leslie took care of me. He said my fever broke this morning at about 3:00 a.m."

One of the officers overheard her name her benefactor and questioned her.

"Mrs. Winslow. Whom are you talking about?"

"Leslie, the man who owns this house. He took me in and put me by the fireplace, and even made me tea."

"No one has lived here in over a hundred years."

"But," Karen began to speak. When she turned back around to look for Leslie she discovered no one there. The fireplace that had been blazing just a moment ago was cold. The warmth of a charming home was suddenly shrouded in the dust of a century of idleness. "But, he was here, and there was a fire blazing in the fireplace. He had made me tea and toast," she coughed again.

"Sweetheart, you've had a high fever for several hours. You sound as if you have pneumonia. Let's get you to a doctor."

Ted walked Karen back to his car. Karen didn't have an explanation for what had happened to her. Maybe she did dream it all. Her fever was very high. Although when she turned back around before getting into her husband's car, she thought she spied Leslie peering through the window smiling at her. She smiled back and then got into the car.

Karen did have pneumonia, and the doctor told Ted that it was a miracle that she didn't die in the night. Karen kept insisting that her benefactor, Leslie, had kept watch over her until Ted arrived. Although the doctor dismissed Karen's claims, Ted couldn't help but wonder if she had been in an Angel's keep.

THE BARROW TROLL

David Drake

Playfully, Ulf Womanslayer twitched the cord bound to his saddlehorn. "Awake, priest? Soon you can get to work."

"My work is saving souls, not being dragged into the wilderness by madmen," Johann muttered under his breath. The other end of the cord was around his neck, not that of his horse. A trickle of blood oozed into his cassock from the reopened scab, but he was afraid to loosen the knot. Ulf might look back. Johann had already seen his captor go into a berserk rage. Over the Northerner's right shoulder rode his axe, a heavy hooked blade on a four foot shaft. Ulf had swung it like a willow-wand when three Christian traders in Schleswig had seen the priest and tried to free him. The memory of the last man in three pieces as head and sword arm sprang from his spouting torso was still enough to roil Johann's stomach.

"We'll have a clear night with a moon, priest; a good night for our business." Ulf stretched and laughed aloud, setting a raven on a fir knot to squawking back at him. The berserker was following a ridge line that divided wooded slopes with a spine too thin-soiled to bear trees. The flanking forests still loomed above the riders. In three days, now, Johann had seen no man but his captor, nor even a tendril of smoke from a lone cabin. Even the route they were taking to Parmavale was no mantrack but an accident of nature.

"So lonely," the priest said aloud.

Ulf hunched hugely in his bearskin and replied, "You soft folk in the south, you live too close anyway. Is it your Christ-god, do you think?"

"Hedeby's a city," the German priest protested, his fingers toying with his torn robe, "and my brother trades to Uppsala.. . . But why bring me to this manless waste?"

"Oh, there were men once, so the tale goes," Ulf said. Here in the empty forest he was more willing for conversation than he had been the first few days of their ride north. "Few enough, and long enough ago. But there were farms in Parmavale, and a lordling of sorts who went a-viking against the Irish. But then the troll came and the men went, and there was nothing left to draw others. So they thought."

"You Northerners believe in trolls, so my brother tells me," said the priest.

"Aye, long before the gold I'd heard of the Parma troll," the berserker agreed. "Ox broad and stronger than ten men, shaggy as a denned bear."

"Like you," Johann said, in a voice more normal than caution would have dictated.

Blood fury glared in Ulf's eyes and he gave a savage jerk on the cord. "You'll think me a troll, priestling, if you don't do just as I say. I'll drink your blood hot if you cross me."

Johann, gagging, could not speak nor wished to.

With the miles the sky became a darker blue, the trees a blacker green. Ulf again broke the hoof-pummeled silence, saying, "No, I knew nothing of the gold until Thora told me."

The priest coughed to clear his throat. "Thora is your wife?" he asked.

"Wife? Ho!" Ulf brayed, his raucous laughter ringing like a demon's. "Wife? She was Hallstein's wife, and I killed her with all her house about her! But before that, she told me of the troll's horde, indeed she did. Would you hear that story?"

Johann nodded, his smile fixed. He was learning to recognize death as it bantered under the axehead.

"So," the huge Northerner began. "There was a bonder, Hallstein Kari's son, who followed the king to war but left his wife, that was Thora, behind to manage the stead. The first day I came by and took a sheep from the herdsman. I told him if he misliked it to send his master to me."

"Why did you do that?" the fat priest asked in surprise.

"Why? Because I'm Ulf, because I wanted the sheep. A woman acting a man's part, it's unnatural anyway.

"The next day I went back to Hallstein's stead, and the flocks had already been driven in. I went into the garth around the buildings and called for the master to come out and fetch me a sheep." The berserker's teeth ground audibly as he remembered. Johann saw his knuckles whiten on the axe helve and stiffened in terror.

"Ho!" Ulf shouted, bringing his left hand down on the shield slung at his horse's flank. The copper boss rang like thunder in the clouds. "She came out," Ulf grated, "and her hair was red. 'All our sheep are penned,' says she, 'but you're in good time for the butchering.' And from out the hall came her three brothers and the men of the stead, ten in all. They were in full armor and their swords were in their hands. And they would have slain me, Ulf Otgeir's son, me, at a woman's word. Forced me to run from a woman!"

The berserker was snarling his words to the forest. Johann knew he watched a scene that had been played a score of times with only the trees to witness. The rage of disgrace burned in Ulf like pitch in a pine faggot, and his mind was lost to everything except the past.

"But I came back," he continued, "in the darkness when all feasted within the hall and drank their ale victory. Behind the hall burned a log fire to roast a sheep. I killed the two there, and

I thrust one of the logs half-burnt up under the eaves. Then at the door I waited until those within noticed the heat and Thora looked outside.

" 'Greetings, Thora,' " I said. " 'You would not give me mutton, so I must roast men tonight.' She asked me for speech. I knew she was fey, so I listened to her. And she told me of the Parma lord and the treasure he brought back from Ireland, gold and gems. And she said it was cursed that a troll should guard it, and that I must needs have a mass priest, for the troll could not cross a Christian's fire and I should slay him then."

"Didn't you spare her for that?" Johann quavered, more fearful of silence than he was of misspeaking.

"Spare her? No, nor any of her house," Ulf thundered back. "She might better have asked the flames for mercy, as she knew. The fire was at her hair. I struck her, and never was woman better made for an axe to bite—she cleft like a waxen doll, and I threw the pieces back. Her brothers came then, but one and one and one through the doorway, and I killed each in his turn. No more came. When the roof fell, I left them with the ash for a headstone and went my way to find a mass priest—to find you, priestling." Ulf, restored to good humor by the climax of his own tale, tweaked the lead cord again.

Johann choked onto his horse's neck, nauseated as much by the story as by the noose. At last he said, thick-voiced, "Why do you trust her tale if she knew you would kill her with it or not?"

"She was fey," Ulf chuckled, as if that explained everything. "Who knows what a man will do when his death is upon him? Or a woman," he added more thoughtfully.

They rode on in growing darkness. With no breath of wind to stir them, the trees stood as dead as the rocks underfoot.

"Will you know the place?" the German asked suddenly. "Shouldn't we camp now and go on in the morning?"

"I'll know it," Ulf grunted. "We're not far now—we're going downhill, can't you feel?" He tossed his bare haystack of hair, silvered into a false sheen of age by the moon. He continued, "The Parma lord sacked a dozen churches, so they say, and then one more with more of gold than the twelve besides, but also the curse. And he brought it back with him to Parma, and there it rests in his barrow, the troll guarding it. That I have on Thora's word."

"But she hated you!"

"She was fey."

They were into the trees, and looking to either side Johann could see hill slopes rising away from them. They were in a valley, Parma or another. Scraps of wattle and daub, the remains of a house or a garth fence, thrust up to the right. The firs that had grown through it were generations old. Johann's stubbled tonsure crawled in the night air.

"She said there was a clearing," the berserker muttered, more to himself than his companion. Johann's horse stumbled. The priest clutched the cord reflexively as it tightened. When he looked up at his captor, he saw the huge Northerner fumbling at his shield's fastenings. For the first time that evening, a breeze stirred. It stank of death.

"Others have been here before us," said Ulf needlessly.

A row of skulls, at least a score of them, stared blank-eyed from atop stakes rammed through the spinal openings. To one, dried sinew still held the lower jaw in a ghastly rictus; the others had fallen away into the general scatter of bones whitening the ground. All of them were human or could have been. They were mixed with occasional glimmers of buttons and rust smears. The freshest of the grisly trophies was very old, perhaps decades old. Too old to explain the reek of decay.

Ulf wrapped his left fist around the twin handles of his shield. It was a heavy circle of linden wood, faced with leather. Its rim and central boss were of copper, and rivets of bronze and copper decorated the face in a serpent pattern.

"Good that the moon is full," Ulf said, glancing at the bright orb still tangled in the fir branches. "I fight best in the moonlight. We'll let her rise the rest of the way, I think."

Johann was trembling. He joined his hands about his saddle horn to keep from falling off the horse. He knew Ulf might let him jerk and strangle there, even after dragging him across half the northlands. The humor of the idea might strike him. Johann's rosary, his crucifix—everything he had brought from Germany or purchased in Schleswig save his robe—had been left behind in Hedeby when the berserker awakened him in his bed. Ulf had jerked a noose to near-lethal tautness and whispered that he needed a priest, that this one would do, but that there were others should this one prefer to feed crows. The disinterested blood-lust in Ulf's tone had been more terrifying than the threat itself. Johann had followed in silence to the waiting horses. In despair, he wondered again if a quick death would not have been better than this lingering one that had ridden for weeks a mood away from him.

"It looks like a palisade for a house," the priest said aloud in what he pretended was a normal voice.

"That's right," Ulf replied, giving his axe and exploratory heft that sent shivers of moonlight across the blade. "There was a hall here, a big one. Did it burn, do you think?" His knees sent his roan gelding forward in a shambling walk past the line of skulls. Johann followed of necessity.

"No, rotted away," the berserker said, bending over to study the post holes.

"You said it was deserted a long time," the priest commented. His eyes were fixed straight forward. One of the skulls was level with his waist and close enough to bite him, could it turn on its stake.

"There was time for the house to fall in, the ground is damp," Ulf agreed. "But the stakes, then, have been replaced. Our troll keeps his front fence new, preistling."

Johann swallowed, said nothing.

Ulf gestured briefly. "Come on, you have to get your fire ready. I want it really holy."

"But we don't sacrifice with fires. I don't know how—"

"Then learn!" the berserker snarled with a vicious yank that drew blood and a gasp from the German. "I've seen how you Christ-shouters love to bless things. You'll bless me a fire, that's all. And if anything goes wrong and the troll spare you—I won't, priestling. I'll rive you apart if I have to come off a stake to do it!"

The horses walked slowly forward through brush and soggy rubble that had been a hall. The odor of decay grew stronger. The priest himself tried to ignore it, but his horse began to balk. The second time he was too slow with a heel to its ribs, and the cord nearly decapitated him. "Wait!" he wheezed. "Let me get down."

Ulf looked back at him, flateyed. At last he gave a brief crow-peck nod and swung himself out of the saddle. He looped both sets of reins on a small fir. Then, while Johann dismounted clumsily, he loosed the cord from his saddle and took it in his axe hand The men walked forward without speaking.

"There . . . ," Ulf breathed.

The barrow was only a black-mouthed swell in the ground, its size denied by its lack of features. Such trees as had tried to grow on it had been broken off short over a period of years. Some of the stumps had wasted into crumbling depressions, while from others the wood fibers still twisted raggedly. Only when Johann matched the trees on the other side of the tomb to those beside him did he realize the scale on which the barrow was built: its entrance tunnel would pass a man walking upright, even a man Ulf's height.

"Lay your fire at the tunnel mouth," the berserker said, his voice subdued. "He'll be inside."

"You'll have to let me go—"

"I'll have to nothing!" Ulf was breathing hard. "We'll go closer, you and I, and you'll make a fire of the dead trees from the ground. Yes..."

The Northerner slid forward in a pace that was cat soft and never left the ground a finger's breadth. Strewn about them as if flung idly from the barrow mouth were scraps and gobbets of animals, the source of the fetid reek that filled the clearing. As his captor paused for a moment, Johann toed one of the bits over with his sandal. It was the hide and paws of something chisel-toothed, whether rabbit or other was impossible to say in the moonlight and state of decay. The skin was in tendrils, and the skull had been opened to empty the brains. Most of the other bits seemed of the same sort, little beasts, although a rank blotch on the mound's slope could have been a wolf hide. Whatever killed and feasted here was not fastidious.

"He stays close to hunt," Ulf rumbled. Then he added, "The long bones by the fence; they were cracked."

"Umm?"

"For marrow."

Quivering, the priest began gathering broken-off trees, none of them over a few feet high. They had been twisted off near the ground, save for a few whose roots lay bare in wizened fists. The crisp scales cut Johann's hands. He did not mind the pain. Under his breath he was praying that God would punish him, would torture him, but at least would save him free of this horrid demon that had snatched him away.

"Pile it there," Ulf directed, his axe head nodding toward the stone lip of the barrow. The entrance was corbelled out of heavy stones, then covered over with dirt and sods. Like the beast fragments around it, the opening was dead and stinking. Biting his tongue, Johann dumped his pile of brush and scurried back. "There's light back down there," he whispered.

"Fire?"

"No, look—it's pale, it's moonlight. There's a hole in the roof of the tomb."

"Light for me to kill by," Ulf said with a stark grin. He looked over the low fireset, then knelt. His steel sparked into a nest of dry moss. When the tinder was properly alight, he touched a pitchy faggot to it. He dropped his end of the cord. The torchlight glinted from his face, white and coarse-pored where the tangles of hair and beard did not cover it. "Bless the fire, mass-priest," the berserker ordered in a quiet, terrible voice.

Stiff-featured and unblinking, Johann crossed the brushwood and said, "In nomine Patris, et Filii, et Spiritus Sancti, Amen."

Don't light it yet," Ulf said. He handed Johann the torch. "It may be," the berserker added, "that you think to run if you get the chance. There is no Hell so deep that I will not come for you from it."

The priest nodded, white-lipped.

Ulf shrugged his shoulders to loosen his, muscles and the bear hide that clothed them. Axe and shield rose and dipped like ships in a high sea.

"Ho! Troll! Barrow fouler! Corpse licker! Come and fight me, troll!"

There was no sound from the tomb.

Ulf's eyes began to glaze. He slashed his axe twice across the empty air and shouted again, "Troll! I'll spit on your corpse, I'll lay with your dog mother. Come and fight me, troll, or I'll wall you up like a rat with your filth!"

Johann stood frozen, oblivious even to the drop of pitch that sizzled on the web of his hand. The berserker bellowed again, wordlessly, gnashing at the rim of his shield so that the sound bubbled and boomed in the night.

And the tomb roared back to the challenge, a thunderous BAR BAR BAR even deeper than Ulf's.

Berserk, the Northerner leaped the brush pile and ran down the tunnel, his axe thrust out in front of him to clear the stone arches.

The tunnel sloped for a dozen paces into a timber-vaulted chamber too broad to leap across. Moonlight spilled through a circular opening onto flags slimy with damp and liquescence. Ulf, maddened, chopped high at the light. The axe burred inanely beneath the timbers.

Swinging a pair of swords, the troll leaped at Ulf. It was the size of a bear, grizzled in the moonlight. Its eyes burned red.

"Hi!" shouted Ulf and blocked the first sword in a shower of sparks on his axehead. The second blade bit into the shield rim, shaving a hand's length of copper and a curl of yellow linden from beneath it. Ulf thrust straight-armed, a blow that would have smashed like a battering ram had the troll not darted back. Both the combatants were shouting; their voices were dreadful in the circular chamber.

The troll jumped backward again. Ulf sprang toward him and only the song of the blades scissoring from either side warned him. The berserker threw himself down. The troll had leaped onto a rotting chest along the wall of the tomb and cut unexpectedly from above Ulf's shield. The big man's boots flew out from under him and he struck the floor on his back. His shield still covered his body.

The troll hurtled down splay-legged with a cry of triumph. Both bare feet slammed on Ulf's shield. The troll was even heavier than Ulf. Shrieking, the berserker pistoned his shield arm upward.

The monster flew off, smashing against the timbered ceiling and caroming down into another of the chests. The rotted wood exploded under the weight in a flash of shimmering gold. The berserker rolled to his feet and struck over-arm in the same motion. His lunge carried the axehead too far, into the rock wall in a flower of blue sparks.

The troll was up. The two killers eyed each other, edging sideways in the dimness. Ulf's right arm was numb to the shoulder. He did not realize it. The shaggy monster leaped with another double flashing and the axe moved too slowly to counter. Both edges spat chunks of linden as they withdrew. Ulf frowned, backed a step. His boot trod on an ewer that spun away from him. As he cried out, the troll grinned and hacked again like Death the Reaper. The shield-orb flattened as the top third of it split away. Ulf snarled and chopped at the troll's knees. It leaped above the steel and cut left-handed, its blade nocking the shaft an inch from Ulf's hand.

The berserker flung the useless remainder of his shield in the troll's face and ran. Johann's torch was an orange pulse in the triangular opening. Behind Ulf a swordedge went *sring*! as it danced on the corbels. Ulf jumped the brush and whirled. "Now!" he cried to the priest, and Johann hurled his torch into the resin-jeweled wood.

The needles crackled up in the troll's face like a net of orange silk. The flames bellied out at the creature's rush but licked back caressingly over its mats of hair. The troll's swords cut at the fire. A shower of coals spit and crackled and made the beast howl.

"Burn, dog-spew!" Ulf shouted. "Burn, fish-guts!"

The troll's blades rang together, once and again. For a moment it stood, a hillock of stained gray, as broad as the tunnel arches. Then it strode forward into the white heart of the blaze. The fire bloomed up, its roar leaping over the troll's shriek of agony. Ulf stepped forward. He held his axe with both hands. The flames sucked down from the motionless troll, and as they did the shimmering arc of the axehead chopped into the beast's collarbone. One sword dropped and the left arm slumped loose.

The berserker's axe was buried to the helve in the troll's shoulder. The faggots were scattered, but the troll's hair was burning all over its body. Ulf pulled at his axe. The troll staggered, moaning. Its remaining sword pointed down at the ground. Ulf yanked againat his weapon and it slurped free. A thick velvet curtain of blood followed it. Ulf raised his dripping axe for another blow, but the troll tilted toward the withdrawn weapon, leaning forward, a smouldering rock. The body hit the ground, then flopped so that it lay on its back. The right arm was flung out an angle.

"It was a man," Johann was whispering. He caught up a brand and held it close to the troll's face. "Look, look!" he demanded excitedly, "It's just an old man in bearskin. Just a man."

Ulf sagged over his axe as if it were a stake impaling him. His frame shuddered as he dragged air into it. Neither of the troll's swords had touched him, but reaction had left him weak as one death-wounded. "Go in," he wheezed. "Get a torch and lead me in."

"But…why—" the priest said in sudden fear. His eyes met the berserker's and he swallowed back the rest of his protest. The torch threw highlights on the walls and flags as he trotted down the tunnel. Ulf's boots were ominous behind him.

The central chamber was austerely simple and furnished only with the six chests lining the back of it. There was no corpse, nor even a slab for one. The floor was gelatinous with decades' accumulation of foulness. The skidding tracks left by the recent combat marked paving long undisturbed. Only from the entrance to the chests was a path, back against the slime of decay, worn. It was upon the broken container and the objects which had spilled from it that the priest's eyes focussed.

"Gold," he murmured. Then, "Gold! There must—the others—in God's name, there are five more and perhaps all of them—"

"Gold," Ulf grated terribly.

Johann ran to the nearest chest and opened it one-handed. The lid sagged wetly, but frequent use had kept it from swelling tight to the side panels. "Look at this crucifix!" the priest marveled. "And the torque, it must weight pounds. And Lord in heaven, this—"

"Gold," the berserker repeated.

Johann saw the axe as it started to swing. He was turning with a chalice ornamented in enamel and pink gold. It hung in the air as he darted for safety. His scream and the dull belling of the cup as the axe divided it were simultaneous, but the priest was clear and Ulf was off balance. The berserker backhanded with force enough to drive the peen of his axehead through a sapling. His strength was too great for his footing. His feet skidded, and this time his head rang on the wall of the tomb.

Groggy, the huge berserker staggered upright. The priest was a scurrying blur against the tunnel entrance. "Priest!" Ulf shouted at the suddenly empty moonlight. He thudded up the flags of the tunnel. "Priest!" he shouted again.

The clearing was empty except for the corpse. Nearby, Ulf heard his roan whicker. He started for it, then paused. The priest—he could still be hiding in the darkness. While Ulf searched for him, he could be rifling the barrow, carrying off the gold behind his back. "Gold," Ulf said again. No one must take his gold. No one ever must find it unguarded.

"I'll kill you!" he screamed into the night. "I'll kill you all!"

He turned back to his barrow. At the entrance, still smoking, waited the body of what had been the troll.

I Look Forward to Remembering You

Mur Lafferty

The time whore - time escort, he'd insisted - stood in front of Susan Apple while she surveyed his virtues and flaws. She studied the ridges of his abdominals and the curve of his buttocks. He was thin and wiry, with tight muscles creating a compact frame devoid of any unnecessary bulk. The young man looked to be about twenty, with firm, pale skin. Susan looked him over for a good five minutes, instructed him to turn a couple of times, and finally to remove his boxer shorts.

She smiled at last and gave a satisfied little sigh. He was just as she'd ordered. Without raising her eyes to his face, she asked, "So when do we begin?"

"We just have some paperwork to go over," he said. He bent over to pick up his bathrobe and Susan stared as his muscles flexed. Kevin slipped the robe on with the slow grace of someone who was unashamed of his nakedness. "Once we take care of that, I'll go back to headquarters and take my trip back to 1992, find your younger self, and seduce her."

"Excellent, Kevin," she said. She imagined saying his name after a night of sweaty sex, and it felt wrong. "Kevin. That won't work for me. I'd rather have you be Paul," she said.

He nodded. "I'll introduce myself to you as Paul, then." He paused. "As long as there is no one in your past called Paul. That may cause confusion for your younger self."

She kept her face straight. "No one."

Kevin picked up his briefcase that he'd left by the door with his folded khakis and sweater. "We need to go over the paperwork before you sign, Ms. Apple." He walked to Susan's heavy oak dining room table and pulled a chair out for her.

Susan gripped the sides of her chair and pulled herself to her feet. Her bad knee, injured twenty years ago in China, wobbled and threatened to give out. She hissed and it seemed to rethink its direction. She silently cursed her vanity that caused her to leave her cane in the other room. He was a whore; she didn't need to impress him. And anyway, she wouldn't be sleeping with him in her current state. She shuffled over to the table and took the proffered chair with a smile of thanks. Up close, he smelled of musk.

Kevin looked quite businesslike and official in his bathrobe (complete with the monogrammed logo "TEI"—for "Time Escorts, Inc."). He put his briefcase on the table and leaned over her shoulder. His scent was more pervasive, and heat drifted off his skin as he slid a paper in front of her, brushing her arm. Susan swallowed.

"I have been sterilized by both a vasectomy and a Nano Vas. I am tested for disease after every mission - you can see the documentation here." He pointed at the lines on the paper, which repeated his statements in more businesslike terms. She initialed the bottom of the page.

"Here our are guarantees," he said, whisking the paper away and producing another one. "They protect you from time paradox, possible mental anguish, and a full money-back and experience-deleting guarantee."

"That was what made me finally decide to do this," Susan admitted. She felt heat rise to her wrinkled cheeks for the first time that day.

Kevin smiled, and she felt hotter. "That's what most of our clients say. We offer the best guarantee in the business. If you experience mental anguish, disease, family grief, physical harm or death due to this service, the experience will be erased and your money returned to you," he said.

Susan stared at the legal jargon on the page and couldn't make heads or tails of it.

"By signing this, however, you do acknowledge that there may be unavoidable changes to your current way of life," Kevin continued. "While we do cover drastic changes in the life path, we do not cover minor ones. You could wake up tomorrow morning wearing a different color of nightgown or be close friends with someone you currently hate. You will remember both paths of your lives, although the previous path—your current path, that is—will fade over time."

Susan put up her hand. "Wait just a minute. Are you saying that I could wake up tomorrow a different person?"

Kevin put a diagram in front of her. "Everything we do in life affects everything else. Your cat knocks your keys off the table and you take five minutes to find them. You leave later than you'd intended, and are not there when a bus driver loses control and kills three pedestrians. That tiny detail saved your life and you didn't even know it. We do everything in our power - with your help - to schedule the sexual encounter during a time in your life when it will affect the fewest number of outside events, but we cannot guarantee small changes won't happen. Not to mention how losing your virginity at 19 will change your life and make you take a different path than you are currently on."

Susan made a face. This wasn't sounding as good as before. "What if I don't like the changes? Can I erase the encounter then?"

"Of course," the escort said, smiling a charming grin. One of his front teeth was crooked. Susan felt a thrill of both excitement and anxiety; this guy was good. He knew his stuff. "We can modify the time continuum a second time if you are not satisfied with the outcome. These modifications do come with an additional fee, however." He handed her a rate card.

Susan's eyes widened. She could have the encounter, then have it erased for double. That was unexpected. She looked into the fireplace across the room and her eyes drifted to the mantle. Pictures of her aiding children in Africa, meeting the UN Secretary to receive a humanitarian award, going walkabout in Australia, hiking in the Rockies. She was alone or with friends, never with a lover. She'd experienced nearly everything in life. Nearly.

"Fine. Where do I sign?"

—·—

Kevin had promised to leave for 1992 that night at six o'clock. Susan had an early dinner of soup and soft bread - she could no longer chew the crunchy loaves she'd loved in her youth - and settled in front of the fire with a glass of wine. The memories should start flowing in around six-thirty, and by tomorrow morning she would remember everything about her sexual encounter with the handsome Paul that she had when she was nineteen. Plus anything that had changed due to the encounter.

She sipped the wine and leaned back. Images, memories and smells began flowing to her, feeling recent as her mind processed the new memories. A bad day in college. She had been dumped by Bruce, her boyfriend who was turned off by her intelligence and her social awkwardness. He had been a bad kisser, she had told herself, crying as she walked across campus to her dorm. Then she had met a kind man, someone named Paul, who showed his concern for her by slowly and deliciously initiating her in the glories of the flesh.

———•———

Kevin thought that the young Susan wasn't that bad looking. He sat on the steps of the Foreign Languages building and waited for her to get closer. She held herself awkwardly, hunching over and hiding her form. She hadn't yet achieved the sharp intelligent confidence that the elderly Susan had; her intelligence was a hindrance to her, something that made others dislike and mistrust her. He had read Susan's account of her college years thoroughly and had run her journals through their personality computer. He knew just how to approach the young woman to begin the encounter.

His employers had developed the personality matrix software. Even if people wanted to change their past to include more and better sexual encounters, their selves in the past wouldn't know what was coming. The encounter could fail at a costly loss for the company - traveling through time was not cheap, and they couldn't afford many refunds - or could even be construed as harassment or rape. Kevin did not know of any circumstances where this had happened, but the trainers at Time Escorts heavily emphasized the psychology of seduction to fit the person.

She was crying, just as he'd expected. He took a deep breath - the first meeting was the hardest - and fell into step beside her as she scuttled past. He was so intent on catching up with her naturally that he didn't see the woman coming the other way. They brushed shoulders and she stumbled. Kevin excused himself quickly and fell into stop beside the sobbing woman.

"Hey, are you OK?" he asked, putting concern into his voice.

She sniffled and looked up at him. "What? Oh, I'm fine, yes, thank you. Yes."

He smiled and saw her mouth hang open a moment. "You don't look fine to me. Fine people don't take a stroll on campus while crying their eyes out. What happened?"

Her lower lip trembled and more tears spilled over her cheeks as she looked away.

"Is it a guy?" he asked. She nodded.

"Do you want to get some coffee and talk about it? I'm a good listener," he said. "My treat."

She looked at him for a moment, and he saw her calculating the safety involved. *This is it.* "Do I know you?" she asked.

"I've seen you in my Econ 10 class. I usually sit in the back," he said. He'd looked for the biggest class on her schedule, the easiest to get lost in. Most freshmen took that class. "I'm Paul." He extended his hand.

She took it, and he let his fingers trace across her palm lightly after they had shaken hands. "Erica," she said.

———•———

Asshole, fucker, shitface, bastard, um, asshole. Susan ran through all of the swear words she knew, and when she was done, she repeated them. So she wasn't social enough, was she? She wasn't pretty enough, studied too much, partied too little, and wouldn't let him touch her *there*.

"Maybe I wouldn't let you touch me there because you kiss so poorly that I'm afraid what you might do elsewhere!" she'd screamed at him before leaving. At least she'd gotten the last word in.

She'd stopped by her Japanese TA's office to check her mid-term grade and then got plowed into by some shmoe who said, "Sorry!" before running after some girl.

Yeah, always they're chasing someone else. Fuckers. All of them. She rubbed her shoulder and decided to go back to her dorm by way of the Student Union. Walking her usual way would have her following the jerk and his girlfriend, and she really didn't feel like putting someone else's problems on her shoulders. It was her night to feel sorry for herself, dammit, and she was going to treat herself to a donut or three.

She trudged to the Union, purchased her donut, and went to the TV lounge to see what was on the big screen. She stayed near the back, hoping no one would notice her blotchy face and her tear-streaked eyes.

"Susan?" the voice said from behind her.

She gasped, sucked in a bit of donut, and went into a coughing fit. A hand thumped her on the back and she was free of the offending pastry. She wheezed a bit and straightened up.

"Oh man, I'm sorry, didn't mean to startle you!" It was Paul, her lab partner in geology. She avoided his blue eyes, as always, and looked directly at his slightly crooked teeth.

"That's OK, I just didn't hear you come up," she said, trying to regain her composure. Aware of her swollen eyes and crumby mouth, she passed a hand down her face. Unfortunately, the hand had more sugar from the donut and she just succeeded in getting more stuff on her face.

"Are you OK? You look, ah, upset," he said.

"Oh, yeah, just had a bad night. Thanks. Just, stuff. You know," she gestured vaguely with her donut then dropped it in a wastebasket. She turned and grabbed for some napkins from the condiment table.

Nonchalantly cleaning her hands and face, she attempted a smile at him. He still stared at her. "So, uh, what are you up to tonight?" she asked.

"I was supposed to meet the anime club in a basement room, but no one showed, now I'm stuck with a bunch of tapes and some AV equipment. I just came up here to grab a Coke before having my own private viewing," he said, waving the bottle of Coke at her.

"Do you like anime?" he asked.

"Well, I've never seen any," she said, hoping he couldn't hear her thundering heart. "But I'm an International Studies major and hope to study in Japan in a couple of semesters."

"Then you should watch some!" he said. "Come on!" He walked off towards the stairs without looking behind him.

Men. Always expecting you to do what they say. She tried to think this with acidity, but it felt hollow. She'd nursed a crush on Paul all semester, but squashed it because of her relationship with Bruce. And hell, she knew she wasn't a catch.

She followed.

———•———

Kevin's voice caught in his throat. This wasn't Susan, and he didn't know where she was. If he had missed her, he had no idea where she would end up. He'd have to try her dorm.

But there was the problem of this girl. She looked up at him with wet brown eyes, taking in the natural charm he had inadvertently oozed at her. *Shit, I'm so going to lose my job for this.*

He checked his watch and gasped. "Oh, crap, I'm sorry Erica, I forgot I'm late for a study group. I'm so sorry to leave you like this. Can we get that coffee in an hour? I'll meet you at the Daily Grind—I'll buy you the biggest double chocolate mocha you can drink."

She bought it. "All right, thanks Paul. I really need someone to talk to now."

Kevin dashed off towards Susan's dorm, pulling a map from his pocket.

———•———

Two episodes of Ranma 1/2 and Susan was hooked. Paul had insisted on watching in Japanese with subtitles, and she told him where the translation differed from what the characters really said. They sat next to each other on folding chairs and every once in a while their knees touched.

While changing tapes, Paul looked at her. "So why were you crying? Really."

"I just got dumped," she said, looking at the floor.

"Aw shit, I'm sorry. You were with that guy for, what, four months?"

"Yes, how did you know?" she looked up at him.

"Well," Paul focused his attention on the VCR. "I was going to ask you out, but you came to lab all excited about this new guy you were dating. So it kinda stuck in my mind."

"Oh."

"So what happened between you guys?" he hit a button and returned to his seat.

"I am not enough of a party girl for him. Not pretty enough, not fun enough, not, you know, physical enough." She fiddled with the zipper on her jacket. Her ears were hot.

"Oh, so you were a smart girl who wouldn't put out, right?" His voice was mocking.

"What's wrong with that?" she asked.

"Nothing at all. Just that he was a retard who didn't see what he had.

"Check this out, there's a new character in this one." He pointed to the TV. "A guy who always gets lost."

The opening credits came on, the chirpy Japanese theme song circling the confusion and excitement somewhere in Susan's middle.

Susan didn't answer the phone at her dorm, and no one would let Kevin through the locked doors to get up to her room without an escort. Had elderly Susan said something about sexual assaults going up that year? He couldn't get his focus.

Where else? Susan was smart. Libraries. She was upset. Coffee shops or Student Union. She was heartbroken. Boyfriend's dorm? He had no idea. It was obvious his appearance had already changed something in the timeline; Susan was supposed to go from her boyfriend's dorm to her dorm, where she lived in a single room. Kevin was going to seduce her there with no interruptions. It was supposed to have been easy. Find the girl, console the girl, fuck the girl, get out. Easy money. He'd never messed up like this.

With hope, he could still catch her. He checked his map again and went off at a run towards the library.

———•———

Halfway through the second tape, Paul took Susan's hand. She didn't withdraw it, even though his palm was hot and sweaty. After putting in the third tape, Paul closed the door to the room and returned to sit with her.

"So is it too soon to ask you out?" he asked. His face was red. "I mean, it's not soon to me. I've been waiting for months. But soon after your breakup, I mean."

She surprised herself by kissing him. He surprised her by sliding his arms around her middle and holding her tightly. His lips were soft and electrifying, nothing wet or insistent or Bruce-like about them.

More surprising things happened, all of them quite good. The most surprising thing was that she initiated most of them. He let her lead, and she ended up on top of him, watching the animated heroine lose her ponytail during a battle scene.

———•———

Kevin had no idea what to do if he found her. Losing his seductive nature in his frantic search, he interrupted several people in the library looking for her. Inside the Student Union, he searched the top two floors and paused to rest on the way to the basement.

What was he qualified to do if he lost this job? He had been trained in avoiding paradoxes, extreme time management, all the levels of seduction. Perhaps they would put him on a desk job. Less exciting, but at least he could still eat. Maybe he could find a wealthy older woman who wanted a boy toy. Heck, Susan had seemed to like his looks. The thought repulsed him.

He got up, determined to finish the job, and descended the stairs. Susan now, so he wouldn't have to do Susan later.

———•———

They were experimenting again, this time letting Paul take a turn on top, when the door opened. Susan gasped. Paul swore and rolled off her. The lights were off, so there was only a silhouette of a man in the hallway.

"Whoops," the man said. "Um, Susan?"

Fuck. "Yeah, what?" she said.

"Hey, it's Paul, you know, from… Econ 10… I needed, uh, to borrow some notes. But, crap, never mind. Sorry." The door closed.

"Who the hell?" asked Paul.

"I have no idea." she said.

"Well. This isn't the most private place, now, is it?" he said, the still-running anime lighting up his wicked grin.

She returned his smile. "I have a single room. It has a door that locks."

———•———

Kevin trudged out of the Student Union, head hanging. He could find no way to fix this now. He couldn't sneak back to the home office and use the machine without his superiors' knowledge. The time travel machine was a complicated device that required seven people to operate, and there was no unofficial company business to be conducted with it. He was fired for sure. Unless Susan didn't like the way this turned out … but she had seemed pretty damn happy when he'd walked in on them.

Not paying attention to his direction, he heard someone yell, "Paul!" It took him a moment before Kevin remembered to turn. *Susan?*

He'd passed right in front of the outside coffee bar. Erica sat at a table, waving at him. He studied her for a moment, then checked his watch. One hour until the device would call him home. He had time to kill. Might as well enjoy his job while he still had it.

————•————

It was seven-thirty when Susan gasped, realizing that the memories that were flooding her mind had nothing to do with Kevin. Had she even met him? She had requested someone who had looked like Paul, someone who took the name Paul, without ever remembering her old college crush. Tears sprang to her eyes as her new past wove itself in her mind's eye. Paul. Their time together in college. Their letters when she traveled the world, studying other cultures and eventually getting work as a diplomat.

She stood uncertainly - was her knee stronger? She couldn't tell. The pictures on her mantle were fading and changing. The picture of her shaking hands with Chen Chua Xing, the UN Secretary, morphed into a picture of her and an older Paul in front of a temple in China. She smiled. He had studied kung fu during the months that she served at the American embassy. The picture of her hiking in the Rockies didn't change at all, but she remembered that Paul had taken it. Instead of aiding children in Africa, she was passing out food crates to earthquake survivors in southeast Asia. And there was no walkabout picture at all; there was a statue of an open hand; an award for humanitarian aid that she and Paul had won.

She smiled, tears streaming down her face. Her life was unchanged, only enriched by the man she'd chosen to spend it with. This was better than anything she could have expected. It took up to twelve hours for the current timeline to catch up to the restructured past, so she went to bed, looking forward to waking up beside her husband.

The memories hit her before she even opened her eyes the next morning, causing her to cry out. The hostage situation ten years ago. Paul had been planning on leaving Indonesia with the other aid workers - she had been in Australia on the walkabout she'd always wanted to experience - when the terrorists had grabbed him and twelve others. He'd been the first beheaded when the Australians hadn't complied with the demands.

She wept, the pain that had dimmed in the past ten years suddenly new and fresh. She cried and screamed into her pillow until she fell into an exhausted sleep.

She spent the afternoon flipping through photo albums and going through her house to find remnants of him. He had been a spearhead of humanitarian Internet news radio, and she discovered multiple CD's of his programs. She listened to several, laughing at the inside jokes he inserted for her.

That night, there was a knock at her door. Sniffling, she shuffled to the door and opened it.

Damn, but Kevin looked like Paul. She wondered if she had chosen him because of this, but couldn't remember. He glanced at her face and looked down at the floor. "Can I come in?"

She held the door open.

"This was all my fault. I … missed you and found another girl who looked like you, who was also crying. And I guess I caused you to find that guy. You aren't going to die a virgin like you feared, but this was not what you paid for. My company is here to offer you a money-back guarantee and an experience erase, free of charge." He looked as if he were going to cry.

"You were the guy who bumped into me before I went to the Union," she said, her eyes widening. "I was going to go back to my dorm before you ran into me."

He nodded. "I am so sorry. It looks like I really screwed up."

She looked at the crumpled, moist tissue in her hand. Remembering what it was for, she dabbed her eyes again. "We got married after college. Traveled the world together. He died ten years ago."

Kevin stared at her, stricken. "We can fix all of this. Really. For free."

Susan looked at the apartment that still seemed new to her, a world of a man she never got a chance to experience. She focused on the throb within her chest, the ache that she remembered took two years to heal and still flared up on holidays and whenever she saw old anime. All she had wanted was not to die a virgin. She hadn't asked for this.

She went to an open photo album that focused on their work with inner city children. Paul was hugging one of the many children they had sponsored, a girl who had shown a gift for languages and they'd padded her few scholarships so she could follow in Susan's footsteps in International Studies. She pointed to the photo.

"What do you think will happen to her if Paul disappears from her life? Gunned down in a drive-by? Raped? Under appreciated in a minimum-wage job? There's no way of telling." She stared at the girl who grinned widely in the picture. Tasha still visited during some holidays, like most of the children they had helped out of bad situations. Having no children of their own, they had loved all they could of those who needed it.

"I can't do it," she said quietly. "I can't remove him from their lives. I can't remove him from mine." She looked at Kevin's face. He was pale. "Are you going to get in trouble for this?"

"I - they didn't say. I had to come here and offer a refund and fix. Then, I don't know," he admitted. "I'm still so sorry."

"Don't be," she said. "It was a good life. Not what I expected, but then life never is, is it? I'm surprised this doesn't happen more often. Butterfly wings causing hurricanes and all that. If you'd like, I will contact your employers and give you a recommendation. What I had with Paul was more fulfilling than a one-night-stand ever could have been."

Kevin sighed, visibly relieved. "I can't tell you what that means to me. Thanks a lot. Is there anything I can do personally to make it up to you?"

Susan motioned for him to follow her to the kitchen. She took two beers from the fridge and handed one to him. "I am curious.

My college friend Erica told me that she, too, slept with a dark-haired, blue-eyed Paul the same night I did. We joked that we were Eskimo sisters, that my Paul had somehow made it into her bed after mine. But now I wonder…"

Kevin smiled at last. "Mrs. Apple, I never give private information about my clients."

Isabelle's Prince

Elizabeth Blue

Alma stood at the bay window in the living room looking out into the black night. She wrung her hands, massaged her arthritic knuckles as best she could, wishing she could, for once, will the pain away. She didn't need the distraction right then. Isabelle, her sister, had disappeared, and Alma dreaded something terrible had happened.

Isabelle had gone outside for a smoke. She had taken up the filthy habit on her eightieth birthday saying she had made it far enough in life to do whatever she pleased, and if the tobacco killed her, then at least she would die having had at least one vice. Alma didn't want the smell of smoke or the vile butts in the house they had shared since childhood, so she had insisted Isabelle smoke outside.

She was afraid Isabelle's vice had finally done her in, albeit indirectly.

She had been gone for thirty minutes. Alma called out to her from the upstairs window but gotten no answer. She hadn't wanted to open the front door and accidentally let in a billow of choking smoke along with a blast of arctic air. Opening the front bedroom window a couple of inches was bad enough.

Isabelle had been acting odd the past couple of weeks. Alma wondered at first if her sister had Alzheimer's, but she knew that couldn't be the case—she had her wits, and she wasn't forgetful in the least. She had simply taken up some strange new habits and had been saying weird things.

She had been talking about her prince, her knight in shining armor, who would be coming for her. Talking about how she had, after eighty years of life, finally figured out how to snare a man. She spent long hours in her bedroom writing in a journal rather than sitting in the parlor with Alma drinking tea and eating scones like they had done most afternoons. She spent a lot of time gazing out of the windows as if searching for something, probably her imaginary prince, Alma thought.

"Oh, he's quite handsome," Isabelle had said when Alma asked about him. "But he's got his ugly side, too."

"Whatever do you want with him, then?" Alma had asked, not understanding why Isabelle even felt the need for a man after all these years.

"Because he can make all my dreams come true." Isabelle had giggled and blushed like a teenager.

"Well, what about his ugly side?"

Isabelle's smile had faded, and she'd looked away from Alma, giving Alma the impression that whatever this man's secret was, she was ashamed of it. Or afraid.

She had leaned forward in her seat and whispered to Alma, "He has a dark side, I suppose you could say."

"Do you mean he's a criminal?" Alma had asked.

Isabelle had laughed. "Oh, no. Nothing like that. It's just that— he isn't exactly what one would call human."

"Oh, for pete's sake, Isabelle. You're talking nonsense."

"I most certainly am not. You'll see when he arrives."

Alma had forgotten all about her sister's silly, imaginative story until she hadn't come back in after having her cigarette. Usually it took her only ten minutes. Less time when it was cold out, and it certainly was that. A cold front had moved in the night before, making Alma's arthritis act up ferociously.

When no answer came in response to her calls, Alma worried. Could the man Isabelle had spoken of be real? Could some "prince" have come and whisked her away just as Isabelle imagined he would?

No, she told herself. Isabelle had simply been engaging herself in a fantasy. God only knew why, but she had. Besides, Isabelle had said he wasn't human, and that was simply not possible.

When ten more minutes passed with no sign of her sister, Alma realized she had no choice but to go outside and look for her. Something could have happened to her.

She put on her coat and buttoned it to her neck, pulled on a pair of gloves and her hat. Then she stepped outside into the biting cold.

The wind stung her face, and she wished she had one of those stocking caps bank robbers wore —the kind that covered the entire face with openings only for the mouth and nose. She cupped her gloved hands around her mouth and called her sister's name.

Her voice sounded muffled to her, like the air froze the sound before it could travel far.

Isabelle will never hear me, she thought. *Why on earth did she wander off?*

She decided to check the old chicken coop. They hadn't kept animals on their property in two decades, but the chicken coop still stood in the back yard. Perhaps Isabelle had gone there to smoke and stay out of the cold. Alma saw the old wooden structure loom into view when she opened the back gate.

"Isabelle!" she called.

The wind whipped her words away and carried them off to who knew where. She limped toward the coop, the arthritis taking control of her hips and knees now, too. The frozen ground crunched beneath her feet. She saw her breath plume out in front of her, obscuring her view.

"Isabelle! This isn't one bit funny!"

She reached the chicken coop and jerked open the door.

The small building was empty.

Goosebumps crawled over her arms and legs, and a chill crept up her spine. The icy wind gnawed at her face as she whirled around, suddenly feeling eyes upon her.

"Isabelle? Where are you? What sort of game are you playing with me?"

Alma looked left, then right, seeing no one.

"Isabelle! Why are you hiding from me? Have you lost your mind?"

No one answered.

"Well, I haven't. I'm going back inside. I don't have time for this foolishness. If you know what's good for you, you'll come back in, too."

Alma's fear for her sister's safety gave way to anger. She couldn't imagine what Isabelle was up to, but she refused to play along with such nonsense.

"Let the old bat freeze out here, then," she said under her breath as she stomped off toward the house despite the pain in both her legs. "And don't I feel like a fool for falling into her silly, childish trap. Ha!"

As she neared the gate again something caught her eye among the crabapple trees in the side yard. She stopped. A hard gust of wind made the bare limbs of the trees flap around like bony arms. She stared hard into the shadows, seeing nothing at first, then realizing she was looking at a face.

Isabelle's face.

Alma gasped.

The rest of Isabelle's body lay on the ground. Her head had been propped up in the crook of a tree limb.

Alma screamed. Isabelle's eyes stared blankly at her, and Alma saw that her mouth had frozen in the shape of an O, as if she, too, had been screaming, her voice cut short by whoever had done this to her. Alma stepped backward, unable to tear her eyes from the sight of her sister's face. Somehow that was easier than looking at her body.

The feeling of being watched crept up on her again, and she knew she must run, get back to the safety of the house. Something, a monster, a demon, something, had attacked Isabelle, and Alma knew it would get her next. She forced herself to turn away, willed her old, achy legs to move, run—something she had not asked of them in many years.

As she turned, she felt hands on her shoulders. Fingers dug into her flesh, squeezed her bones so hard she cried out. Then she screamed. A man stood before her. Isabelle's "prince", she knew at that moment. But he was not a prince at all. Not even a man. His red eyes blazed with hatred, and she could almost feel their heat on her face.

Oh, God, help me, she thought. *He's real.*

He opened his mouth, which looked like that of an animal—a cow or bull—and bared two rows of sharp teeth. Alma smelled his rotten breath. He roared at her, and the sound was so deafening Alma thought her eardrums might burst.

She heard her own shrill screams as he pulled her close to him. She shoved him hard in the chest. The effort sent sharp jabs of pain through both of her hands and into her forearms. She spit in his face, and saw his skin bubble where her saliva landed.

He grabbed her by the neck and lifted her off the ground. His tight grip around her throat made it impossible to scream, but she thrashed her arms and legs, feeling energy she hadn't had in years course through her. He carried her into the crabapple trees, unfazed by her blows. He snorted and tossed her to the ground. She hit the frozen dirt on her back. The impact knocked the breath out of her. She struggled to suck in air as the monster stood over her.

Alma noticed he had thrown her beside her sister's body. She had no doubt he would do the same thing to her that he had done to Isabelle. She pulled her feet underneath her and fought to stand up. Ignoring the pain and the numbness that was beginning to seep into her extremities, she scrambled up. The creature shrieked, and she realized she had taken him by surprise. He hadn't expected her to try to escape.

Get away, she told herself. *Run.*

She dodged his arm just as he reached out, her own agility amazing her. She ran, adrenaline pumping through her veins. She headed back for the chicken coop; it was closer than the house. She didn't know what shelter the building would provide, but she hoped it would buy her at least a few more minutes. Perhaps she would pass out from the exertion and he would kill her while she was unconscious. She prayed Isabelle had not suffered, that she had not been conscious when he had killed her.

Oh, Isabelle, she thought. As she ran across the yard, a pang of sadness hit her, but the knowledge that the creature was only seconds from grabbing her again overcame her grief.

The door to the chicken coop stood open, and the wind banged it against the wall. She expected the beast to jerk her back at any moment, but didn't dare look over her shoulder for fear she would lose her balance and fall.

Still free of him, she reached the open door and ran inside. When she turned to grab the handle, she was afraid he would be there, but she saw only darkness. She pulled the door shut then slammed the latch into place.

Her whole body shook with cold and fear. She dropped to the floor and crawled into the far corner of the chicken coop. That thing would be coming for her any minute. The best she could do was hide and pray it couldn't get in and find her.

A moment later, the chicken coop rocked as the creature slammed into the side wall. Alma heard wood splinter. She squeezed her eyes shut. Tears leaked out and ran down her cheeks. She slapped a hand over her mouth to muffle a cry as another crash shook the coop. The wall buckled and wood slats broke free.

Oh, what do I do? God, help me, how do I get away from this thing? she thought.

She saw his muzzle poke through the hole. She couldn't tell if he saw her or not. Surely he would catch her scent and know where she was. She tried to make herself small, to will herself to just disappear into the wall. Her heart beat so hard she knew he must be able to hear it.

A roar came from outside, and the creature crashed into the wall again. Planks of wood flew inward. A piece slid across the floor and bounced off Alma's shoe. She grabbed it.

Maybe, she thought.

The piece of wood felt like ice in her hands. The blunt end was smooth, but the broken end was pointed—not sharp, but maybe pointed enough to stab the monster. Alma stood, knowing she would have no leverage if she remained crouched on the floor.

The coop rocked again, and the creature's fist widened the hole. He reached in and knocked away broken pieces of wood. He stuck his head in and looked right at Alma. His mouth formed something like a grin. She saw his tongue hang out, drool dripping from it. The sight turned her stomach.

You don't have time to be sick, she told herself. She lunged forward, her weapon held out in front of her. She bashed the creature on the side of his head. He howled and spit at her. She reared back and stabbed the pointed end of the wood into his face. She felt the resistance as the wood hit. She pulled back and stabbed at his face again. Blood gushed from his left eye.

The monster stepped back and rammed the wall again. This time more wood flew free, and he was able to step through. Alma smacked the wood against his nose. Then she aimed for his crotch. She jabbed the pointed end between his legs. The creature screamed. He fell to his knees. Alma beat him on his head with the wood. She saw the skin split and blood drain from the wounds she made. The sight both sickened and energized her. She hit him harder.

The creature toppled over and lay on the floor, his legs sticking out of the hole he had made in the wall. Alma saw that he was breathing, so she knew he wasn't dead. But he was wounded. Maybe she could get away. Maybe she could make it to the house. She darted around the monster's still form and ran from the chicken coop.

As she neared the back gate she couldn't help but glance in the direction in which she had first seen poor Isabelle. The sight she saw stopped her in her tracks.

Isabelle's head had fallen out of the tree. It lay on the ground near her body, as if still attached, the face turned in Alma's direction, the blank eyes staring, imploring.

A wave of sadness washed over Alma. Tears sprung to her eyes. Isabelle was gone. Her best friend in the whole world was gone. She suddenly felt weak and tired, the stress on her octogenarian body catching up to her. She thought how nice it would be to lie down on the frozen ground beside her sister and simply go to sleep.

Alma took a step closer, tempted, then stopped. Something about Isabelle didn't look right. She was smiling, her mouth full of glistening, sharp teeth.

Her head had been placed back on her body.

No, not placed, thought Alma. *Reattached.*

This can't be, she thought. *This must be a nightmare.* She shook her head, tried to wake up, but knew deep inside it was no dream

Isabelle sat up slowly, then stood. Her smile widened. Her eyes blazed red, just like those of the monster prince.

She's become like him, Alma thought. "What has he done to you?" she shrieked to her sister.

"Why, Alma, he's made me his bride!" Isabelle answered. "I tried to tell you, but you didn't want to listen. You didn't want to believe. My prince came for me just as I told you he would." Isabelle clasped her hands and placed them over her heart.

"But, but—Isabelle, he *killed* you! You're not his bride! You're dead!"

"Not really, sister. Not dead anymore. He remade me. Plucked my head off like a ripe grape! Oh, that hurt at first, but as I healed, I felt so much better. Better than I have in fifty years!"

"Healed? What are you talking about?"

"*He* healed me. Emptied me of all of my human impurities, then put me back together again. It's quite clever, I think."

Alma noticed the pooled blood on the ground where Isabelle's body had lain. "No." She shook her head slowly from side to side and spoke in a shaky voice.

"Don't worry, dear sister. Once upon a time we promised never to leave one another. Remember?"

Alma nodded. Tears streamed down her cheeks.

"I won't break that promise." Isabelle took a step toward Alma. She held out her arms.

Alma backed away. She knew she should run, but she couldn't make her legs move.

"Don't be afraid," said Isabelle, taking a few more steps forward.

Alma shifted her gaze to the chicken coop. She saw only a wide, jagged hole in the wall. The creature was gone. She whirled around, checking every inch of open space around her. He was nowhere to be seen. While Alma glanced away, Isabelle had closed the distance between them. Alma turned and ran, barely dodging Isabelle's outstretched arms. She headed for the house, afraid to let out her breath, to feel too confident or safe, even as she saw herself reaching out for the doorknob.

She swung the door open, her mind registering the slick feel of something wet on the knob at the same moment that she slammed the door shut behind her. She lifted her hand to see what she had touched.

Blood.

Something came into view from the parlor. A hairy, blood-covered face, an animal's muzzle, sharp teeth, red eyes. Blood on his hands, on his chest.

Isabelle's blood.

THE IMPORTANCE OF UNDERGARMENTS & SCIENCE FICTION CONVENTIONS

Tony Ruggiero

I h ave the bra to prove she was real. It is the only credible piece of evidence that is keeping me from going insane.

Although the chain of events is somewhat convoluted in my mind, there are certain things I remember for sure—such as the bra, but we will come back to that later. I am going to try and explain what happened using these specific instances that I can recall as markers so as to keep the timeline of events in order as best I can. You may at times question the validity of the events I am going to discuss and I am asking that you take a leap of faith to believe that at least some of these things could have happened. I'm not giving to lying or even fantasizing—well maybe a little, but not about what happened. Not this time.

I remember I was in my car driving with a semi-naked woman. I have her bra to prove it. I know I already mentioned that but I want to keep that in the forefront of your thoughts because it's very important. It is black in color, one of those types without the straps. Specifics and details are always important in any given setting however, the fact that the bra was black and did not have any straps is not really important unless you are taking personal preferences into consideration. But even in that consideration, this is not the most exciting or bizarre part of the story. That comes later.

Like I was saying, I was driving and it was night. I was on the interstate on the way back from a science fiction convention. Emyra, I still don't feel right using that name because I'm not really sure if that *was* her real name, but I guess it's the only proper way to identify her rather than by saying *she* all the time.

So there I am driving and the next thing that happened was Emyra leaned over my seat and rested her head on my thigh. This was after she had taken her bra off. It was hanging on my rear view mirror. I remember the part about the bra well because: (a) its such a rare occurrence and (b) she smiled that grin she seemed to always be able to summon on demand. I thought of it as an evil grin but never complained, *why ruin a good thing right?* She said it was a souvenir to remember her by. I thought the words were harmless at the time, you know, just having some fun and making a coy comment and all. Later I realized it wasn't.

So here I am driving with her head in my lap getting all snugly and comfortable. Is the suspense killing you yet? Well it was killing me at the time this was happening. But that was one of the many strange things that kept on occurring. I say *things* because there are so many but right now I am just referring to this one particular instance.

Well after a few minutes she stopped moving. I thought she had died or something but when she started snoring I realized that she had only fallen asleep. Some of you may be wondering what effect her falling asleep had on my male ego, but after you hear the rest of the events, you will learn that this was the least of my concerns in comparison to the police, the psychiatrists, the dwarfs, the snarky women—a regular cast of thousands. But all that comes later. *I may be pushing the envelope a little with the dwarfs but the rest is pretty solid.*

The drive back was obviously after the convention so I probably need to go back to the beginning. I was at a science fiction convention. Now before you go into convulsions and start waving the Vulcan "V" symbol with your hand and everything, it's not that kind of convention. While we're on the subject, let's also dispel another nasty rumor that always comes up when someone says they go to science fiction conventions—I am not what I would call a geek—maybe you would but I don't think so. I have a life outside of this activity as well thank you very much and I do not live in my parents' basement although I do know many that do fit into this category, but that's another story *(see the Panel from Hell blog that hasn't been written yet).* But even that is not going to compare with what happened to me that weekend.

The conventions I go to are more about the books and media. I go to conventions because I like science fiction, fantasy, and horror stuff. I also go to hang out with my friends and have some fun talking about the latest trends or whatever else we feel like. Fans of these genres may seem a little odd or strange, but they are usually quite intelligent and caring people. There are always exceptions, such as the panel infamously known as the "Evil Panel." If you want to know more about that one, it will cost you a few beers.

So like I was saying, there I was at the convention and it was a Saturday night. I was sitting in the bar relaxing and having a beer as I perused the programming schedule to see what I wanted to do next. People I know were passing by and saying hello—just the usual things that happen at a con. But then the unusual happened.

The voice came from somewhere but I wasn't actually sure where. It was as if the voice came from a home theater system—the sound simply resonating all around me.

"May I join you?" a woman's voice said.

I looked up and saw this woman, well a goddess actually was my first thought, standing next to my little table and looking at me. Now first impressions are usually important in terms of understanding events. Let me explain, she was wearing this *very slinky black evening dress*... you know the kind with the little straps that look like if you pull on them they will fall apart. The first thought that came into my mind was that she was not attending the convention—convention goers are usually not known for their selection of formal wear or dinner dress apparel (*disclaimer: most—not all*).

The rest of her that was tucked into this little dress was quite interesting... okay she was *freaking gorgeous!* Long brown hair that tickled her shoulders and a face that not only could launch a thousand ships, but which could launch an entire universe for that matter. Blue eyes that glittered with the reflection of light that gave the impression of a flickering candle. Soft smooth cheeks that seemed to beckon to be touched... and often. That's when I should have realized... *I was in trouble.*

When my heart settled back into place, it was then that I realized that *she was talking to me*. So naturally I did the manly thing and ushered out in my most charismatic tone possible the first coolest words I could imagine at the moment.

"Excuse me, are you speaking to me?" I asked. (*I said it was at the moment, what did you expect.*)

"Yes," she replied with a smile that fused the rubber soles of the Payless shoes I was wearing to the floor.

"Yes, I was talking to you," she said again.

Ding (bell rings)... Insert Moment of Decision Time.

Do I stay or do I go, (some song lyric which I can't remember the title to). I actually thought, for a very brief instance, of going off to a panel and giving the table to her. *But then an epiphany of extraordinary proportion rocked my world!* Maybe, just maybe she wants to sit here because *I* am here. Yeah I know what you're thinking…me too. I almost choked on my own thought which is actually harder and more dangerous than choking on actual words. Try it sometime and you will see what I mean. Anyway I figured why not? I didn't have anything to lose considering that the panel selection of the hour mainly consisted of drum circles or a reading by Tee and John…somebody (*only kidding guys*).

I quickly looked around the bar to see if anyone I knew was there to ensure that if I got dumped in vivid color, they wouldn't see it and then have the details show up in somebody's blog or something. *People that go to conventions will blog about anything (consider yourself warned)!* Finally when I realized that she was still standing there, (of course remember that all of these thoughts were a blur of mere seconds in my mind), I spoke, "Sure," I said loudly so that anyone nearby could see what was happening in case I woke up the next day with no recollection of the event. Proof is always important in these situations, like the bra, as you will see as this story progresses.

"Thank you," she said and staring at me as she sat down. There she remained not saying a word and just continuing to look at me.

"So," I began, "you're obviously not here for the convention judging by your attire, which I might add looks really nice. So, are you here for another event, a party or something?"

"No," she said, "*I am here* for the convention. I want to observe the rituals of the gathering."

"The what?" I stammered.

"The ritual," she repeated. "I've heard that these events are quite popular so I wanted to see what it was comprised of."

"Ah, okay," I said wondering what the heck she was talking about. I assumed she was a foreigner or something from a country where they didn't have any conventions. But she didn't have any accent that I could discern. Could she be pulling my leg? Maybe she was just one of those snarky women that go to cons and prey on innocent men like myself and watch dwarf mud wrestling competition for thrills—(*sorry for the image—but they are out there*).

"Are they not popular?" she asked sounding disappointed and interrupting my most pessimistic thoughts of impending rejection of the absurd.

"They are, it's just that … well the way you are dressed, you kind of standout at a convention. Is this your first one?"

"Yes it is."

"A con virgin," I said without even thinking and wished I could take it back. Not only did I insert foot in mouth—but numerous other anatomical parts as well.

"A virgin," she said, "a young woman who has never had sexual intercourse. I don't understand the correlation of the two? Can you *please* explain that comment?"

"Ah … yes, well con virgin." I began as I searched for my metaphorical tap dancing shoes. "Sorry, it's just a term for people attending their first con and then there's the other meaning … well we don't need to go into that. You're not from around here are you?

"Yes I am," she countered.

"So you're local then?"

"Well not at the moment. I like to think of it in relative terms. I'm from the 4th floor."

"I'm confused," I said trying to sound lighthearted but the truth of the matter was that I really was confused.

"That's not really important," she said.

"Right, you want to observe the … ritual as you said."

"Will you help me?"

"Sure. What do you want to know?"

"Everything. I want to be…how do you say…I want to be intimate with the ritual so that I have a complete understanding."

"Intimate," I said as my mind immediately went in the wrong direction with the word. Now here is another of those moments when you either say something really slick or you fall completely on your face in embarrassment by making a bad joke. Being me, I of course chose option number 2.

"Intimate," I repeated, "shouldn't we get to know one another a little first? My name is Mike and you are?"

"Emyra," she said and then appeared to think over what I had just said.

I felt the impending cloud of doom settle upon me as I waited for her to either slap me or pour the contents of her drink into my crotch. Myself preservation instinct kicked in and I tried to change the subject so that I could try and cover my butt with that last remark I made.

"So Emyra, that's a pretty name. What is its origin?"

She didn't answer. It was as if she was communing with the silence or deciding how she was going to kill me. I could deal with option one but not two. I prepared for a hasty departure or a ruthless physical attack.

"Of course," she finally said in a tone that flowed assuredly as if she had just discovered some exiting medical breakthrough or something. "Now I understand your earlier reference to virgin."

"Huh?" I said totally confused. I removed my hands from my groin area where they had gone into the defensive mode. "What do you understand?"

"You wish to have sex first? This is part of the ritual? Is this where the naked chef comes in or is it the card game?"

Ding (more like a gong sound)…Another Moment of Decision Time.

Okay…now here I was sitting in the bar with this gorgeous woman who appeared to be lacking in the brain department, but made up for it in the other sundry areas with room to spare. But she seemed to be…well clueless doesn't even come close to defining her mental capability. So one *could* tell her about the misconception she has or someone *could* take shameless advantage of it for their own personal gain.

I chose to do the right thing and point out her misconception. I really did. Honest and cross my heart and all that stuff (for about a millisecond anyway). Don't shake your head or say *tsk…tsk… tsk* as you wag your finger at the printed page or computer screen. You would have done the same thing I did and *you know it*. At conventions there is an implied leeway to the rules of decorum… you check them at the lobby and that's where they stay. You know the saying…what happens in Vegas stays in Vegas. Well at conventions it's sort of the same thing except it's just a lot less glamorous or if you prefer another term… *spiffy (I know there are a few eyss out there rolling at that one—deal with it).*

Okay, back to the conversation. After overcoming my shock at giving any thought to refusing this offer, I found my voice and continued.

"Emyra, I'm not sure about the naked chef thing or the card game, but the sex is a big YES in order to truly experience the convention and all its subtle nuances."

"But the naked chef thing, I thought that was important to? If you lost the bet playing cards you had to cook dinner—naked?"

"Honey *w-h-a-t-e-v-e-r.* But you must have your wires crossed with the Food Network or some combination of those wacky reality shows. I don't know about the naked chef thing or the card thing, but if that is a requirement for you—well then I'm all for it. I'm sure I could find an apron and a deck of cards, after all it is a convention and weirdness abounds in every corner and crevice. It's just the way it is…"

Suddenly she reached out and grabbed my wrist. I was shocked and yet at the same time I felt a surge of goose bumps envelop my entire body… I say again… *my entire body!* For a few seconds she didn't say anything but just looked at me intently. I felt as if I couldn't move, but then I didn't want to anyway.

Maintaining that grip, she said, "I'm confused."

"Well join the club darlin," I answered. "Everyone here is confused in some way or another. That's part of the con experience. We come to escape."

Her stare seemed to become vacant for a few moments as if she was thinking about something completely distant or she was having dinner with Elvis. Yet she maintained her grip on me and I have to admit… I was pretty excited about it. My name is Bond… James Bond…

Finally she spoke, "I am sensing your elevated hormones which are focusing on the sexual aspect."

"Say what?" I said aloud and then I muttered numerous and sundry silent curses. I too was feeling the elevation…so to speak. I felt very transparent and a wee bit embarrassed. I crossed my legs.

"Yet," she continued, "I sense that there is much more you are not telling me. Where I am wrong in my information?"

Her hand slid from my wrist and down to my hand where she maintained a firm grip. Her hand was warm and very inviting. I was about to grasp it with my other free hand (*Yes, I was still plying the sex angle—damn it!*) when she spoke.

"Tell me," she said again. "How is my information incorrect?"

"Well your information isn't really wrong," I said starting to back pedal quickly before I ruined an all too good to be true scenario. "Let's start from the beginning. Maybe you can tell me where you got your information from?" I asked.

"Well, I read about it the literature on the table in the hallway. The one where there are stacks of paper which are free."

"The freebie table?"

"Yes," she said and then acquired a puzzled look on her face. "The name is curious. In terms of slang, it constitutes an act between a man and woman—"

"Not exactly," I said and then added quickly, "Look, a Klingon," I said pointing at someone at the bar. I needed a few moments to regroup and … reorganize. I was beginning to feel like I was on a game show: *What's Your Most Embarrassing Moment* or *How to Screw Up an Opportune Moment … where is she getting this stuff from!*

"Interesting," she said as she returned her glance back to me, "more of the experience as you say? Is sex with a Klingon—"

"Hold that thought," I stammered not wanting to go there. "Where did you say you were from again?"

"The 4th floor," she said casually.

"But that's just where you are— oh never mind," I said not wanting to tempt fate any further. This conversation was becoming like the Abbott and Costello routine: Who's on First? (For you "younger folks" you haven't lived until you have. Search the web and you'll find it and don't skip it if you have not heard it because it really really sums this moment help extremely well).

"So you were saying earlier?" I asked.

"You were explaining the true significance of the freebie table."

"Right," I agreed. "Well you can't believe everything you read over there … there's a lot of stuff there that doesn't have an ounce of truth to it."

"Then why is it there if it contains incorrect information?"

"Well maybe incorrect is not the right word," I said. "The table is a place for people that might be marketing either an event, like another convention, or there are things there from writers that are marketing their own work. There are magazines, buttons, pens and a whole bunch of stuff. But you have to keep in mind, it's all self serving so there might be some truth stretching going on."

"Ah I see now how I may have made the wrong assertion," she said.

"I'm almost afraid to ask what else did you read from there?"

"Well there was this magazine I picked up, the title was a temperature reference or something, and I was reading a story about a man and woman that drove into a parking lot. She asked him to park in a dark area and—"

"Whoa…" I exclaimed, not wanting to go there…well at least not yet anyway. I needed a distraction. Then as if a miracle *(insert heavenly music here)* was beamed down from wherever they come from, I saw one. My miracle came in the simple version of a paper flyer which was posted on the wall.

"Ah and the parties are a very important part of the true con experience. You don't want to miss out on any of them," I said.

"Party?" she said and then recited, "A body of persons united for some common purpose…this is an important part of the ritual?"

"Important! Why of course. You see, there are the daytime activities and then there are the *night time* activities. Parties are a common theme at most conventions."

"Describe them more," she said.

I felt her hand tighten on mine—must be really into this touching thing I thought—keep that in mind for later consideration.

"Well let's see, there are a few that are regulars such as the barnymphs, dwarf pirates, the should have stayed home and don't want to see group, other conventions prostituting themselves," I rambled off the top of my head quickly.

"Bar-nymphs? This terminology is very conflicting. A bar is a place of drink or similar social activity, but nymph may refer to maidens or the young of insects? Please explain," she said as that perplexed look that I was becoming accustomed to came over her face…again.

"Well, it's just a group of fun folks that get together and have a good time."

"Specifics please"—she said firmly as her grip on my hand squeezed tighter. "I need to understand the terminology."

"Ah…let's see," I began, "I'm not really that sure about the connotation behind the name, perhaps they start off as the insect version of nymphs and end up as maidens? Alcohol can be a wonderful transformation tool if you know what I mean?"

"I do not," she said, "how can insects turn into maidens?"

"You missed my attempt at humor," I said.

"Apparently," she agreed readily.

"Look, it's just a group of people. They're fun and entertaining—well most of them anyway."

As I waited for her response, she tilted her head to one side and kind of looked off into that distant place she had a habit of going to. But this time it was different than before. Her face held a bemused look as if she was …I don't know how to explain it—before she had that look…very vague and indistinct. Earlier I coined it as she was off somewhere having dinner with Elvis or something. But now it was as if she was communing with Elvis… or worse. She had this mischievous look on her face that well… both scared me and delighted me.

"Hello?" I said.

"What about the dwarf-pirates?" she asked surprising me by coming out of her trance and changing the topic away from the bar-nymph issue. "What do pirates have to do with a science fiction convention?"

"Ah … good question. Never really thought about it before but I guess they play in the fantasy realm enough to qualify," I answered. "Regardless they are still a very fun crowd and some of the wenches … well we'll save that for another time."

"As you wish," she said simply.

At this point I am starting to wonder why she is agreeing with me and letting this stuff go by without any further explanation. Something had changed. But if she was going to be agreeable—this seemed like an opportune time to suggest some extracurricular activity of my own. But I needed to ease into it somehow.

"Can I get you another drink?" I suggested.

"Do you want me to change—like your bar-nymphs?" she asked.

Hmmm … I said to myself. Was that a touch of *Snarkism* I detect? That's new. Maybe she has this alter personality going on or something. Maybe it's time to ratchet this up a notch and—

"We shall go to the 4th floor," she said. "Now! I am ready!"

"Ready for—" I began as she snatched me out of my chair and shoved me in the direction of the elevator.

"In a hurry are we?" I asked.

"Yes," she simply said with no explanation. "We must get to the 4th floor."

As she ushered me into the elevator she placed her arms around me and kissed me … deeply. I say again … deeply. So I literally was along for the ride yet had no complaints—no complaints whatsoever. However, as for the other people in the elevator, that might be a different story. Did I mention that there were people on the elevator?

The people were the definitive con-goers of all shapes and sizes. Of course you will ask: *Well how did you know—didn't you have your eyes closed when you were kissing her.* There could be several dignified answers to that question but I will just have to say no. No, I did not have my eyes closed. *It was in an elevator for God sakes.* Who closes their eyes when on an elevator? Besides, don't you remember what happened in "Fatal Attraction"…never mind.

Anyway, there was someone dressed up as a Wookiee—and a darned good one too—it was so good I could feel the hairball forming in my throat. It just tilted its head in my direction and with its furry hands and gave me the proverbial and very hairy thumbs up.

Then there was a woman who was dressed up as…well I guess it was as "Blade" or something *(why would a woman dress up like a man…never mind)*. She wasn't smiling though—she just stroked the sword that was encased on her back…which I hoped was not real. Next there was a…you guessed it a dwarf pirate…dressed as none other than Captain Jack Sparrow (with of course the height differential), he winked at me showing me a full mouth of gold—more than I cared to see. Lastly, and for the coup de grace, there was the poor mundane couple. A plain ordinary middle aged couple, probably from Kansas who for sure had 2.5 kids and two cars of which one was an import—you can just tell these things sometimes as well as their candid reaction to unfortunately being at a hotel where there was a convention going on. They were wide eyed and slunk as far back in the elevator as they could get from all of us.

Well when I regained enough of my composure to try and communicate this fact to Emyra she seemed to already sense my trepidation and she broke away from the kiss while still remaining in my arms. (No resistance from me either.) But as she backed away from me she looked *different* somehow. At first I couldn't describe it but when she spoke it rocked my world…again.

She turned toward the Wookiee and said: "That must be hot as hell, huh?" And then without missing a beat she turned to the woman dressed as Blade and said, "You need to reexamine your feminine side," and of course the dwarf pirate was not left unscathed as she fired a broadside at him, "I bet you don't know any good pirate pick up lines—do you?"

That left only the normal mundane people to which I assumed would be left alone. *Wrong.* She looked at them and said, "I bet someone is going to get lucky tonight? Come on admit it, the costumes are kind of kinky aren't they?"

Okay so at this point I figured that someone *switched* the girl I had been talking with earlier because this was certainly not the unsure and naïve girl I remembered. This girl was *Miss SNARKY, circa 2007.*

"Emyra," I said not sure if I was stating or asking it. "Are you alright?"

"Of course." she said. "The update is working fine."

"The what?" I asked.

"Never mind," she said.

I could feel her winding up for a next assault on the poor people and tried to think of some way to not have her decimate them. So I did the first thing that came to my mind and placed a lip lock on her that left her unable to speak. I kept her that way as we hit the second and third floor amidst the applause and comments of getting a room.

On the second floor the mundane couple got off the elevator trying to seem very cool with the whole scenario they found themselves in, yet failing miserably. As con-goers you get used to this kind of thing and it really doesn't faze you anymore. On the third floor the rest of the people got off as well heading off to one of the con parties—a usual Saturday night.

I released Emyra from my grasp and made a move to get off the elevator. But she pulled me back in.

"What?" I asked. "Are we going back down?"

"No," she said calmly, "we have one more floor to go."

Now I have to admit that I had been paying absolutely no attention to the elevator keypad and the circles of numbers. But at that moment something told me to look. When I finished my thorough examination I returned my attention to Emyra.

"Emyra, there are only three floors. There is no *4th* floor. And what was that about back there when you said all that weird stuff?"

"No 4th floor—is that what you think?" She said in a purring sound that sent a complete armada of goose bumps on my body into motion. Then she grabbed me and…well…let's just leave it at that and fade to black. If you want to read that kind of stuff, you're in the wrong market at least as far as I am concerned. Now, back to the elevator. There comes a day in our lives when something both bizarre and wonderful happens. And I think that night in the elevator at that moment, it was my time. Call it fate, destiny, or whatever word works for you. The event changes us forever as it molds and shapes us into what we were meant to be. That was what happened to me that night, that much I am sure of. My epiphany had finally arrived…the only problem is that I don't remember a damned thing!

I awoke in my hotel room on Sunday morning. I was naked and my body felt as if I had been run over by a tractor trailer…several times and whoever had been driving had enjoyed themselves immensely in the act. The sound of the shower running indicated that I was not alone. A few minutes later Emyra came out of the bathroom.

"Good morning," I said.

"Good morning to you sweetie," she said. "Sleep well," she said and then winked at me.

"Ah … well I'm not sure," I said because well … I wasn't sure of much of anything at the moment.

"You should have," she said with a very provocative edge to her voice. "You were very much *on target* last night."

"Well that's good," I said without knowing what the hell she was talking about. Of course one could associate that comment with the act of … well you know what. But at this point if I had not learned anything else, I had learned to not take anything at face value with Emyra.

"Did we … ah—"

"Yes," she continued, "you were quite helpful to a needy woman last night. You made my convention experience complete. I now understand it all."

Trying to be subtle I asked, "So this *on target* was a good thing?"

"Oh yes," she purred, "a very good thing and several times while we were on the 4th floor."

"The 4th floor…" I said remembering the elevator and the button that only went to the three floors that the hotel claimed to have.

"Yes," she answered.

"Ah … and because of what happened on the 4th floor, you now have a complete understanding of the convention experience?"

"Oh yes, and all thanks to you."

Okay that was it. If this wasn't a complete role reversal and the most bizarre occurrence I have ever had … or anyone else for that matter I don't know what is. I had come to the con, scored with a beautiful woman, and couldn't remember any of what I did on a floor that doesn't exist. Yet here was Emyra with this complete and utter look of contentment on her face and if she felt any more

fulfilled she was going to need another room to fit her dispos-
ition in. Talk about not being fair—and yes I know what fair is—a
place for cotton candy and rides, but I wanted my due. I wanted a
memory of the convention and *I was going to have it.*

"Well," I began in my best James Bond voice, "how about you
come back to bed and—"

"We can't honey, the 4th floor no longer exists," she said matter
of fact like.

"And it did last night?" I asked.

"Of course it did. Don't you remember?"

"Emyra, I don't remember anything past the elevator," I said as
my frustration peaked to new heights. "I really want to understand
all this—what happened last night—who the hell you are—and
what is really going on here!"

"Oh, that's right," she said. "Sorry about that—it's all part of
the process honey."

"The process?" I asked. "I thought it was about you and experiencing the con?"

"Well sort of," she started hesitantly. "I don't think you quite
understand what is happening here."

"Well, that's an understatement," I agreed.

"You see—I'm your con fairy."

"My what?"

"I'm your convention fairy and I am here for your convention
experience—not mine."

"Whoa … back up Emyra my head is spinning!"

And it really was spinning. The room felt as if it was going 80
miles per hour and the G-forces were pinning me to the walls, but
in this the case the walls weren't just drywall and plaster but a new
reality of some sort.

"How can I explain this," she began. "You see, this is a new program that was initiated by the Fairies Customer Service Branch for the Betterment of all Mankind FCSBM, to show our appreciation to those like you that go to conventions. You keep us alive and vivid in the imaginations of thousands. So to show our appreciation in a way for all that you people do, we thought it would be appropriate to thank you by giving YOU a real life fantasy for a change."

"This is a joke right? Someone at the convention is putting you up to this? Either that or one of us is suffering delusions from consuming too much Nth degree tea at the party which I also do not remember attending." (But if I can't remember attending—then how do I remember I drank the tea? Just go with me on this one—its fantasy for crying out loud.)

"No hon, no tea—no party—this is as real as it gets considering it still fantasy."

"Okay," I began, "then if that is the case, why can't I remember anything from last night?"

"Well you will, but not yet."

"Huh?"

"I am a fairy. I live in your dreams—not in the real world. So when we were on the *4th floor*, which is really the area between the fantasy world and real life, what we experienced there will come to you in your dreams."

"But you are physically here. I remember your grip on me—that wasn't fantasy."

"You're correct. This physical shape you see before you is real, but only a mere shell of life with a very limited span of time. My real essence lies in that realm of—"

"The 4th floor…" I said as my voice trailed off and my thoughts beckoned to the dream part of my mind for answers.

"Yes," she agreed. "And it was very special night, of that I assure you. As a fairy I can experience not only physically, but also your emotional psyche. You're a very special guy, in another world or dimension I think I could easily fall in love with you."

"I wish I could…understand what happened," I said.

She stepped to within a few feet of me and placed her hand upon my forehead.

"Close your eyes," she said.

I closed them and within a few seconds I was overcome by a warmth and sensation that I could only describe as an emotional drowning in good way. She was there and I could feel her touch on me which both comforted and excited me. I had never known such feeling or emotional contact with anyone else. Was this how love felt? I don't know. All I knew was that it was a feeling I did not want to part from. I stroked her face with my hands and bathed in the luxurious feel of her flesh. I kissed her fingers and held them to my own face feeling their softness in such stark contrast to my own.

I felt her remove her hand from my forehead and the euphoria I experienced dissipated immediately leaving me feeling empty.

"In your dreams I will come to you," she said.

"But I don't know if that will be enough," I answered. "This is too wonderful to just leave to my dreams. There must be some-thing else that can be done."

"There will be other conventions," she said and then smiled that grin that was somewhere between evil and innocence. "You never know…"

"But…suppose…" I grappled to find the words to ask the right question to get the answer I wanted. "Suppose I want to give you a rose or something…" (at this point for some reason I don't think I will ever comprehend, the Meatloaf song of *"You took the words right out of my mouth,"* came into my thoughts and ever since has been imbedded there.) I continued my line of thought "…how would I get it to you?"

"Just leave them where you will and I will find them," she said. Then she kissed me and finished getting dressed.

I watched her dress, not out of any sexual gratification, but out of the sheer enjoyment of watching her every movement. We didn't talk for those few moments, it was as if we had tele-pathically agreed to not talk as we sorted everything into its place—or at least some form of temporary holding cell for later contemplation.

When she had finished dressing she said: "I must be on my way and you must drive me."

"To where," I asked.

"It doesn't matter," she said, "my time is almost done," and offered nothing more.

From the time we left the hotel and during the drive home, we talked about everything as if we had known each other for a long period of time. We held hands, we kissed, and just simply enjoyed the moment. I felt like asking the clichéd question, "Is this heaven?" but the thought that someone would say, "No, and that it was Iowa," encouraged me to leave well enough alone.

So this brings us back to the beginning of this story. As I said, I was driving down the road and she had placed her head in my lap. She had fallen asleep, as evidenced by the snoring that emanated from her. I have to admit that the fact that fairies snore was a little disturbing, but it was also a fact that I could easily overlook in this instance.

As she slept, I looked at the souvenir she had given me earlier which hung from my rearview mirror, the black bra. I couldn't help but snicker about the whole affair. As I did so, I actually experienced a dream flashback to what I had experienced earlier in the hotel when she had touched my forehead. The euphoria was momentary but oh so gratifying and any attempt to place into words would be meaningless. But emotions and feelings may be transformed into words and I heard her words clearly… as well as the words that softly crept across my lips … *I love you too …*

This euphoria was quickly replaced by the sound of a siren and the flashing of blue and red lights in my rearview mirror—a State Trooper. A quick glance at the speedometer confirmed I was going about ten miles over the speed limit. I began to decelerate and pull off onto the shoulder.

"Emyra," I said as I gently shook her, "Wake up."

She looked up at me with those blue eyes. Her eyes were the brightest blue I had ever seen and as they grew brighter and brighter until the front seat of the car was encompassed in a blue-white light. Then it suddenly went dark leaving my vision full of those white spots you see when a flash goes off directly in your line of sight.

"Sir, can I see your license and registration," the officer's voice boomed into my consciousness.

I ignored the voice as my eyes cleared and saw that Emyra was no longer here with me. My eyes told me she was gone but my mind refused to accept the fact because it simply did not want to.

"Sir, can I see your license and registration," the officer repeated.

"She's gone," I said.

"Who is gone sir?" the officer asked.

"Emyra," I answered. "She's gone."

The officer shined his light into the interior of my car. The beam stopped on the bra.

"Sir, can you step out of the vehicle," the officer said in a more authoritative voice. "Do you want to tell me what "that" (referring to the bra) is about?"

149

In moments of despair or anguish, we take much comfort in strangers. I relayed the entire story to the police officer. After I had finished I was asked to sit in the police car and was later transported to the police station. After retelling the story again, I was evaluated by the police psychiatrist on duty. He placed me on an overnight hold due to possible suicidal tendencies due to an emotional breakdown. I was released the next day into the custody of my parents and court ordered to seek professional assistance in dealing with an undetermined trauma.

That was about nine months ago. Since that time I have had many sessions with a psychiatrist and have been deemed no risk to society. Talking with the shrink the goal was for me to rationalize what happened with Emyra, the shrink's answer was that it was all a fantasy that I had played out in my mind.

"So what about the bra?" I asked? "It *is* physical evidence that proves her existence?"

"It is much more probable," the shrink began, "that you went out and bought it subconsciously as part of your fantasy and somehow managed to block it from your mind. It's the only reasonable and plausible answer."

This seemed to be a sticking point so I thought it best to just agree with him and move along. Once I did, I was deemed fit to return to my meager existence of life as I knew it. I agreed readily with the shrink because he could not touch those dreams that were locked up in my head. Those were mine and I kept and cherished them.

I still go to conventions and I haven't changed my routine very much while there. I go to panels, talk with friends, and just hang out. I sit in the bar and have a drink. I will grab a table that has two chairs and make sure that the other chair is left unoccupied. I leave a rose at the front desk at each hotel for Emyra. I don't know if they are ever picked up or not but I leave them anyway. If the shrink knew I was doing this he probably bring me in for my counseling so let's just keep this between us … okay?

As to my own theory as to what happened that weekend … I keep it in my heart and my dreams. As to what is real and what is not— when it comes to a matter of the heart, those things are best left alone and you just follow them where they lead you in life. As to the bra—well I still have it … and the assortment of colors it comes in.

THE END

Alternate Ending 2

I still go to conventions and I haven't changed my routine very much while there. I go to panels, talk with friends, and just hang out. I sit in the bar and have a drink. But there is one thing I do differently since all of this happened. But before I get to that I need to warn you that it might sound a little bizarre, but if you had experienced what I had, then perhaps you would feel somewhat differently about it. So let me go through this before you decide anything.

When I am at a convention, I carry my small carry bag with me. Inside of the bag wrapped up in tissue paper I carry the bra. When it's late and most of the people have gone to bed and things are quiet, I take the bra out of the bag and place it on my head and snap the clasps under my chin so that the cups face upward toward the ceiling. I am not a pervert nor do I have a women's clothing fetish—there is a logical reason for this you will see as you read on so withhold judgment until the end.

I figure Emyra had to have left the bra for a reason other than just a souvenir, perhaps it is some kind of lightning rod that points upwards … perhaps even toward the 4th floor. That fabulous place that I can see only when I sleep and it comes to my dreams. It truly is a fantastical place where only the most wondrous things happen or have happened—not sure which really applies but I guess it doesn't really matter.

As I was saying, the cups point upward. I figure maybe…just maybe if all of this is true, then perhaps there is some way that Emyra can tell I'm here and waiting for her to come back. Perhaps the bra acts as some form of fairy GPS system or something. After all, with all the conventions that go on all around the world, even fairies are bound to get lost sometimes. It makes sense to me, heck, I get lost going around the block sometimes so it's only fair to assume that fairies might have the same kind of challenges at times.

So if you are one of those folks that can't sleep and you wander down to the bar in the wee hours of the morning at a convention and you see someone in the bar sitting there quietly having a drink and wearing a bra on the top of their head, don't be so fast to judge. But rather if you have the time to stop and sit and have a drink, I will tell you the story of *The Importance of Undergarments at a Science Fiction Convention*. Getting the story in person is always better than in writing. You get to hear all those subtle nuances in the voice rather than supplying your own in your mind. And for those who do stop by and chat for a bit, maybe I can put in a a good word for you the next time I see Emyra and maybe she can pull some strings for you and get you a con-fairy experience as well.

Now, I can imagine what you're thinking. Guys will read this story and think that if they come to the bar and place a bra on their head, they too can attempt to have their own con-fairy experience. Then before you know it there will be a bunch of men sitting in the bar with bras on their heads and then the women will join in with their own assortment of men's undergarments such as briefs, boxers, and perhaps even the dreaded banana hangers or something and it will look like the most ridiculous thing anyone has ever seen and there goes the whole con experience thing. But then again, if you think about it, it is a science fiction convention and you know what—probably no one will notice. And if any of the mundanes do notice we will just tell them that there is a Victoria Secrets or Fredericks or GQ or whatever gathering is going on and they will nod in agreement and with complete understanding accompanied by a very sly grin on their faces from both men and women alike. And if they don't well that's okay too.

So after all this you might ask yourself at some point if *any of this* makes any sense. Some will say no, and others will just silently nod their heads in agreement. As for me, I am off in my own little world and for all I know I may be the only person that has made it to the fourth floor... after all I have the bra to prove it. Oh and one other thing, did I mention the label inside the bra? The one that reads: *"100% cotton mixed with magic fairy dust for enhanced lift-both physically and mentally."*

I guess I forgot to mention that.

THE END

Alternate Ending 3

I still go to conventions and I haven't changed my routine very much while there. I go to panels, talk with friends, and just hang out. I sit in the bar and have a drink. I will grab a table that has two chairs and make sure that the other chair is left unoccupied. I leave a rose at the front desk at each hotel for Emyra. I don't know if they are ever picked up or not but I leave them anyway.

It's been a while, maybe a few years since that weekend and I was doing my usual routine at a convention and toasting the memory. I was sipping my third or fourth drink of the evening when suddenly there was a flash of light and the seat in front of me was filled with a shape. In a few moments the form stabilized and Emyra was there.

"Hey," she said.

"Hey," I answered as I looked upon her image and then added, "I missed you."

"And I have missed you," she said as she leaned closer and placed her hand upon mine. When her hand touched my own it was like someone had opened a floodgate and the warmth that it contained washed over me.

"Thanks for the roses," she said, "I have them all."

"You're very welcome. I just wanted to do something nice for you."

"That's what I like about you…so honest and simple. Your heart is so open."

"For you it is always…" I said allowing my words to trail off.

She let her hand trace the outline of my face. "So silly and yet so sweet." When her hand returned to mine she said, "I've watched you sit and have these drinks late at night."

"You have? Why didn't you come to me earlier then?"

"Rules. There are only certain things we fairies are allowed to do. Actually I m breaking a quite a few right now by coming to you."

"Emyra—I don't want you to get in any—"

"Hush," she said and placed her fingers to my lips. "I am here because I want to be here. I wanted to see you."

"Well in that case then, I guess I won't argue," I said and felt myself satisfying grin stretch from ear to ear.

"Good, we never have argued and I don't want to start one now—besides you would lose anyway."

"Ah…I see you still have that snarky streak after all this time."

"You seem to bring it out in me," she countered and smiled that grin that drove me crazy—the oh so innocent and yet oh so evil mixture that only she could do.

"Glad to know I'm good for something besides entertainment," I said.

"Entertainment? Where did that come from?" she asked.

"You know…us mere mortals. We must be amusing with our daily lives as compared to you fairy folk."

"Ah…I see," she said, "is that what you *really think*?"

Her question and serious tone of voice caught me off guard.

"Well I don't know."

"It's actually quite the reverse," she said emphatically. "I…or rather we can't experience the same joy that you do. We have in a way become immune to it after so long of a period of time."

"Emyra I'm so sorry. I didn't know."

"Of course you didn't," she said sincerely. "But that's why I have been keeping my eye on you."

"Oh?"

"You see, ever since we were together. I have been grounded so to speak because I behaved abnormally when I left you the… ah…item."

"Item? Oh—you mean the bra."

"Yes. That is against the rules. You see why obviously."

"No," I said adamantly. "If it wasn't for the bra, I would have questioned the entire…" My voice trailed off as I saw what she meant now. "Oh…I get it."

"That's exactly the reason," she said. "It can have an adverse affect on humans and cause emotional stress. It's not supposed to seem like it was real but rather just a dream of something that might have been."

"I see," I said. My voice reflecting my disappointment.

"But I'm glad I did. And the way you have kept that time in your heart is what convinced me."

"Convinced you of what?" I asked.

"I'm staying this time."

"What?"

"I'm staying."

"Emyra I'm so glad to hear that but … can you do that?"

"If I give up my immortality, I can."

"That's a lot to give up," I said.

"Well a woman has to do what she must," she said and smiled. "Besides … you're worth it and I only have so many bras."

"I don't know what to say," I said.

"That's a good start to a relationship. Let me do all the talking."

"Snarky," I said.

"Yes it comes from years of experience and of course genetics as well," she proudly stated.

"By the way," I began, "now that you brought it up, seeing as how you were immortal, how old are you anyway?"

"Don't you know you should never ask a woman's age—shame on you."

"Well I was just curious—it doesn't really matter."

"And you may keep that curiosity to yourself young man unless it deals with a more physical nature as to where I am concerned."

"Well then, shall we adjourn to the 4th floor?" I said.

"We can't go there anymore," she said looking sadly at me. "We have to—"

"Emyra *this hotel* has six floors …"

"Well then," she said, "don't you need to work on that undergarment collection of yours?"

THE END

Alternate Ending 4

Since that eventful weekend, I still go to conventions and I haven't changed my routine very much while there. I go to panels, talk with friends, and just hang out. I sit in the bar and have a drink. I will grab a table that has two chairs and make sure that the other chair is left unoccupied. I leave a rose at the front desk at each hotel for Emyra. I don't know if they are ever picked up or not but I leave them anyway.

It's been a few years now and I still honor the ritual I started. I always tell myself…just one more convention and then I should stop, but there always seem to be one more convention and one more ritual of hope to go through. So I do it.

I was at another convention sitting at a table sipping my drink as usual when there was the flash of light that blinded me as something settled into the empty chair next to me. In a few seconds my eyes cleared and then I blinked them several times not believing what I saw.

"Whoa…" I said. "You're an awfully big ostrich!"

"Of course I am," the large bird said nonchalantly.

"And you talk as well," I said as I reached into my pocket for my cigarettes but then realized I had quit smoking about ten days ago. So instead of the comforting feel of a pack of smokes, I came up with the little square piece of nicotine gum. I quickly took one and stuffed it into my mouth and chewed it until I could feel the nicotine.

"Correct again," the ostrich said.

Not seeing too much of a choice of ignoring whatever it was that sat next to me, and of course not having any previous interaction with such a creature, I asked the obvious question. "So what do I call you?"

"My name is Nora."

"Well by the way…er…Nora," I began trying to keep my voice calm, "ostriches can't talk. Which means you aren't real. I don't know what you are…maybe you are an hallucination of some kind brought on by my nicotine deprived state or a result of the pain killers I am taking for my…injury." (*The injury was a result of an intergalactic slide…well that will all become clear later.*)

"Is that what you r-e-a-l-l-y believe?" she asked in a very snark-isk manner.

Is it me or is this snarkish thing becoming a trend or something lately?

"Well there isn't another rational explanation is there?" I asked. "I mean how often is it that an ostrich shows up in a bar for a bit of conversation?"

"I see," she said and grinned as if she knew something about me but wanted to lure it out of me. "You talk of rationality," she continued, "yet you sit here waiting for something that is not rational either—isn't that so?"

"What?" I said acting as if I didn't know what she meant.

"You don't lie well," she said with a sly smile. "Your eyes give you away. I know you're waiting for a fairy."

"Now how do you know that?' I asked trying to keep the surprise out of my throat.

"I know a lot about you," she said. "I have the ability—"

"Wait a minute," I protested, "if you know that, then that only proves my point about you being an hallucination from my own thoughts."

"Maybe," she said in a very neutral tone. "And maybe not."

"That's not much of an answer," I said.

"But does it really matter," she said. "If I am a hallucination, then you are really just talking to yourself. No harm there because you do that already."

"True," I agreed.

"And if I am not an hallucination, and I am just an ostrich, well then you are just having a conversation and there is no harm in that is there?"

"Well I…," I tried to come up with an answer but couldn't.

"But to make you feel better, we can just go along with your assumption that I am an hallucination brought on by your deprived state. Feel better?"

"I suppose," I said but I really did feel better. I mean which is easier to explain—that I was talking to myself via an hallucination or I was really having a conversation with an ostrich? Chances are the first one would get you some odd looks but the second one would get you thrown into a psych ward. So I decided what the heck and just went along.

"So what was her name?" the ostrich asked.

"He name is…wait a minute…you should know her name."

"Well I do, but I want to hear you say it."

"Well…her name is Emyra," I said and felt the warmth well up inside me as the syllables crossed my lips.

"So…what would you do with her?" she asked. "If she showed up here right now?"

"Well there's a short and a long answer to that question" I said.

"Which might be?"

"That's a pretty personal question from an ostrich that I don't really know," I said.

"Are we going to go through that again," she said as she cocked her head to one side.

"No," I smiled. "But still that's…"

"Oh…so it's for her ears only—is that it?"

"Kind of," I agreed.

"Well I think I know what it is," she said and smiled what I assumed was a sly grin … for an ostrich. "And she thinks the same?"

"Well I … think so." I said and then added, "No, I'm sure she feels the same way."

"You have such faith—that is good," she said.

"Sometimes it's all we have," I said.

"And sometimes it is enough," she said. "Just enough … but now I must be going. I wish you luck in your search and what you are looking for."

"Thanks and …" There was a sudden flash of light and the ostrich was gone. I felt an emptiness at her departure. In the short time we conversed I felt as if I had known her in an odd sort of way. But of course if it was an hallucination—then I should know her because it was really myself. This gets kind of confusing … eh?

These thoughts about Emyra made me really want a cigarette very badly. I got up and made my way toward the doors which led out into the street. There was a little convent store I remembered where I could get a pack of cigarettes and calm my nerves.

As I stepped out of the hotel and into the street, there was the usual transition as the vortex swept me back to my own world. My mind received the neural input that rearranged the other information that had been implanted in order for me to function in that past environment. Now the two information streams intermingled and the purpose of the trip became clear; the date was 200 years in the future of the period I had just come from.

"So how did it go?" the man standing at the console asked.

"No joy this trip. But the other problem … it's getting bad," I said. "I'm seeing the ostrich more and more. It must be some form of interplanetary dementia caused by vortex interference during the time travel. But the summoning device to call me back, the need for a cigarette, worked fine. "

"Well you were in there for quite a while, a number of years according to their time so I ratcheted up the craving to draw you out. What about the woman? Did you see her?"

"No. Not this trip," I said.

"Do you think she really exists?" he asked.

"Yeah I do," I said. "The story we uncovered about her and the man she fell in love with is one of the greatest stories our world knows."

"But don't you ever wonder if it was just a fictional story? Maybe it was just something that was made up."

"No…I don't believe so. Besides with a title like that, The Importance of Undergarments—it has to be true. Why else would anyone write something as ridiculous as that?"

"I suppose," the operator agreed.

"Going back into time is the only way to find out for sure," I said. "If I can duplicate the exact situation by doing what he did, I might get the chance to meet her."

The operator looked up from the control console he monitored, "The vortex is becoming unstable. It's time."

"Close the gateway," I said. But I will find her…someday."

THE END—OF ALL THE ENDINGS

This story is dedicated to the many people who I have met at conventions. You're all great! The friends and memories that I have from conventions are of the type that shall always remain with me especially when I have been drinking heavily.

And of course, this story would not be possible without special thanks to a very special woman. This one is for you Mary, aka Emrya, Nora…and of course—the ostrich!

I hoped you enjoyed *The Importance of Undergarments & Science Fiction Conventions.* Now it's your turn to pick which ending you like best. Please drop me a email at aruggs@aol.com or visit my website at www.tonyruggiero.com to vote on which ending you liked the best.

———•———

Disclaimer: This story is an obvious work of fiction meant to be fun and entertaining. The liberties I have taken with individual stereotypes and groups is purely fun and whimsical—and not a political or social statement of any kind. I think that those of you who know me and my sense of humor will understand that. For those of you that don't—well tough (that was a joke).

THIS IS REALLY THE END

SO TURN THE PAGE AND GET ON WITH YOUR LIFE—TIL NEXT TIME.

Disconnected

Christiana Ellis

J*anie, do not be afraid."*
Janie Doucétte was lost in thought when the woman walked in front of her car. Lurching out of daydream, she slammed on the brakes. The tires squealed in protest and the car began to fishtail. A shuddering vibration traveled up through the steering wheel and her illusion of control slipped away entirely. The car, stronger than her will, skidded toward the crosswalk, pulling her along as a powerless hostage.

In a peculiar optical illusion, the woman's face seemed to rush at Janie right through the windshield, past her brittle veneer and into her darkest thoughts. Then she was gone. A pseudo-infinity, over in an instant, and the car finally came to a stop.

Janie's hands clutched the wheel with a strength that frightened her, trembling with something she couldn't identify. Either it was the engine, still running in a vulgar display of impropriety, or it was her own fear, coursing through her fingertips.

Her insides churned through nausea and hyperventilation while she sat rigid, staring straight ahead. The woman was no longer visible, but Janie couldn't bring herself to look around. The pedestrian didn't exist, had *never* existed. The whole thing had been in her head.

A loud thump jerked her to attention, and she turned to see the woman pounding on her driver-side window. "You dumb bitch! Don't you pay attention?"

Janie recoiled from the window, unable to reply, afraid and relieved and angry and ashamed. The woman's fury overwhelmed Janie's awareness, stripping away all her defenses, grabbing her by the heart and shaking. After a moment, the woman kicked the door and stormed away from the car.

Janie watched her go, and finally raised a hand from the steering wheel to brush a hot tear from her cheek. Her thoughts flirted with the reality of what had just happened, but pushed it away. Then she felt a subtle flicker, as though the universe had just blinked.

A car horn squawked from behind her and she stiffened in her seat. *How long had she been sitting there? And why? The woman didn't exist. Had never existed.*

Janie put the car into gear and drove away.

At home, the cable was out.

Janie glared at the TV. The screen glowed a soft gray and produced nothing but a bland hiss from the speakers.

Brushing away another tear, she shuffled down the hall to exchange her slacks and blouse for sweat pants and a T-shirt. Next, she picked up the phone and dialed Chinese delivery from memory. Soon her sesame chicken was on its way.

Pulling a chair from the cluttered kitchen table, she surveyed the stacks of stuff in her 'To-Do' pile and went from tired to exhausted. She buried her head in her arms for a moment, but a red 'Second Notice' stamp seemed convincing, so she tried to lose herself in the mindless action of opening envelopes, writing checks, and making sure that addresses appeared in little paper windows.

She set the phone bill aside. Thanks to her now-*ex*-roommate, she could not yet afford to pay it.

The whole roommate experiment had been a disaster. Her mother had suggested that living with someone would keep her from getting lonely. After weeks of nagging, Janie had placed an ad in the newspaper. Sally gave all the right answers to all the right questions: no drugs, no smoking, no pets, pay the rent on time. She was even willing to provide references, though Janie didn't bother with them.

At first, it had been kind of nice. Someone to come home to, to talk to, to brighten up the place. But soon came the loud music, the awful TV shows, and the obnoxious parties thrown without warning. Before, she had been alone in her apartment. With Sally around, she had been driven into hiding, confined to her bedroom.

That had continued until one day Sally announced that she was moving out. She packed her bags and left the next day.

"It's too depressing around here," she'd said. She left no forwarding address, and Janie didn't ask for one.

A knock at the door startled her. She swallowed a brief flash of anxiety and got up from the table. Standing on tiptoe, she peered through the tiny peephole.

A filmy haze of unknown origin obscured the view, so she settled back onto her heels with a frown. "Who is it?" she called.

"Delivery," said an unfamiliar voice. "Wu's Chinese."

Her chest tightened and she swallowed hard. "Just a second." She jogged down the hall and leaned against her bedroom wall, peering through the window at an acute angle. Through it, though distorted, she saw a young man holding a white plastic bag. He wasn't the usual guy, but the car at the sidewalk had a "Wu's Chinese" sign on the antenna. It seemed okay, and after all, who else would know that she had ordered food? Unless someone intercepted her phone call…

The guy knocked on the door again. She heard a muffled "Hello?" through the window.

She grimaced, clenching her fists and forcing long deep breaths, then she walked back down the hallway and opened the door.

"Did you order Chinese food?" The young man's bored expression and relaxed body language didn't seem threatening. He was tall, somewhat attractive actually, though conspicuously *not* Chinese.

"That's twelve fifty-three," he said.

A flush of warmth crept over her face when she realized that she had not yet written out the check. She accepted the food and asked him to wait. He smiled at her, with an unjustified condescension.

She set the bag on the table and walked around the other side to get her checkbook. As she was considering the tip, the guy began making little sports-guy noises. "Oh," "Aww," "Get'im," and the like. She turned and raised an eyebrow. He glanced back from the television with a sheepish grin.

"You like the Knicks?"

She furrowed her brow. "What?"

"Oh, well, I saw you had the game on…" He gestured toward the screen, which remained an undistinguished gray. "I just assumed you were a Knicks girl. I like the Pacers myself, but when it comes to B-ball, I'll watch anything." He gave her what he must have thought was a winning smile.

It was returned to him unopened.

"What are you talking about?"

The guy shifted his weight, his confidence fading. "I saw that you were watching the game." He pointed at the TV again. "And I was just wondering who you were rooting for."

"I'm not watching anything. The cable's out."

"What, you can't get anything but the game?"

"I can't get anything, period. The cable's out."

"But…" He frowned. "But, look at the TV."

166

She did. It was still blank. The heat returned to her face and she scowled. "Are you making fun of me?"

"What? No, I'm just saying that I can see…"

"You can see *what?*"

"I can see the-"

Her patience broke. "You can see a blank screen, and see this? It's your money. And this? It's me with my food. Your work here is done." With that, she held open the door, and glared, willing him out of her apartment.

His hand dropped back to his side. "Fine." He sneered as he walked out. "Bitch."

She slammed the door behind him and stood there, shocked and afraid. Her eyes suddenly welled with tears and she slid down the wall to the floor, knees pulled to her chest. After a few stifled cries, she shook the tears away.

She stood up, indignant and angry, and considered calling his supervisor, but the passion drained away like a leaky bucket. They wouldn't do anything about it. With a sigh, she walked to the couch and collapsed into it, covering her face with both hands.

Are they all *jerks,* she wondered, *or are they just all jerks to* me*?*

Kevin had seemed different at first. He proofread her paper on "Taming of the Shrew," and gave her insight and advice. He took her to dinner and gave her wit and sincerity. He dated her and gave her warmth and sensitivity. He slept with her and gave her love and tenderness. Then he dumped her and gave her insecurity and despair.

"I can't wait for you forever," he had said.

But Janie tried not to think too much about it.

Looking at the plastic bag with its cardboard containers, she lost all enthusiasm for it, so she stuck it in the fridge and wandered off to bed.

The next morning, she woke to static from her clock radio, the same bland hiss she had gotten from the television. After rubbing her eyes, she fiddled with the dials, but neither 'Tuning' nor 'Volume' had any effect. Dragging herself out of bed, she made her way to the shower.

She turned the faucet and yawned, scratching her ribs and waiting for the water to get hot. But after several minutes, the spray remained lukewarm. She turned the faucet all the way to hot, but it had no effect. She scowled.

A glance at the clock pressed the issue, so she turned the faucet back to her normal setting, in case the hot water suddenly returned, and climbed under the spray.

The hot water didn't return, but it wasn't *unpleasant* exactly, not *too* cold really. Just… wet. She finished quickly, then dried and dressed. She thought about calling her landlord about the water, but didn't pick up the phone.

On her way out the door, she tried to remember if she had anything due at work. No, she decided. Only some filing and database maintenance. Nothing pressing.

Documentation support for a pharmaceutical company was not exactly where she had pictured herself during college. Not that her predictions had ever been particularly specific. Could be worse. Besides, nobody *likes* their job. At least she worked mostly on her own and did not depend on other people to get her job done.

Her car wouldn't start. With the key in the ignition, the car seemed to have power; the radio was on, though it played nothing but soft white noise. Turning the key did nothing at all. No engine turning over, no grinding noises, nothing. She pounded the steering wheel with her hands until they throbbed and ached. Then she felt it had learned its lesson and got out of the car.

It was a chilly, overcast day, with the kind of frigid wind that easily pierced her thin jacket and chilled her to the bone, like a ghost just passing through. She almost walked right back inside and back to bed, but told herself that getting fired would not help fix her car. Until then, she was stuck with public transportation.

Though she ran for the last block, the bus left the stop without her, and she huddled into her jacket, leaning against the sign to wait. She looked at other people. Most of them bundled behind bland overcoats, pulled up collars, and windbreaker hoods. With only the upper halves of their faces visible, eyes all squinted against the wind, everyone looked strangely alike. Janie shivered, wishing that she had her heavy coat.

It was in a storage locker. She had left it at the old house last spring and her father had boxed it up with everything else when he sold the place. He never called about it, but she supposed that his new job kept him busy.

Her mother's new boyfriend kept *her* busy. The last conversation had been a couple of weeks ago, a rushed exchange of idle small talk. Janie started to ask about the dog, but she was interrupted by call waiting. "Oh, sorry, honey," said her mom. "I have to take this. You feel better, okay?"

When the bus arrived, Janie deposited sixty cents in the slot and took a seat in the back. They had changed the seats since the last time. Hard gray plastic instead of ratty, smelly upholstery. A lateral move, as far as Janie was concerned.

The bus pulled away from the stop and trundled past cinderblock apartment complexes and chain convenience stores. Round and round it went on its perpetual route, forever going in circles and passing the same old stops over and over again. *Sounds familiar,* she thought.

"You have chosen this life."

"Huh?" She looked around, but there was no one else on the bus, and the driver was yards away, singing something to himself. She sighed and muttered under her breath. "Great, even my imagination is giving me a hard time."

After taking a moment for wry self-pity, Janie frowned. Something was wrong. Glancing around again, she could see what looked like an ordinary bus with no obvious anomalies, but something remained amiss.

She had already noticed the seats, and as she looked, she realized that the bus interior had been painted to match, but neither item satisfied her disquiet. She didn't see anything unusual.

It came upon her like a flash. There were no ads. Usually, a number of ads ran along the top of the aisle on either side. Advertisements for a local travel agent, a new restaurant, or discount bus passes. Little things to look at while you ride. The metal strip meant to hold the ads was empty. When she looked forward, she saw that even the normal instruction signs were missing. The "No food/drink" sign, the "Please stay behind yellow line" sign, even the yellow line. All gone.

Her eyes went wide and her heart began to pound. Did she get on the wrong bus by mistake? She swallowed the lump in her throat and called out to the driver. "Um, excuse me? Is this the 227 route?"

The driver turned in his seat and smiled back at her for a moment before facing the road again. "Sure is. That the one you want?"

"Yeah," she said, frowning at the empty ad strip again. She wanted to ask about the signs, but her feeling of discomfort continued to grow. What if this wasn't the real bus? What if this guy had stolen it and now he was kidnapping… Her breath came faster. *No. No, that's stupid.* But she couldn't control herself. Before she knew what she was doing, she pushed the stop-signal strip.

The route had taken her downtown, to the park, and the bus pulled up to the next stop and opened the door. She kept her eyes to the ground as she made her way back up the aisle and off the bus. As it pulled away, she covered her face with both hands. "What am I doing? Now I'm just going to be even *later!*"

Finally, she took a deep breath and looked across the street to the park. She came here sometimes. On slow workdays, when she could get away with taking a long lunch, she sometimes got a sandwich from a nearby deli and ate on a quiet bench off the main path. She decided that she wasn't feeling well, and should call in sick, but instead of finding a payphone, she bought a turkey sandwich from the corner deli, crossed the street and walked into the park.

Her bench was gone.

There was nothing in its place. Even the concrete base that had served as its foundation was gone. Briefly disoriented, she turned, looking up and down the path, and established that she was, in fact, where she thought she was. The bench was not.

Janie stood there, frowning in consternation. Had it been stolen as an act of vandalism? Was it being replaced? Repaired? She glanced around, looking for the other benches. They were all still in place, but all occupied as well. *Why did they have to take* my *bench?* It was too cold to sit on the ground under a tree. The sky was still overcast, an almost featureless plane of gray; the sun was nowhere to be found. The breeze from earlier had gone, and the air was very still. After deliberating for a moment, she decided to put up with sharing a bench.

Janie selected one occupied only by a middle-aged woman reading a book and eating bits off the top of a ridiculously oversized muffin. She seemed to Janie to be the one least likely to try and start up a conversation. Janie sat, and unwrapped her sandwich.

She took a bite and made a face. The turkey was very bland today. It didn't taste spoiled exactly, it just didn't taste like anything.

Out of the corner of her eye, she saw the middle-aged woman tear off a chunk of her muffin, toss it on the ground, and smile at it.

Janie stared at the small lump of muffin resting on the concrete, then looked up at the woman.

The woman blushed a little and smiled, as though Janie had caught her at something. "I know I shouldn't feed them, but they're just so cute, I can't help it."

Janie turned back to the small fragment of muffin, which clearly wasn't feeding anything. It sat there on the ground all alone. There were no birds or animals to be seen.

"Oh, look, now he's got a little friend."

Janie turned back to the woman, incredulity written all over her face.

The woman looked up from the pavement, a frown of confusion lining her face. "What is it? Don't you like squirrels?"

"What squirrels?"

The woman pointed to the sidewalk again, where the chunk of muffin had gone, probably blown away by a gust of wind or something. "Those squirrels." She paused. "Right there."

Janie turned away and tried to stare at anything other than the woman's worried face, but the only things she could find were her tasteless sandwich and the muffin crumbs. Neither one seemed acceptable.

Was it some sort of prank? She glanced around cautiously, looking for a camera. Risking a furtive glance at the woman, Janie saw a large brooch on her lapel. Was it a tiny video transmitter? She was mortified to think that her confused expression might find its way onto television screens, to be laughed at by housewives and tax attorneys.

She imagined the delivery boy pointing her out to the cooks in the Chinese restaurant. 'I delivered once to that bitch.' Her mother would drop anything she was doing and rush to the phone as fast as she could in order to tell Janie that it was 'no big deal'. Her ex-roommate Sally, giggling hysterically into her boyfriend's chest.

Almost before she knew it, she leapt to her feet and seized the brooch. The synthetic material of the woman's collar made a high tearing sound as it gave way to Janie's desperate fingers. The woman shrieked in surprise, and sat cowering on the bench, her eyes wide and afraid, her hands shaking. Her muffin had fallen off her lap on to the ground, crumbling into pieces on impact.

Janie stood motionless, unable to comprehend her own actions. She held the brooch in her palm, feeling the patch of smooth material that had torn loose with the bauble. She squeezed it tight, and felt the sharp metal pin poking the skin of her ring finger.

She threw the trinket to the ground and ran down the path, away from the crazy squirrel woman. They needed your permission to put you on the air, didn't they? Maybe the woman was crazy. But… the delivery guy had done the same thing. And the missing ads on the bus. She stopped short. Her car. Her television! They had been inside her apartment!

Janie didn't go to work. Instead, she waited for the next bus, but when she saw no ad on the side, she didn't get on. It left without her, and as she watched it go, she grew stern. She was being silly. Why would anyone go to all this trouble to play pranks on *her*? She was nobody!

When the next bus came, again without ads, she forced herself to climb aboard. For a while, she found herself stealing covert glances at the other passengers, trying to catch them watching her, but no one looked suspicious. She sagged deeper into her seat.

The squirrel-woman was just crazy after all. Totally nuts, it was that simple. And the bench? Probably damaged by vandals and off being repaired. Or moved to another spot. All perfectly logical. Just a series of coincidences.

By that time, she was nearly home, so she tried to press the pressure strip that signaled the driver to stop. She pressed it hard, but whether from the cold or from sheer nervous energy, her hands felt numb and insensitive. The strip didn't chime, or make any signal that she could see. She pounded it again and again until the driver yelled at her to stop.

Janie got off the bus and walked home. As she passed her car, she reminded herself to call the mechanic. As soon as she phoned work to say she wasn't coming in. And her landlord. She made a mental list of necessary calls and ran through it over and over in her head, repeating it like a mantra.

Inside, she grabbed the beige plastic handset of her cordless phone and had already started to dial before realizing that the phone was dead.

She felt a quick flash of frustration but stopped herself from throwing the handset across the room. She giggled involuntarily and felt tears in the corners of her eyes. Fighting to calm herself, she set the phone down on the table in a slow, deliberate motion, and coaxed her hand into relaxing its grip. When she pulled away, she left a bright red smear on the plastic. She examined her hand and found it bleeding, probably from the brooch. *Funny*, she thought, poking at the small hole in her finger. It didn't even hurt. She was bleeding and it didn't even hurt.

She shook her hands, opening and closing her fists. She didn't have any trouble controlling her fingers, but they felt like they were wrapped in a layer of foam, robbed of any texture and all sensation was muted. She pinched the end of her index finger hard between her fingernails and was rewarded with a small twinge of pain.

She pinched harder and smiled at a sharper, more intense flash. She idly glanced up at the kitchen knives on the counter, and wondered if…

But a rumble in her stomach interrupted the thought.

Lunchtime? The clocks on both her VCR and microwave were blank. She had lost her sandwich in the park, so she went to the refrigerator and retrieved her uneaten Chinese food. Sitting down at the table with a cola and cold sesame chicken, she took a bite.

And spit it out. No taste at all. It may as well have been a piece of damp sponge. She stared in astonishment at the chicken speared on her fork, then down at the rest of her meal. She nudged off the first piece and speared another one, this one dripping with dark orange sauce and sesame seeds. Nothing. The cola was in an unopened can. Surely it couldn't have been… She opened it and sipped a flat, flavorless liquid.

She dropped the can and leapt to her feet. The sudden motion sent her chair skittering across the hardwood floor, where it crashed into an end table. She glanced at the noise, but returned to glare at the food. The soda can rolled across the table and onto the floor, pouring its contents into spattered puddles.

Drugged. She'd been drugged. Her breath raced in and out of her lungs, moving too quickly to do its job, and her heart felt ready to explode. Practically before she knew it, she had packed an overnight bag and fled.

Outside, the sky was still overcast, but not so dark as before, instead, it was an almost uniform gray. She started for the bus stop, walking in long, hurried strides, but realization stopped her short. They controlled the buses. She broke into a run and sprinted down a small alley between two neighboring buildings.

When she emerged on the next street over, she saw a cab waiting and started to enter it, but realized, that too might be part of their plan. She froze, doing nothing but breathing hard. "Why are they doing this to me?" she whispered.

"You are doing it to yourself."

Her eyes went wide and she looked around. A few people stood watching her from the sidewalk and she ran in the other direction. She sprinted back up the alley and down the street, the weight of her bag nearly toppling her and her breath rushing, until she spotted a gas station across the street.

She hurried to the pay phone in front. She intended to call a random cab company from the phone book and confirm the car number before hanging up. The phone was in use by a thirty-something man in gray coveralls. They were the type that might be used by a mechanic, but there was not a spot of grease on them.

"Please!" she shouted. "I need to use that phone!"

He jumped at the sound of her voice, and turned around with an annoyed expression. She glared at him, and after meeting her eyes, the anger vanished from his face and he swallowed. "I'll have to call you back," he said into the phone, then he hung up and backed away. "There you go," he said. "Go right ahead."

She watched him go. Why had he been looking at her that way? She seized the receiver and put it to her shoulder, then grabbed the phone book. All the pages were blank. It belatedly occurred to her that there was no dial tone coming from the handset.

She dropped the receiver and phone book as if bitten. The man who had just been talking on it was nowhere in sight. He had been part of it! Rage bubbled up from her gut and she clenched both hands into fists. With barely a conscious intent, she turned and ran into the gas station.

Everything was blank. Everything in the store was a plain gray, with no printing or pictures of any kind. She saw rows of plain, gray aluminum cans. Stacks of plain, gray boxes. Racks of plain, gray bags. Gray floor, gray ceiling. She looked behind the counter at the cashier, dressed in a plain, gray uniform, wiping the gray counter with a gray rag. His nametag was blank.

With a surge of fury, she seized a magazine. Pulling it open, she found blank pages all the way down to blank insert cards. She stormed over to the cashier and threw it at him. "What the hell is going on? Why are you people doing this to me?"

The man took a few steps back from the counter, eyes wide and mouth open. He looked down at the magazine, then up at Janie. "Um… doing what?"

"You're part of this too, you… You know *exactly* what I'm talking about! The magazines! The packages!" She gestured around the store. "Why are they all blank?"

"Blank? Lady, are you okay?"

She grabbed a double-handful of blank candy-bars and threw them to the ground. "No, I'm not fucking okay!"

"I'm going to call the police," he said, with a shaky voice.

"The police? Right. 'The police.' Fine! Call them! See if I care! Whatever you people are doing, why don't you stop messing with me and tell me what the hell is going on!"

"Lady, I'll tell you whatever you want, but first you're going to have to calm down and tell me what the problem is. Blank what?"

"I'm sick of this," she shouted. "The signs! The boxes! The magazines! Why are they blank? What are you people trying to do to me?"

"Janie, be still."

Janie whirled in place to see who had spoken but no one was there.

"What is it now?" asked the clerk.

"Who else is here?" she demanded. Her voice shook, and hot stinging tears began to stream from her eyes. "Who said that?"

"I don't know what you mean," said the clerk. "No one else is here. Just try to—"

Janie turned and ran out the door, only to stop short at what she found outside.

Everything… *Everything* was blank, gray, and smooth. All detail, all color, all texture… gone. She looked for the pay phone she had tried to use just a few moments ago but it had disappeared, leaving a smooth blank wall. There were no cars, and no people; all plants and trees had vanished. A smooth gray surface stretched across what had, only a moment ago, been the street. A short distance away, it met a smooth gray wall that had been a building.

"Janie, be still."

She beat on both temples with dull fists. "Who's saying that?" she demanded. "Why are you doing this to me?"

She turned back the way she had come and faced another featureless gray wall. She reached out her hand, to touch the smooth surface. It wasn't cold, it wasn't hot, it wasn't anything. She realized that she was hyperventilating again, but could not stop, could not catch her breath. Her stomach lurched and she felt as though some invisible force were compressing her chest. When she turned again, even the featureless block of the building across the street was gone. Turning again, the convenience store was missing.

"No! Stop it!" she screamed. "Stop doing this to me! Why can't you just leave me alone?" Looking all around, her breath rasping hot and painful through a closed throat, she could see nothing but a flat gray plane, imperceptibly merging into a blank horizon. She took a few shaky steps, and reeled. She tried to catch her breath, but after a few more steps, she fell to her knees, and couldn't feel it. Her clothes were all gray. Then nothing.

———•———

"Janie, do not be afraid."

Janie opened her eyes with a start. When she saw nothing but gray, she closed them again, breathing hard and fast. She tentatively reached out one hand, probing, but found nothing. She opened her eyes again.

Nothing but grayness. Even the horizon had faded away, leaving no distinction between featureless plain and monotonous sky. There was no object, no feature, no landmark she could see. Only waving a hand before her face showed that she had not gone blind.

The invisible foam around her fingers remained, and she gasped to discover that her clothes had been replaced by a thin garment like a hospital gown, colored to match everything else.

She swallowed, and with a desire to stand, she found herself standing, despite the absence of anything to stand on. Hovering in the void, she was able to dip her toes through the invisible plane that otherwise seemed able to support her.

She walked a few steps, feeling nothing under her feet, holding her hands out in front, fingers spread wide, lest she run into some invisible obstacle. Though she felt a sense of forward motion, nothing in her surroundings showed any change. She began to feel tears pricking at her eyes again, but she continued forward, closer to sobbing with every step.

And what of the still, small voice? Had she imagined it? Something about it seemed familiar. She began to tremble.

"Janie… Do not be afraid."

She jumped in spite of herself. "Hello?" she called. The lump in her throat made it hard to speak. "Who's there? What is this place?"

"This is not a place." The voice came from everywhere. From nowhere.

"Not a… Where am I?"

"Nothing."

"What am I doing here?"

"You have brought yourself here."

"What? No! I didn't! Something is happening to me!"

"The world is too large to push away. You can only push yourself away from the world."

The words shook her, and Janie fell to her hands and knees, struggling to retain control. "What do you mean? I don't understand! Why is this happening to me?"

"You understand."

"No, I don't!" she shouted. "I *don't* understand. I don't know what's happening to me. I—"

"Janie, do not be afraid."

A sob escaped her throat. "But I *am* afraid!" she said, then curled into a ball, drawing her arms and legs in around her like a shield. "I *am* afraid."

"There is no need. I am with you."

Janie cried, shaking, feeling hollow, as though she might collapse in on herself at any moment. "I just want all this to stop!"

"All is as one. Do not harden your heart."

"Why are you doing this to me? Why can't you just leave me alone?"

"You are loved."

"Just go away!" she shouted. "I don't want to be loved, I want it all to be over!"

"You have a purpose."

"I don't want it! Just leave me alone!"

"You are never alone."

She collapsed into sobbing, great heaving spasms that shook her to the core, tears trailing hot-cool streaks down her face.

Slowly, as she lay there, she began to feel something embrace her. She was wrapped in warmth, but not just on the outside. It moved through her, permeating her, absorbing her, connecting her to something larger, something infinite.

She stared at nothing in wide-eyed wonder, the tears still streaming down her face. It seemed as though time had stopped, the universe pausing in its constant expansion, taking a moment just for her. Then, as gently as it had slowed, time began moving again, and the universe resumed its progress, carrying her aloft on its shoulders.

Who are you?

I care for you.

What's going to happen to me?

There is a plan.

But what do I *do*?

That decision is yours.

She thought for a moment, absorbing that. At last, she said, "I just … I want to go back, but I don't know how."

"Love."

"Love," she repeated, turning the word over in her mind. It was as though she had heard it for the first time. Janie looked up and saw something in the distance. "Hello?" She stood, feeling stiff, and wiped her eyes and nose on the short sleeve of her light gown. She walked toward the object, vaguely aware of floor tiles, cool and rough beneath her bare feet. Walls faded into her peripheral vision. Her gaze remained fixed on the thing until she was upon it.

It was a bundle of flowers. A riot of color, reds and pinks and yellows and greens, all seeming to glow with an inner light. She leaned closer, inhaling the sweet fragrance with a deep even breath. The light, the fragrance, filled her with an echo of the presence that had lifted her, embraced her. Staring at the flowers, unaware of anything else, she sat on the strange, railed bed that she hadn't noticed appearing, and lay down.

The card read: "You are never alone. Get Well Soon."

It was signed simply "Love."

Janie laughed. It was small and soft, but genuine. She laid back on the bed, and when she spoke, her voice was just a whisper. "Thank you."

She closed her eyes and felt sunlight on her face.

The Cat's Pajamas

James Marrow

"All politics is local politics."
— Tip O'Neill

The eighteenth-century Enlightenment was still in our faces, fetishizing the rational intellect and ramming technocracy down our throats, so I said to Vickie, "Screw it. This isn't for us. Let's hop in the car and drive to romanticism, or maybe even to preindustrial paganism, or possibly all the way to hunter-gatherer utopianism." But we only got as far as Pennsylvania.

I knew that the idea of spending all summer on the road would appeal to Vickie. Most of her affections, including her unbridled *wanderlust*, are familiar to me. Not only had we lived together for six years, we also worked at the same New Jersey high school—Vickie teaching American history, me offering a souped-up eleventh-grade Humanities course—with the result that both our screaming matches and our flashes of rapport drew upon a fund of shared experiences. And so it was that the first day of summer vacation found us rattling down Route 80 in our decrepit VW bus, listening to Crash Test Dummies CDs and pretending that our impulsive westward flight somehow partook of political subversion, though we sensed it was really just an extended camping trip.

Despite being an *épater le bourgeois* sort of woman, Vickie had spent the previous two years promoting the idea of holy matrimony, an institution that has consistently failed to enchant me. Nevertheless, when we reached the Delaware Water Gap, I turned to her and said, "Here's a challenge for us. Let's see if we can't become man and wife by this time tomorrow afternoon." It's important, I feel, to suffuse a relationship with a certain level of unpredictability, if not outright caprice. "Vows, rings, music, all of it."

"You're crazy," she said, brightening. She's got a killer smile, sharp at the edges, luminous at the center. "It takes a week just to get the blood-test results."

"I was reading in *Newsweek* that there's a portable analyzer on the market. If we can find a technologically advanced justice of the peace, we'll meet the deadline with time to spare."

"Deadline?" She tightened her grip on the steering wheel. "Jeez, Blake, this isn't a *game*. We're talking about a *marriage*."

"It's a game and a gamble—I know from experience. But with you, sweetheart, I'm ready to bet the farm."

She laughed and said, "I love you."

· — · — ·

We spent the night in a motel outside a pastoral Pennsylvania borough called Greenbriar, got up at ten, made distracted love, and began scanning the yellow pages for a properly outfitted magistrate. By noon we had our man, District Justice George Stratus, proud owner of a brand new Sorrel-130 blood analyzer. It so happened that Judge Stratus was something of a specialist in instant marriage. For a hundred dollars flat, he informed me over the phone, we could have "the nanosecond nuptial package," including blood test, license, certificate, and a bottle of Taylor's champagne. I told him it sounded like a bargain.

To get there, we had to drive down a sinuous band of dirt and gravel called Spring Valley Road, past the asparagus fields, apple orchards, and cow pastures of Pollifex Farm. We arrived in a billowing nimbus of dust. Judge Stratus turned out to be a fat and affable paragon of efficiency. He immediately set about pricking our fingers and feeding the blood to his Sorrel-130, which took only sixty seconds to endorse our DNA even as it acquitted us of venereal misadventures. He faxed the results to the county courthouse, signed the marriage certificate, and poured us each a glass of champagne. By three o'clock, Vickie and I were legally entitled to partake of connubial bliss.

I think Judge Stratus noticed my pained expression when I handed over the hundred dollars, because he suggested that if we were short on cash, we should stop by the farm and talk to Andre Pollifex. "He's always looking for asparagus pickers this time of year." In point of fact, my divorce from Irene had cost me plenty, making a shambles of both my bank account and my credit record, and Vickie's fondness for upper-middle-class counterculture artifacts, solar powered trash compacters and so on, had depleted her resources as well. We had funds enough for the moment, though, so I told Stratus we probably wouldn't be joining the migrant worker pool before August.

"Well, sweetheart, we've done it," I said as we climbed back into the bus. "Mr. and Mrs. Blake Meeshaw."

"The price was certainly right," said Vickie, "even though the husband involved is a fixer-upper."

"You've got quite a few loose shingles yourself," I said.

"I'll be hammering and plastering all summer."

Although we had no plans to stop at Pollifex Farm, when we got there an enormous flock of sheep was crossing the road. Vickie hit the brakes just in time to avoid making mutton of a stray ewe, and we resigned ourselves to watching the woolly parade, which promised to be as dull as a passing freight train. Eventually a swarthy man appeared gripping a silver-tipped shepherd's crook. He advanced at a pronounced stoop, like a denizen of Dante's Purgatory balancing a millstone on his neck.

A full minute elapsed before Vickie and I realized that the sheep were moving in a loop, like wooden horses on a carousel. With an impatience bordering on hysteria, I leaped from the van and strode toward the obnoxious herdsman. What possible explanation could he offer for erecting this perpetual barricade?

Nearing the flock, I realized that the scene's strangest aspect was neither the grotesque shepherd nor the tautological road-block, but the sheep themselves. Every third or fourth animal was a mutant, its head distinctly humanoid, though the facial features seemed melted together, as if they'd been cast in wax and abandoned to the summer sun. The sooner we were out of here, I decided, the better.

"What the hell do you think you're doing?" I shouted. "Get these animals off the road!"

The shepherd hobbled up to me and pulled a tranquilizer pistol from his belt with a manifest intention of rendering me unconscious.

"Welcome to Pollifex Farm," he said.

The gun went off, the dart found my chest, and the world turned black.

———•———

Regaining consciousness, I discovered than someone—the violent shepherd? Andre Pollifex?—had relocated my assaulted self to a small bright room perhaps twelve feet square. Dust motes rode the sunlit air. Sections of yellow wallpaper buckled outward from the sheetrock like spritsails puffed with wind. I lay on a mildewed mattress, elevated by a box-spring framed in steel. A turban of bandages encircled my head. Beside me stood a second bed, as uninviting as my own, its bare mattress littered with artifacts that I soon recognized as Vickie's—comb, hand mirror, travel alarm, ankh earrings, well thumbed paperback of *Zen and the Art of Motorcycle Maintenance*.

It took me at least five minutes, perhaps as many as ten, before I realized that my brain had been removed from my cranium and that the pink, throbbing, convoluted mass of tissue on the nearby library cart was in fact my own thinking apparatus. Disturbing and unorthodox as this arrangement was, I could not deny its actuality. Every time I tapped my skull, a hollow sound came forth, as if I were knocking on an empty casserole dish. Fortunately, the physicians responsible for my condition had worked hard to guarantee that it would entail no functional deficits. Not only was my brain protected by a large Plexiglas jar filled with a clear, acrid fluid, it also retained its normal connection to my heart and spinal cord. A ropy mass of neurons, interlaced with augmentations of my jugular vein and my two carotid arteries, extended from beneath my orphaned medulla and stretched across four feet of empty space before disappearing into my reopened fontanel, the whole arrangement shielded from microbial contamination by a flexible plastic tube. I was thankful for my surgeons' conscientiousness, but also—I don't mind telling you—extremely frightened and upset.

My brain's extramural location naturally complicated the procedure, but in a matter of minutes I managed to transport both myself and the library cart into the next room, an unappointed parlor bedecked in cobwebs, and from there to an enclosed porch, all the while calling Vickie's name. She didn't answer. I opened the door and shuffled into the putrid air of Pollifex Farm. Everywhere I turned, disorder prospered. The cottage in which I'd awoken seemed ready to collapse under its own weight. The adjacent windmill canted more radically than Pisa's Leaning Tower. Scabs of leprous white paint mottled the sides of the main farmhouse. No building was without its unhinged door, its shattered window, its sunken roof, its disintegrating wall—a hundred instances of entropy mirroring the biological derangement that lay within.

I did not linger in the stables, home to six human-headed horses. Until this moment, I had thought the centaurial form intrinsically beautiful, but with their bony backs and twisted faces these monsters soon deprived me of that supposition. Nor did I remain long in the chicken coop, habitat of four gigantic human-headed hens, each the size of a German shepherd. Nor did the pig shed detain me, for seven human-headed hogs is not a spectacle that improves upon contemplation. Instead I hurried toward an immense barn, lured by a spirited performance of Tchaikovsky's Piano Concerto No. 1 wafting through a crooked doorway right out of *The Cabinet of Dr. Caligari.*

Cautiously I entered. Spacious and high roofed, the barn was a kind of agrarian cathedral, the Chartres of animal husbandry. In the far corner, hunched over a baby grand piano, sat a humanoid bull: blunt nose, gaping nostrils, a long tapering horn projecting from either side of his head. Whereas his hind legs were of the bovine variety, his forelegs ended in a pair of human hands that skated gracefully along the keyboard. He shared his bench with my wife, and even at this distance I could see that the bull man's virtuosity had brought her to the brink of rapture.

Cerebrum in tow, I made my way across the barn. With each step, my apprehension deepened, my confusion increased, and my anger toward Vickie intensified. Apprehension, confusion, anger: while I was not yet accustomed to experiencing such sensations in a location other than my head, the phenomenon now seemed less peculiar than when I'd first returned to sentience.

"I know what you're thinking," said Vickie, acknowledging my presence. "Why am I sitting here when I should be helping you recover from the operation? Please believe me: Karl said the anesthesia wouldn't wear off for another four hours."

She proceeded to explain that Karl was the shepherd who'd tranquilized me on the road, subsequently convincing her to follow him onto the farm rather than suffer the identical fate. But Karl's name was the least of what Vickie had learned during the past forty-eight hours. Our present difficulties, she elaborated, traced to the VD screening we'd received on Wednesday. In exchange for a substantial payment, Judge Stratus had promised to alert his patrons at Pollifex Farm the instant he happened upon a blood sample bearing the deoxyribonucleic acid component known as QZ-11-4. Once in possession of this gene—or, more specifically, once in possession of a human brain whose in utero maturation had been influenced by this gene—Dr. Pollifex's biological investigations could go forward.

"Oh, Blake, they're doing absolutely *wonderful* work here." Vickie rose from the bench, came toward me, and, taking care not to become entangled in my spinal cord, gave me a mildly concupiscent hug. "An external brain to go with your external genitalia—I think it's very sexy."

"Stop talking nonsense, Vickie!" I said. "I've been *mutilated*!"

She stroked my bandaged forehead and said, "Once you hear the whole story, you'll realize that your bilateral hemispherectomy serves a greater good."

"Call me Maxwell," said the bull man, lifting his fingers from the keyboard. "Maxwell Taurus." His voice reminded me of Charles

Laughton's. "I must congratulate you on your choice of marriage partner, Blake. Vickie has a refreshingly open mind."

"And I have a depressingly vacant skull," I replied. "Take me to this lunatic Pollifex so I can get my brain put back where it belongs."

"The doctor would never agree to that." Maxwell fixed me with his stare, his eyes all wet and brown like newly created caramel apples. "He requires round-the-clock access to your anterior cortex."

A flock of human-headed geese fluttered into the barn, raced toward a battered aluminum trough full of grain, and began to eat. Unlike Maxwell, the geese did not possess the power of speech—either that, or they simply had nothing to say to each other.

I sighed and leaned against my library cart. "So what, exactly, does QZ-11-4 *do*?"

"Dr. Pollifex calls it the integrity gene, wellspring of decency, empathy, and compassionate foresight," said Maxwell. "Francis of Assisi had it. So did Charles Darwin, Clara Barton, Mahatma Gandhi, Florence Nightingale, Albert Schweitzer, and Susan B. Anthony. And now—now that Dr. Pollifex has started injecting me with a serum derived from your hypertrophic superego—now *I've* got it too."

Although my vanity took a certain satisfaction in Maxwell's words, I realized that I'd lost the thread of his logic. "At the risk of sounding disingenuously modest, I'd have to say I'm not a particularly ethical individual."

"Even if a person inherits QZ-11-4, it doesn't necessarily enjoy expression. And even if the gene enjoys expression"—Maxwell offered me a semantically freighted stare—"the beneficiary doesn't always learn to use his talent. Indeed, among Dr. Pollifex's earliest discoveries was the fact that complete QZ-11-4 actualization is impossible in a purely human species. The serum—we call it Altruoid—the serum reliably engenders ethical superiority only in people who've been genetically melded with domesticated birds and mammals."

"You mean—you used to be … human?"

"For twenty years I sold life insurance under the name Lewis Phelps. Have no fear, Blake. We are not harvesting your cerebrum in vain. I shall employ my Altruoid allotment to bestow great boons on Greenbriar."

"You might fancy yourself a moral giant," I told the bull man, "but as far as I'm concerned, you're a terrorist and a brain thief, and I intend to bring this matter to the police."

"You will find that strategy difficult to implement." Maxwell left his piano and, walking upright on his hooves, approached my library cart. "Pollifex Farm is enclosed by a barbed-wire fence twelve feet high. I suggest you try making the best of your situation."

The thought of punching Maxwell in the face now occurred to me, but I dared not risk uprooting my arteries and spinal cord. "If Pollifex continues pilfering my cortex, how long before I become a basket case?"

"Never. The doctor happens to be the world's greatest neuro-cartographer. He'll bring exquisite taste and sensitivity to each extraction. During the next three years, you'll lose only trivial knowledge, useless skills, and unpleasant memories."

"Three years?" I howled. "You bastards plan to keep me here *three years*?"

"Give or take a month. Once that interval has passed, my peers and I shall have reached the absolute apex of vertebrate ethical development."

"See, Blake, they've thought of *everything*," said Vickie. "These people are *visionaries*."

"These people are Nazis," I said.

"Really, sir, name calling is unnecessary," said Maxwell with a snort. "There's no reason we can't all be friends." He rested an affirming hand on my shoulder. "We've given you a great deal of information to absorb. I suggest you spend tomorrow afternoon in quiet contemplation. Come evening, we'll all be joining the doctor for dinner. It's a meal you're certain to remember."

———•———

My new bride and I passed the night in our depressing little cottage beside the windmill. Much to my relief, I discovered that my sexual functioning had survived the bilateral hemispherectomy. We had to exercise caution, of course, lest we snap the vital link between medulla and cord, with the result that the whole encounter quickly devolved into a kind of slow-motion ballet. Vickie said it was like mating with a china figurine, the first negative remark I'd heard her make concerning my predicament.

At ten o'clock the next morning, one of Karl's human-headed sheep entered the bedroom, walking upright and carrying a wicker tray on which rested two covered dishes. When I asked the sheep how long she'd been living at Pollifex Farm, her expression became as vacant as a cake of soap. I concluded that the power of articulation was reserved only to those mutants on an Altruoid regimen.

The sheep bowed graciously and left, and we set about devouring our scrambled eggs, hot coffee, and buttered toast. Upon consuming her final mouthful, Vickie announced that she would spend the day reading two scientific treatises she'd received from Maxwell, both by Dr. Pollifex: *On the Mutability of Species* and *The Descent of Morals*. I told her I had a different agenda. If there was a way out of this bucolic asylum, I was by-God going to find it.

Before I could take leave of my wife, Karl himself appeared, clutching a black leather satchel to his chest as a mother might hold a baby. He told me he deeply regretted Wednesday's assault—I must admit, I detected no guile in his apology—then explained that he'd come to collect the day's specimen. From the satchel he removed a glass-and-steel syringe, using it to suck up a small quantity of anterior cortex and transfer it to a test tube. When I told Karl that I felt nothing during the procedure, he reminded me that the human brain is an insensate organ, nerveless as a stone.

I commenced my explorations. Pollifex's domain was vaster than I'd imagined, though most of its fields and pastures were deserted. True to the bull man's claim, a fence hemmed the entire farm, the barbed-wire strands woven into a kind of demonic tennis net and strung between steel posts rising from a concrete foundation. In the northeast corner lay a barn as large as Maxwell's concert hall, and it was here, clearly, that Andre Pollifex perpetuated his various crimes against nature. The doors were barred, the windows occluded, but by staring through the cracks in the walls I managed to catch glimpses of hospital gurneys, surgical lights, and three enormous glass beakers in which sallow, teratoid fetuses drifted like pickles in brine.

About twenty paces from Pollifex's laboratory, a crumbling tool shed sat atop a hill of naked dirt. I gave the door a hard shove—not too hard, given my neurological vulnerability—and it pivoted open on protesting hinges. A shaft of afternoon sunlight struck the interior, revealing an assortment of rakes, shovels, and pitchforks, plus a dozen bags of fertilizer—but, alas, no wire cutters.

My perambulations proved exhausting, both mentally and physically, and I returned to the cottage for a much needed nap. That afternoon, my brain tormented me with the notorious "student's dream." I'd enrolled in an advanced biology course at my old alma mater, Rutgers, but I hadn't attended a single class or handed in even one assignment. And now I was expected to take the final exam.

Vickie, my brain, and I were the last to arrive at Andre Pollifex's dinner party, which occurred in an airy glass-roofed conservatory attached to the back of the farmhouse. The room smelled only slightly better than the piano barn. At the head of the table presided our host, a disarmingly ordinary looking man, weak of jaw, slight of build, distinguished primarily by his small black moustache and complementary goatee. His face was pale and flaccid, as if he'd been raised in a cave. The instant he opened his mouth to greet us, though, I apprehended something of his glamour, for he had the most majestic voice I've ever heard outside of New York's Metropolitan Opera House.

"Welcome, Mr. and Mrs. Meeshaw," he said. "May I call you Blake and Vickie?"

"Of course," said Vickie.

"May I call you Joseph Mengele?" I said.

Pollifex's white countenance contracted into a scowl. "I can appreciate your distress, Blake. Your sacrifice has been great. I believe I speak for everyone here when I say that our gratitude knows no bounds."

Karl directed us into adjacent seats, then resumed his place next to Pollifex, directly across from the bull man. I found myself facing a pig woman whose large ears flopped about like college pennants and whose snout suggested an oversized button. Vickie sat opposite a goat man with a tapering white beard dangling from his chin and two corrugated horns sprouting from his brow.

"I'm Serge Milkovich," said the goat man, shaking first Vickie's hand, then mine. "In my former life I was Bud Frye, plumbing contractor."

"Call me Juliana Sowers," said the pig woman, enacting the same ritual. "At one time I was Doris Owens of Owens Real Estate, but then I found a higher calling. I cannot begin to thank you for the contribution you're making to science, philosophy, and local politics."

"Local politics?" I said.

"We three beneficiaries of QZ-11-4 form the core of the new Common Sense Party," said Juliana. "We intend to transform Greenbriar into the most livable community in America."

"I'm running for Borough Council," said Serge. "Should my campaign prove successful, I shall fight to keep our town free of Consumerland discount stores. Their advent is inevitably disastrous for local merchants."

Juliana crammed a handful of hors d'oeuvres into her mouth. "I seek a position on the School Board. My stances won't prove automatically popular—better pay for elementary teachers, sex education starting in grade four—but I'm prepared to support them with passion and statistics."

Vickie grabbed my hand and said, "See what I mean, Blake? They may be mutants, but they have terrific ideas."

"As for me, I've got my eye on the Planning Commission," said Maxwell, releasing a loud and disconcerting burp. "Did you know there's a scheme afoot to run the Route 80 Extension along our northern boundary, just so it'll be easier for people to get to Penn State football games? Once construction begins, the environmental desecration will be profound."

As Maxwell expounded upon his anti-extension arguments, a half-dozen sheep arrived with our food. In deference to Maxwell and Juliana, the cuisine was vegetarian: tofu, lentils, capellini with meatless marinara sauce. It was all quite tasty, but the highlight of the meal was surely the venerable and exquisite vintages from Pollifex's cellar. After my first few swallows of Brunello di Montalcino, I worried that Pollifex's scalpel had denied me the pleasures of intoxication, but eventually the expected sensation arrived. (I attributed the hiatus to the extra distance my blood had to travel along my extended arteries.) By the time the sheep were serving dessert, I was quite tipsy, though my bursts of euphoria alternated uncontrollably with spasms of anxiety.

"Know what I think?" I said, locking on Pollifex as I struggled to prevent my brain from slurring my words. "I think you're trying to turn me into a zombie."

The doctor proffered a heartening smile. "Your discomfort is understandable, Blake, but I can assure you all my interventions have been innocuous thus far—and will be in the future. Tell me, what two classroom pets did your second-grade teacher, Mrs. Hines, keep beside her desk, and what were their names?"

"I have no idea."

"Of course you don't. That useless memory vanished with the first extraction. A hamster and a chameleon. Florence and Charlie. Now tell me about the time you threw up on your date for the senior prom."

"That never happened."

"Yes it did, but I have spared you any recollection of the event. Nor will you ever again be haunted by the memory of forgetting your lines during the Cransford Community Theater production of *A Moon for the Misbegotten*. Now please recite Joyce Kilmer's 'Trees.'"

"All right, all right, you've made your point," I said. "But you still have no right to mess with my head." I swallowed more wine. "As for this ridiculous Common Sense Party—okay, sure, these candidates might get *my* vote—I'm for better schools and free enterprise and all that—but the average Greenbriar citizen..." In lieu of stating the obvious, I finished my wine.

"What *about* the average Greenbriar citizen?" said Juliana huffily.

"The average Greenbriar citizen will find us morphologically unacceptable?" said Serge haughtily.

"Well ... yes," I replied.

"Unpleasantly odiferous?" said Maxwell snippily.

"That too."

"Homely?" said Juliana defensively.

"I wouldn't be surprised."

The sheep served dessert—raspberry and lemon sorbet—and the seven of us ate in silence, painfully aware that mutual understanding between myself and the Common Sense Party would be a long time coming.

⸺·⸺

During the final two weeks of June, Karl siphoned fourteen additional specimens from my superego, one extraction per day. On the Fourth of July, the shepherd unwound my bandages. Although I disbelieved his assertion to be a trained nurse, I decided to humor him. When he pronounced that my head was healing satisfactorily, I praised his expertise, then listened intently as he told me how to maintain the incision, an ugly ring of scabs and sutures circumscribing my cranium like a crown of thorns.

As the hot, humid, enervating month elapsed, the Common Sense candidates finished devising their strategies, and the campaign began in earnest. The piano barn soon overflowed with shipping crates full of leaflets, brochures, metal buttons, t-shirts, bumper stickers, and pork-pie hats. With each passing day, my skepticism intensified. A goat running for Borough Council? A pig on the School Board? A bull guiding the Planning Commission? Pollifex's menagerie didn't stand a chance.

My doubts received particularly vivid corroboration on July 20th, when the doctor staged a combination cocktail party and fund-raiser at the farmhouse. From among the small but ardent population of political progressives inhabiting Greenbriar, Pollifex had identified thirty of the wealthiest. Two dozen accepted his invitation. Although these potential contributors were clearly appalled by my bifurcation, they seemed to accept Pollifex's explanation. (I suffered from a rare neurological disorder amenable only to the most radical surgery.) But then the candidates themselves sauntered into the living room, and Pollifex's guests immediately lost their powers of concentration.

It wasn't so much that Maxwell, Juliana, and Serge looked like an incompetent demiurge's roughest drafts. The real problem was that they'd retained so many traits of the creatures to which they'd been grafted. Throughout the entire event, Juliana stuffed her face with canapés and petit-fours. Whenever Serge engaged a potential donor in conversation, he crudely emphasized his points by ramming his horns into the listener's chest. Maxwell, meanwhile, kept defecating on the living room carpet, a behavior not redeemed by the mildly pleasant fragrance that a vegetarian diet imparts to bovine manure. By the time the mutants were ready to deliver their formal speeches, the pledges stood at a mere fifty dollars, and every guest had manufactured an excuse to leave.

"Your idea is never going to work," I told Pollifex after the candidates had returned to their respective barns. We were sitting in the doctor's kitchen, consuming mugs of French roast coffee. The door stood open. A thousand crickets sang in the meadow.

"This is a setback, not a catastrophe," said Pollifex brushing crumbs from his white dinner jacket. "Maxwell is a major Confucius scholar, with strong Kantian credentials as well. He can surely become housebroken. Juliana is probably the finest utilitarian philosopher since John Stuart Mill. For such a mind, table manners will prove a snap. If you ask Serge about the Sermon on the Mount, he'll recite the King James translation without a fluff. Once I explain how uncouth he's being, he'll learn to control his butting urge."

"Nobody wants to vote for a candidate with horns."

"It will take a while—quite a while—before Greenbriar's citizens appreciate this slate, but eventually they'll hop on the bandwagon." Pollifex poured himself a second cup of French roast. "Do you doubt that my mutants are ethical geniuses? Can you imagine, for example, how they responded to the Prisoner's Dilemma?

For three years running, I had used the Prisoner's Dilemma in my Introduction to Philosophy class. It's a situation-ethics classic, first devised in 1951 by Merrill Flood of the RAND Corporation. Imagine that you and a stranger have been arrested as accomplices in manslaughter. You are both innocent. The state's case is weak. Even though you don't know each other, you and the stranger form a pact. You will both stonewall it, maintaining your innocence no matter what deals the prosecutor may offer.

Each of you is questioned privately. Upon entering the interrogation room, the prosecutor lays out four possibilities. If you and your presumed accomplice hang tough, confessing to nothing, you will each get a short sentence, a mere seven months in prison.

If you admit your guilt and implicate your fellow prisoner, you will go scot free—and your presumed accomplice will serve a life sentence. If you hang tough and your fellow prisoner confesses-and-implicates, *he* will go scot free—and *you* will serve a life sentence. Finally, if you and your fellow prisoner both confess-and-implicate, you will each get a medium sentence, four years behind bars.

It doesn't take my students long to realize that the most logical course is to break faith with the stranger, thus guaranteeing that you won't spend your life in prison if he also defects. The uplifting-but-uncertain possibility of a short sentence must lose out to the immoral-but-immutable fact of a medium sentence. Cooperation be damned.

"Your mutants probably insist that they would keep faith regardless of the consequences," I said. "They would rather die than violate a trust."

"Their answer is subtler than that," said Pollifex. "They would tell the prosecutor, 'You imagine that my fellow prisoner and I have made a pact, and in that you are correct. You further imagine that you can manipulate us into breaking faith with one another. But given your obsession with betrayal, I must conclude that you are yourself a liar, and that you will ultimately seek to convert our unwilling confessions into life sentences. I refuse to play this game. Let's go to court instead.'"

"An impressive riposte," I said. "But the fact remains …" Reaching for the coffee pot, I let my voice drift away. "Suppose I poured some French roast directly into my jar? Would I be jolted awake?"

"Don't try it," said Pollifex.

"I won't."

The mutant maker scowled strenuously. "You think I'm some sort of mad scientist."

"Restore my brain," I told him. "Leave the farm, get a job at Pfizer, wash your hands of politics."

"I'm a sane scientist, Blake. I'm the last sane scientist in the world."

I looked directly in his eyes. The face that returned my gaze was neither entirely mad nor entirely sane. It was the face of a man who wasn't sleeping well, and it made me want to run away.

———•———

The following morning, my routine wanderings along the farm's perimeter brought me to a broad, swiftly flowing creek about twelve feet wide and three deep. Although the barbed-wire net extended beneath the water, clear to the bottom, I suddenly realized how a man might circumvent it. By redirecting the water's flow via a series of dikes, I could desiccate a large section of the creek bed and subsequently dig my way out of this hellish place. I would need only one of the shovels I'd spotted in the tool shed— a shovel, and a great deal of luck.

Thus it was that I embarked on a secret construction project. Every day at about 11:00 AM, right after Karl took the specimen from my superego, I slunk off to the creek and spent a half-hour adding rocks, logs, and mud to the burgeoning levees, returning to the cottage in time for lunch. Although the creek proved far less pliable than I'd hoped, I eventually became its master. Within two weeks, I figured, possibly three, a large patch of sand and pebbles would lie exposed to the hot summer sun, waiting to receive my shovel.

Naturally I was tempted to tell Vickie of my scheme. Given my handicap, I could certainly have used her assistance in building the levees. But in the end I concluded that, rather than endorsing my bid for freedom, she would regard it as a betrayal of the Common Sense Party and its virtuous agenda.

I knew I'd made the right decision when Vickie entered our cottage late one night in the form of a gigantic mutant hen. Her body had become a bulbous mass of feathers, her legs had transmuted into fleshy stilts, and her face now sported a beak the size of a funnel. Obviously she was running for elective office, but I couldn't imagine which one. She lost no time informing me. Her ambition, she explained, was to become Greenbriar's next mayor.

"I've even got an issue," she said.

"I don't want to hear about it," I replied, looking her up and down. Although she still apparently retained her large and excellent breasts beneath her bikini top, their present context reduced their erotic content considerably.

"Do you know what Greenbriar needs?" she proclaimed. "Traffic diverters at certain key intersections! Our neighborhoods are being suffocated by the automobile!"

"You shouldn't have done this, Vickie," I told her.

"My name is Eva Pullo," she clucked.

"These people have brainwashed you!"

"The Common Sense Party is the hope of the future!"

"You're talking like a fascist!" I said.

"At least I'm not a coward like you!" said the chicken.

For the next half-hour we hurled insults at each other—our first real post-marital fight—and then I left in a huff, eager to continue my arcane labors by the creek. In a peculiar way I still loved Vickie, but I sensed that our relationship was at an end. When I made my momentous escape, I feared, she would not be coming with me.

———•———

Even as I redirected the creek, the four mutant candidates brought off an equally impressive feat—something akin to a miracle, in fact. They got the citizens of Greenbriar to listen to them, and the citizens liked what they heard.

The first breakthrough occurred when Maxwell appeared along with three other Planning Commission candidates—Republican, Democrat, Libertarian—on Greenbriar's local-access cable channel. I watched the broadcast in the farmhouse, sitting on the couch between Vickie and Dr. Pollifex. Although the full-blooded humans on the podium initially refused to take Maxwell seriously, the more he talked about his desire to prevent the Route 80 Extension from wreaking havoc with local ecosystems, the clearer it became that this mutant had charisma. Maxwell's eloquence was breathtaking, his logic impeccable, his sincerity sublime. He committed no fecal faux pas.

"That bull was on his game," I admitted at the end of the transmission.

"The moderator was *enchanted*," enthused Vickie.

"Our boy is going to win," said Pollifex.

Two days later, Juliana kicked off her campaign for School Board. Aided by the ever energetic Vickie, she had outfitted the back of an old yellow school bus with a Pullman car observation platform, the sort of stage from which early twentieth-century presidential candidates campaigned while riding the rails. Juliana and Vickie also transformed the bus's interior, replacing the seats with a coffee bar, a chat lounge, and racks of brochures explaining the pig woman's ambition to expand the sex education program, improve services for special needs children, increase faculty awareness of the misery endured by gay students, and—most audacious of all—invert the salary pyramid so that first-grade teachers would earn more than high-school administrators. Day in, day out, Juliana tooled around Greenbriar in her appealing vehicle, giving out iced cappuccino, addressing crowds from the platform, speaking to citizens privately in the lounge, and somehow managing to check her impulse toward gluttony, all the while exhibiting a caliber of wisdom that eclipsed her unappetizing physiognomy. The tour was a fabulous success—such, at least, was the impression I received from watching the blurry, jerky coverage that Vickie accorded the pig woman's campaign with Pollifex's camcorder. Every time the school bus pulled away from a Juliana Sowers rally, it left behind a thousand tear-stained eyes, so moved were the citizens by her commitment to the glorious ideal of public education.

Serge, meanwhile, participated in a series of "Meet the Candidates" nights along with four other Borough Council hopefuls. Even when mediated by Vickie's shaky videography, the inaugural gathering at Greenbriar Town Hall came across as a powerful piece of political theater. Serge fully suppressed his impulse to butt his opponents—but that was the smallest of his accomplishments. Without slinging mud, flinging innuendo, or indulging in disingenuous rhetoric, he made his fellow candidates look like moral idiots for their unwillingness to stand firm against what he called "the insatiable greed of Consumerland." Before the evening ended, the attending voters stood prepared to tar-and-feather any discount chain executive who might set foot in Greenbriar, and it was obvious they'd also embraced Serge's other ideas for making the Borough Council a friend to local business. If Serge's plans came to fruition, shoppers would eventually flock to the downtown, lured by parking-fee rebates, street performers, bicycle paths, mini-playgrounds, and low-cost supervised day care.

As for Vickie's mayoral campaign—which I soon learned to call Eva Pullo's mayoral campaign—it gained momentum the instant she shed her habit of pecking hecklers on the head. Vickie's commitment to reducing the automobile traffic in residential areas occasioned the grandest rhetorical flights I'd ever heard from her. "A neighborhood should exist for the welfare of its children, not the convenience of its motorists," she told the local chapter of the League of Women Voters. "We must not allow our unconsidered veneration of the automobile to mask our fundamental need for community and connectedness," she advised the Chamber of Commerce. By the middle of August, Vickie had added a dozen other environmentalist planks to her platform, including an ingenious proposal to outfit the town's major highways with underground passageways for raccoons, badgers, woodchucks, skunks, and possums.

You must believe me, reader, when I say that my conversion to the Common Sense Party occurred well before the *Greenbriar Daily Times* published its poll indicating that the entire slate— Maxwell Taurus, Juliana Sowers, Serge Milkovich, Eva Pullo— enjoyed the status of shoo-ins. I was not simply trying to ride with the winners. When I abandoned my plan to dig an escape channel under the fence, I was doing what I thought was right. When I resolved to spend the next three years nursing the Pollifex Farm candidates from my cerebral teat, I was fired by an idealism so intense that the pragmatists among you would blush to behold it.

I left the levees in place, however, just in case I had a change of heart.

———•———

The attack on Pollifex Farm started shortly after 11:00 PM. It was Halloween night, which means that the raiders probably aroused no suspicions whatsoever as, dressed in shrouds and skull masks, they drove their pickup trucks through the streets of Greenbriar and down Spring Valley Road. To this day, I'm not sure who organized and paid for the atrocity. At its core, I suspect, the mob included not only yahoos armed with torches but also conservatives gripped by fear, moderates transfixed by cynicism, liberals in the pay of the *status quo*, libertarians acting out anti-government fantasies, and a few random anarchists looking for a good time. Whatever their conflicting allegiances, the vigilantes stood united in their realization that Andre Pollifex, sane scientist, was about to unleash a reign of enlightenment on Greenbriar. They were having none of it.

I was experiencing yet another version of the student's dream—this time I'd misconnected not simply with one class but with an entire college curriculum—when shouts, gunshots, and the neighing of frightened horses awoke me. Taking hold of the library cart, I roused Vickie by ruffling her feathers, and side by side we stumbled into the parlor. By the time we'd made our way outside, the windmill, tractor shed, corn crib, and centaur stables were all on fire. Although I could not move quickly without risking permanent paralysis, Vickie immediately sprang into action. Transcending her spheroid body, she charged into the burning stables and set the mutant horses free, and she proved equally unflappable when the vigilantes hurled their torches into Maxwell's residence. With little thought for her personal safety, she ran into the flaming piano barn, located the panicked bull man and the equally discombobulated pig woman—in recent months they'd entered into a relationship whose details needn't concern us here—and led them outside right before the roof collapsed in a great red wave of cascading sparks and flying embers.

And still the arsonists continued their assault, blockading the main gate with bales of burning hay, setting fire to the chicken coop, and turning Pollifex's laboratory into a raging inferno. Catching an occasional glimpse of our spectral enemies, their white sheets flashing in the light of the flames, I saw that they would not become hoist by their own petards, for they had equipped themselves with asbestos suits, scuba regulators, and compressed air tanks. As for the inhabitants of Pollifex Farm, it was certain that if we didn't move quickly, we would suffer either incineration, suffocation, or their concurrence in the form of fatally seared lungs.

Although I had never felt so divided, neither the fear spasms in my chest nor the jumbled thoughts in my jar prevented me from realizing what the mutants must do next. I told them to steal shovels from the tool shed, make for the creek, and follow it to the fence. Thanks to my levees, I explained, the bed now lay in the open air. Within twenty minutes or so, they should be able to dig below the barbed-wire net and gouge a dry channel for themselves. The rest of my plan had me bringing up the rear, looking out for Karl, Serge, and Dr. Pollifex so that I might direct them to the secret exit. Vickie kissed my lips, Juliana caressed my cheek, Maxwell embraced by brain, and then all three candidates rushed off into the choking darkness.

Before that terrible night was out, I indeed found the other Party members. Karl lay dead in a mound of straw beside the sheep barn, his forehead blasted away by buckshot. Serge sat on the rear porch of the farmhouse, his left horn broken off and thrust fatally into his chest. Finally I came upon Pollifex. The vigilantes had roped the doctor to a maple tree, subjected him to target practice, and left him for dead. He was as perforated as Saint Sebastian. A mattock, a pitchfork, and two scythes projected from his body like quills from a porcupine.

"Andre, it's me, Blake," I said, approaching.

"Blake?" he muttered. "Blake? Oh, Blake, they killed Serge. They killed Karl."

"I know. Vickie got away, and Maxwell too, and Juliana."

"I was a sane scientist," said Pollifex.

"Of course," I said.

"There are some things that expediency was not meant to tamper with."

"I agree."

"Pullo for Mayor!" he shouted.

"Taurus for Planning Commission!" I replied.

"Milkovich for Borough Council!" he shouted. "Sowers for School Board!" he screamed, and then he died.

There's not much more to tell. Although Vickie, Juliana, Maxwell, and I all escaped the burning farm that night, the formula for the miraculous serum died with Dr. Pollifex. Deprived of their weekly Altruoid injections, the mutants soon lost their talent for practical idealism, and their political careers sputtered out. Greenbriar now boasts a mammoth new Consumerland. The Route 80 extension is almost finished. High-school principals still draw twice the pay of first-grade teachers. Life goes on.

The last time I saw Juliana, she was the opening act at Caesar's Palace in Atlantic City. A few songs, some impersonations, a standup comedy routine—mostly vegetarian humor and animal-rights jokes leavened by a sardonic feminism. The crowd ate it up, and Juliana seemed to be enjoying herself. But, oh, what a formidable School Board member she would've made!

When the Route 80 disaster occurred, Maxwell was devastated—not so much by the extension itself as by his inability to critique it eloquently. These days he plays piano at Emilio's, a seedy bar in Newark. He is by no means the weirdest presence in the place, and he enjoys listening to the customers' troubles. But he is a broken mutant.

Vickie and I did our best to make it work, but in the end we decided that mixed marriages entail insurmountable hurdles, and we split up. Eventually she got a job hosting a preschool children's television show on the Disney Channel, *Arabella's Barnyard Band.* Occasionally she manages to insert a satiric observation about automobiles into her patter.

As for me, after hearing the tenth neurosurgeon declare that I am beyond reassembly, I decided to join the world's eternal vagabonds. I am brother to the Wandering Jew, the Flying Dutchman, and Marley's Ghost. I shuffle around North America, dragging my library cart behind me, exhibiting my fractured self to anyone who's willing to pay. In the past decade, my employers have included three carnivals, four roadside peep shows, two direct-to-video horror movie producers, and an artsy off-Broadway troupe bent on reviving *Le Grand Guignol.*

And always I remain on the lookout for another Andre Pollifex, another scientist who can manufacture QZ-11-4 serum and use it to turn beasts into politicians. I shall not settle for any sort of Pollifex, of course. The actual Pollifex, for example, would not meet my standards. The man bifurcated me without my permission, and I cannot forgive him for that.

The scientist I seek would unflinchingly martyr himself to the Prisoner's Dilemma. As they hauled him away to whatever dungeon is reserved for such saints, he would turn to the crowd and say, "The personal cost was great, but at least I have delivered a fellow human from an unjust imprisonment. And who knows? Perhaps his anguish over breaking faith with me will eventually transform him into a more generous friend, a better parent, or a public benefactor."

Alas, my heart is not in the quest. Only part of me—a small part, I must confess—wants to keep on making useful neurological donations. So even if there is a perfect Pollifex out there somewhere, he will probably never get to fashion a fresh batch of Altruoid. Not unless I father a child—and not unless the child receives the gene—and not unless the gene finds expression—and not unless this descendent of mine donates his superego to science. But as the bull man told me many years ago, QZ-11-4 only rarely gets actualized in the humans who carry it.

I believe I see a way around the problem. The roadside emporium in which I currently display myself also features a llama named Loretta. She can count to ten and solve simple arithmetic problems. I am enchanted by Loretta's liquid eyes, sensuous lips, and splendid form—and I think she has taken a similar interest in me. It's a relationship, I feel, that could lead almost anywhere.

Blood Sacrifices

Valerie Griswold-Ford

April 29, 1995: *11:58*

Two more minutes.

His gaze dropped from the clock ticking peacefully on the wall to the makeshift altar before him, so out of place in the mundane classroom. Three tall black candles as thick as his wrist waited for him on the small piece of marble he'd brought, their flat dark surfaces belying the faintest shimmer of Power hidden deep within them. As the long hand of the clock moved inexorably towards midnight, he picked up a long silver knife and positioned his hand over the first candle.

One more click and midnight arrived. The bells of the nearby Catholic Church tolled the dying of the day; the sound reverberated through him as the blade kissed the skin of his palm. Crimson blood welled out of the cut and dripped carefully onto the candle's wick.

One.

Two.

Three, and the candle burst into flame.

He turned towards the door, the wound in his hand already closing and small tongues of fire caressing the edge of the knife he still carried.

It was time to begin.

Someone had left the T.V. on again. That was the only explanation Shanna Greystone could come up with for why there were white bunnies in storm trooper uniforms lockstepping through random corn fields to the Imperial March. It even made sense, sort of - in that odd way that dreams make sense just before one completely wakes up. Unfortunately, storm bunnies were not conducive to restful sleep; with a groan, she turned over and squinted at her alarm clock.

Six a.m. Someone was going to die for this.

Rolling out of bed and grabbing clothing was done on automatic, as was wandering down the hall to the house's shared living room. She even managed to avoid hitting the wall more than once, a miracle considering her eyes were still mostly shut. It only took her two stabs to kill the T.V. too. The music ended abruptly and Shanna sighed in relief.

"Was it too loud?"

Shanna jumped at the question and spun around, one hand glowing red, ready to defend herself. Luckily, all the inhabitants of St. Mary's Home for Wayward Children, as the house was known, had learned to simply wait for her to recognize who they were, rather than try to move or reason with her. Shanna preferred to shoot first, especially when she was startled.

Adrenaline pushed sleep from her eyes, and she lowered her hand as the familiar face registered. "Holy shit, Rick, you look like hell. What did that silly bitch do this time to keep you up?"

Her housemate winced, running one hand over the dark blonde stubble on his chin. "Nothing. Maddy's still asleep - I had some shitty dreams and decided not to keep her up by tossing and turning. Sorry I woke you - I didn't realize it was that loud."

"You didn't, really." Shanna yawned as her body reminded her it really was six a.m. and that now, since the emergency was over, she should go back to bed. She compromised by dropping into one of the papasan chairs in the living room, curling her legs beneath her. "The storm bunnies did, little bastards."

Her housemate chuckled at that remark and Shanna sighed. –Yet another saying on the quote wall,–she thought ruefully. –Oh well, at least I can read them later, even if I don't remember saying them.–

They sat in silence for a few moments, each lost in their own thoughts, then Rick raised the remote and flicked the T.V. back on, thumbing down the volume a bit. Shanna let the movie wash over her. "At least it was this and not some crappy comedy. The T.V. might not have survived if I'd woken to that."

"Crappy comedy's a little hard to digest this early in the morning," Rick said. "I wanted something familiar."

"When was the last time you slept?" she asked, looking more closely at him. –Because unless I'm very much mistaken, this is more than one night's worth of bad dreams,– she thought to herself, wondering if he'd lie to her.

He shrugged, focusing on the T.V. "I've been busy. Beltane's in two days, you know."

"Don't remind me." Shanna shuddered. "I fully intend to lock myself in my room with a quantity of good alcohol and hide behind the strongest shields I can conjure. The last thing I need is an overdose of sex magic." –Especially since I've got exactly nothing brewing in the relationship department right now.–

"Aw, come on, Shanna." Rick grinned at her. "You mean Dave won't give you a roll in the hay for old time's sake?"

"I wouldn't know," she retorted, wrinkling her nose at the mention of her ex and throwing a pillow at Rick. "I haven't asked him. In fact, I haven't even heard from him since Christmas."

"You've intimidated him."

–You're probably right.– "A loaded revolver wouldn't intimidate him."

Rick cocked his head at her, the light humor in his voice a sharp contrast to the shadows in his amber eyes. "Yeah, but a loaded revolver would only kill him once. You'd kill him, bring him back and kill him again if he pissed you off, and he knows it."

That jab hit a little too close to home. Shanna drew in a deep breath, cutting off a defensive comment, and ran her fingers through her reddish-blond hair instead, pretending to look for split ends while she brought herself back under control. –He doesn't know, leave it alone.– "Don't change the subject," she said finally. "What…"

The telephone rang, interrupting her, and she scowled at it before reaching over and grabbing the receiver from the table. "St. Mary's Home for Wayward Children," she said grumpily. "It's six a.m., so this better be important."

"It is." The voice on the other end of the line made her straighten up quickly, nearly tumbling her from her chair. "I've got a body for you to look at."

"Where?" Shanna snapped her fingers at Rick, pointing urgently at the notebook and pen next to him on the couch. "And what's the situation?"

A gusty sigh echoed over the line and her heart sank. –Oh, this is so going to suck. I can tell.– "It's ugly," he said finally. "Really ugly. Get here quick, so the fire department doesn't howl too loudly, and bring that Sensitive you were telling me about with you."

"Fire department?" –Better and better.– "Where am I going? And do I need to call Justin?"

"Just get here. He's on his way."

She took the address down, hung up the phone and looked at Rick. "Get dressed."

"Me?"

"Yeah." She thought about warning him, but decided not to. –He'll find out soon enough. I just hope he's up for it.– "You're about to find out just what the Greystone kids do for fun."

"Why me?"

"Because I don't argue with the chief of police."

That shut him up. Once he was decent, Shanna herded him into her car and they drove to the address the chief had given her, a small Cape on the outskirts of the college town they called home. As soon as they stepped out from the car, the smell of crisp flesh hit her nostrils, calling up memories she'd hoped never to relive. For a moment, the scene in front of her vanished, and a freshly-charred hand reached out for Shanna again, trying to save her and take her and love her and kill her all at once; a hand that had once wiped tears from her eyes and now promised nothing but damnation, and she couldn't escape…

"Shanna?" Rick's voice shattered the memory into shards of smoke and pain; with a start, she came back to herself. "Are you okay?"

She nodded, not trusting her voice yet, and led him across the grass, passing knots of police officers and fire officials.

"What is that … smell?" Rick whispered as he followed her.

–Death,– her mind said, but she only answered quietly, "It's a body. Someone's burning a body."

He gagged at that, but continued to follow her around the house. They'd had to park down the street because of the fire trucks, but it was readily apparent where the body was; not just from the plume of smoke that rose lazily through the early morning against the pale blue sky, but from the loud conversation between the two men standing next to the burn pit.

"You have to let me pull that body off! It's a health hazard!" the taller of the two was insisting as Shanna and Rick came up. She didn't recognize him, but she did know the other man, who nodded to her before replying.

"Not until these two give the all-clear," he said, his voice rolling over the fire chief's objections. "So shut up and let them do their job."

The other man turned and gave both Shanna and Rick a cursory once-over before turning his back on them. "Them? You made me wait for students, Quinn? Are you insane?"

"Probably," Quinn said, shrugging his massive shoulders. "But when one of my officers says magic's involved, I wait until the experts get here."

"These are your experts?" The fire chief turned to look at them again.

"Yes." Quinn hated wasting words. He jerked his head at the body. "What can you tell me?"

"He's dead," Shanna said, covering her mouth and nose with the sleeve of her sweatshirt as she got close to the edge of the burn pit. "Jesus, Chief, couldn't you at least have pulled the poor bastard off the fire?"

"Not until you give me the okay," he grumbled. "Look closer."

She did, narrowing her eyes to block the smoke, and saw what he was talking about: the faintest sparkle of magic, nearly obscured by the charred skin. The body lay flat on what remained of its back, slowly roasting on a partially-banked bed of coals in a garbage burn pit. "Rick, how much am I going to contaminate the body if I lift it out or damp down the fire?"

"We could wet it down," the fire chief offered, but she shook her head.

"Too dangerous," she said, and he snorted. "I'm serious. Who knows what that web is?"

"What web?"

–I hate mundanes,– she thought, gritting her teeth. –Hate, hate, hate them.– "The one wrapped around that body." She turned to Rick, who was frowning at the scene. "Well?"

Rick was the oddest Sensitive she'd ever met—he could See things most Mages would miss, but he didn't seem to have the same problems as other Sensitives did. He never wore gloves, for example, and it was almost as if he could turn off his gift, tune out the images that bombarded the others constantly. –I could totally blow this scene apart,– she mused, watching him as he crossed his arms over his chest and cocked his head, looking down at the body in disgusted fascination. –But you, my friend, you can quite possibly tell us what did this. And maybe even why. Just from the traces left on the body.–

–Provided, of course, we have a body left.–

"An answer rather quickly might be nice," she suggested when the silence stretched on, broken only by the popping of bodily fluids as they dripped down onto the hot coals. "Before we lose all our evidence?"

"Okay, okay," Rick said, looking down at his boots. "But I need to get closer. At least I've got thick soles on." And before she could stop him, he slid into the pit, deftly avoiding the coals, and laid his hand on the corpse.

"Does he have to touch him?" Quinn asked, and Shanna shuddered.

"Skin-to-skin contact is best," she admitted, glad it wasn't her in that pit.

"He's contaminating my evidence, you know."

"You don't have any evidence, Chief. That's why you called us."

He didn't answer, which meant she was right. Behind her, the fire chief sounded like he was strangling on something. –Probably wigged out at what we're doing,– Shanna mused, trying hard to ignore the memories clawing at the back of her mind. –Hope he doesn't try and interfere. Wonder what Quinn would do if I knocked the fire chief out?–

–Shake your hand?– Her younger brother's voice swam through her mind. –Quinn despises him.–

Shanna turned as he walked up, grateful for an excuse to not watch the body anymore. "What kept you?"

Justin Greystone shrugged, his hazel eyes hooded as he looked down at the pit. "Stuff."

"Singularly unenlightening, little brother," Shanna said, frowning. "Can you …"

"No." His wavy hair was rumpled; he ran a hand through it absently, a vain attempt to smooth it. His shirt was on backwards, too—which gave her a very good idea of what "stuff" he'd been involved with. "What's going on?"

She started to answer, but Rick interrupted them by scrambling out of the pit, barely missing taking Quinn out at the knees. He hit the grass and vomited, nearly falling into it, but Justin caught his shoulder, holding him up. "Blood," Rick choked out. "They took … he … oh, man, I can't do this."

"Take it easy," Justin said, layering a bit of Power into his voice, calming him down. "Let it go, let it come up. Bodies are never easy."

Come it did. Just the mention of the corpse still smoking behind them brought another round of heaves from Rick. Quinn and the fire chief fumed and the body continued to cook, but

Shanna glared at them when they tried to move closer. "Leave him alone, dammit. It's his first body."

"You can pull him out, Shanna," Rick said finally. "He's wrapped in a Blood Magic web. I don't know what kind, but you won't ruin anything."

She turned back to the corpse and concentrated, hoping he was wrong and knowing he probably wasn't. Fingers of dark green Power damped down the coals and then twined around the body and lifted it out. As her magic touched the corpse, she caught a whiff of what Rick had felt and her stomach churned.

"Oh hell, I'd hoped you were wrong," she whispered, setting the ruined body down gently on a plastic sheet Quinn's men had laid on the ground.

"And what about this?" the fire chief demanded, pointing to the pit. "Can I finally do my job?"

"Knock yourself out," Shanna said absently, kneeling beside the sheet. "I need O'Neill."

"You can't have him," Quinn rumbled. "Wife's having a baby." He turned towards the side yard and shouted, "Mal, get your notebook and your ass over here!" Then he turned back to her, florid face thunderous. "Are you going to explain how you failed to notice someone dying by Blood Magic on this campus?"

"Well, we don't know how he died yet," she said, her eyes tracing the interrupted lines of magic on the corpse. "Or that he died here. This looks to me like a dump job. Besides, what do you think I am?"

"The StarChild," he snapped. "Doesn't that tie you in with everything magical?"

"Not quite." –Thank god.– "I'd go insane if it did. Besides, it's nearly Beltane, you know."

"So?"

"So every would-be pagan, witchlet and coven in the state is out playing with sex and fertility magic," Justin said, standing up and helping Rick to his feet. "Gives our killer a hell of a lot of background noise to hide his spells in."

"If we have a killer," Shanna said. Something about the body niggled at her, and she looked over at her younger brother. "What kind of person does a Blood Magic sacrifice on a holiday dedicated to life?"

"A sick one," Rick said, shuddering, and both Justin and Shanna looked sharply at him. "Trust me."

"I hate those words," Quinn grumbled.

"So do I." Shanna looked over at Justin. "You're the psych major. What kind of sick bastard are we dealing with, do you think?"

He ran his hands through his wavy brown hair again, tugging thoughtfully on the curls. "Maybe he's hoping the elementals won't notice what he's doing," Justin said finally. "After all, he did try and destroy the body. The only other thing I can think of is that he's summoning something so big that he just doesn't care who he pisses off."

Rick shivered and Quinn shook his head. "You three got anything GOOD to tell me?"

Shanna sighed. "I hope so. Who's filling in for O'Neill?"

"I am." A young officer skidded to a stop next to her, carrying a sketch pad. "What am I drawing?"

"A web," Shanna said, crooking her finger at him. –Christ, he's a baby,– she marveled. –Barely old enough to wear that uniform.– "Do you have a problem working with Mages, Officer Malcolm?"

"Officer Peters, actually," he corrected her, grinning. The dead body apparently didn't bother him at all, and she envied his easy acceptance of the situation. "Or Mal. And no, my sister's a Mage. Where do you want me?"

–Very good,– came Justin's thought echoing through her mind. –We'll have to remember him; he could be useful.–

–Agreed,– she said silently, pointing to a spot on the other side of the corpse. "Are you ready, Mal?"

"Just a moment." He dropped into a cross-legged position, opened his sketchpad and pulled a pencil from behind his ear. "Okay, what am I drawing?"

"This." Shanna looked over at the smoking corpse, steeling herself for the contact.

Not physical contact, but still—revulsion and memory crawled along her skin as she spread her hands above the corpse and fed Power into the remains of the spells Rick had sensed.

Magic flared, and the body floated up as bright strands of Power wrapped around it in a brilliant spider web of blood, pain and anger that glowed white in the early morning. Shanna could follow the pulsing line of Blood Magic forming a network over the body's cracked, blistered skin; as Malcolm's pencil flew, she memorized the patterning, trying to see what end result had been intended.

"Any ideas?" Justin asked her, and she shook her head in frustration.

"I'm going to have to dig," she said eventually. "I don't recognize it."

"Dig?" Rick asked, and she nodded.

"Dig. Stand back." She gritted her teeth and sank her consciousness into the remains of the victim's mind, hoping to salvage some something; his name, perhaps, or if she was really lucky, the last few minutes of his life. It didn't always work, but she figured it was worth a shot.

Pain. Memories swarmed out of the body and dragged her down, swamping her senses and blotting out everything else. Icy-hot needles erupted out from every inch of her skin, creating the web that a silver knife spun into existence above her and Shanna bit back a scream. The altar beneath her was rough, wooden—long splinters pierced her bare back as she arched upwards, feeding Power to the faceless Mage hovering above her. Leather straps coiled around her wrists and ankles, holding her down as she bled from a thousand cuts, Power and blood and life offered up with joy and pleasure to the one with the knife. The part that was still Shanna recoiled in disgust from the feelings that raced through her, and she wondered how the victim could have reveled so much in his own dying.

–What could have been so horrible that he would have welcomed this?–

"Shanna!" Justin's voice dragged her back up from the well of emotions and memories. She came back to herself collapsed on the ground, the corpse spinning lazily above her. "Who is he?" her brother demanded, as she shivered.

"One sick bastard," she managed to say. "He helped them do this." Then she leaned over and lost complete control of her stomach.

It took her nearly ten minutes to calm down again; the alien emotions had sunk their claws deep into her, tearing into her carefully-constructed walls with a vengeance. When Shanna looked up again, she discovered Justin had pulled down the corpse and it had been taken away. The fire pit had been dowsed and firefighters swarmed over it. Only Rick still sat with her, holding the drawing Mal had made.

"You okay?" she asked him. He was still pale, but more composed, and he nodded. "Good. Let's get the hell out of here. Where's Justin?"

Rick helped her to her feet. "He left with the body. Said he'd call you later."

"Good." Justin's knack for weaseling details out of the Morrisville Police Department had paid off in the past. Maybe he could find out who their body was.

No one stopped them as they exited the crime scene; Shanna at least was well-known, and Rick stuck to her side like a limpet. Once they got into her car, Shanna leaned against the steering wheel and closed her eyes, plotting her next move.

"Now what?" Rick asked quietly.

She sat back up and checked her clock. "I have class at 8," she said finally. "The rest of the day will be spent trying to figure out what that damn web is."

Rick's jaw dropped. "You're going to class?"

"Well, yeah." Shanna started the car, a little amused by his reaction. "That's why I'm here, after all."

"But there's a dead body! And a killer on the loose!"

"You sound like a bad '80s sitcom," she told him as she pulled out onto the road. "And besides, the body isn't going anywhere. He was involved in his death; he welcomed it. I'm not sure Quinn could arrest anyone for murder. Assisted suicide, maybe. And it's only an hour lecture." She nodded at the drawing in his hand. "Do you recognize anything on that?"

"No," Rick said, turning the drawing around. "Then again, my experience with Blood Magic is pretty limited."

"I have a feeling that's about to change."

Shanna dropped him off at the Home, then headed onto campus, her mind still turning the vision of the Blood Magic web over and over. –Why is this so familiar?– she thought, parking the car and grabbing a notebook out of the backseat. –Where have I seen this before?–

Her class was Advanced Magical Theory, a class she normally adored. Shanna sat in the back of the hall and only half-listened, looking instead at the remains of a beautiful, vivacious woman while her brain pondered the body now at the morgue.

Yvaine Boxer had once tall and athletic—now, cancer steadily ate away at her insides, confining her to a wheelchair, her once-tanned skin pale and ghostly. Her voice still crackled with Power as she spoke, but it was the last hurrah of a body that was refusing to go without a fight.

–I wonder why our body didn't fight,– Shanna thought, as the lecture lulled her into a light sleep. –Why did he help them?–

"Ms. Greystone?" The sharp note in Yvaine's voice pulled her upright abruptly. "Are we boring you?"

"Sorry, Professor," Shanna said, blinking. "Long night."

Yvaine tilted her head ever so slightly to the left, an odd gleam in her eyes. "I do not consider pre-Beltane activities an excuse to sleep through class."

–Depends on what they are,– Shanna thought privately, but answered, "No ma'am, me neither. I was working on a project for the police."

"Indeed. Then perhaps I should suggest to Chief Quinn that he won't be needing your skills until after the semester ends."

"Oh, would you?" Shanna asked hopefully, drawing chuckles from the rest of the class. "Then maybe I could sleep later than 6 a.m."

Yvaine's mouth twitched as she tried not to smile. "I would suggest a larger coffee next time he calls you in so early, Ms. Greystone. Now, as I was saying…"

Shanna made it a point to remain awake for the remainder of the class, and stopped by Yvaine's desk at the end. "Professor?"

"Yes, Ms. Greystone?" Yvaine looked up at her; as she stepped closer to the woman, Shanna noticed the fine tremor of her professor's hands and felt a pang.

–That's a new symptom. The cancer must be spreading.– "I wanted to apologize again."

"Apology accepted." Yvaine clasped her hands in her lap. "Do you need me to speak to Chief Quinn?"

Shanna sighed. "No. Hopefully, this won't take too long to figure out and I won't lose too much sleep over it."

"Do you want some help?"

The offer tempted her, but Shanna regretfully shook her head. "I can't discuss police business without permission," she said. "But thank you."

"Let me know if you change your mind." Yvaine turned away, and Shanna hurried out the door.

She barely missed running into a tall man right outside the classroom; he put his hand on her shoulder as he stumbled back. Mumbling an apology, Shanna ducked around him and hurried off. Something prickled on her skin; she stopped as she realized he had set a tag on her.

–Who the hell?– With a slight shiver, Shanna channeled a small bit of Power over her skin, crumbling the small spell, and then looked back. The tall man she'd nearly run over had a sour look on his face; he frowned at her then entered Yvaine's classroom.

"Jerk," Shanna muttered, scrubbing at the spot on her shoulder where he'd touched her and laid the magical tag. "I hate those damn things. And I hate people who think they have the right to know where I am all the time. One of these days, someone's going to tag me, and I'm going to do more than give them a headache when I break it."

The first candle was a mass of molten black wax, the sparkles of magic snuffed in its dying as the wick drowned in its own blood. Only two more hours until midnight tolled again and a new day dawned ripe with potential. The second sacrifice slept, hidden, perfectly innocent. Everything was going according to plan.

The altar, set up in a small grove of trees, was new, pristine – spotless, with no contamination from the previous sacrifice. Each offering had to be untouched by the previous rituals or the spells would fail. Then he would be forced to start over again at the beginning and that would be … awkward, to say the least.

Not to mention expensive. And he'd have to work without all the convenient background noise, unless he waited until the next holiday. And he doubted they had time for that.

His palm itched, and he clenched his fist against the sensation. *This would work.*

It had to.

"Hey, Quinn identified our body!"

Shanna looked up from the drawing in front of her as Justin came into the library. Floor to ceiling bookcases housed a plethora of books on nearly every magical subject imaginable, as well as books on more mundane matters. The center of the room held a large kitchen table; Shanna had nearly every book on Blood Magic she'd been able to find spread out on it, open to various drawings of bodies with various cuts on them, different ways for a Blood Mage to drain a sacrifice. Each pattern yielded a different result – problem was, without knowing what result their Blood

Mage had been looking for, she'd been forced to check each and every pattern for a match.

"Glad he's having more luck than I am," she said dryly, tossing yet another book aside. "Blood Mages are far too creative for their own good. Who was he?"

Justin looked at the papers in his hands, then handed them over to her. "Anthony Brooks. Grad student attached to a Professor Donald Boxer. Says here he was studying political science and magical theory."

"Interesting mix," Shanna said, frowning as she leafed through the short dossier. "Not one you normally see. Then again, if he's attached to Prof. Boxer, it makes sense—he's got doctorates in both Magical Politics and International Relations. I almost took his Magic and Politics class this semester, but it was full."

"They have doctorates in Magical Politics already?" Her brother slid into the chair on the other side of the table and cocked his head at her. "Do you know him?"

"Of course they do," Shanna replied, still reading. "It's been almost twenty years since the elementals showed up in Washington. As far as knowing him—no, I've never met the man. His wife teaches one of my favorite classes, though. Brilliant woman—I was hoping to do some grad work under her, but I doubt that will happen."

"Why not?"

"She's dying," Shanna said, putting the papers down on the table in front of her. "Terminal cancer. Last I heard, both the doctors and the Healers gave her less than a year to live. It's sad, really." She shook her head. "Did Boxer have anything to say about the disappearance?"

"Yeah, he said both of them said they hadn't heard from the victim in several days. In fact, he'd missed his last thesis advisory meeting."

"Curiouser and curiouser." Shanna picked up the papers again. "Did you read this?"

"Of course."

"Did you ask Quinn what the additional charges on the driving violation were last year?" she asked pointedly.

"Yep." Justin sank down deeper into the chair and propped his feet up on the desk, dislodging several books onto the floor. "Transporting hypodermic needles and leeches."

She blinked. "Blood Magic implements? How very interesting, considering cause of death was acute blood loss. What was the story on the dump site, by the way? It was a dump site, yes?"

Justin nodded. "Dead end, too. The burn pit belongs to one Mrs. Clarissa Brown, age 65, who is currently visiting her son and daughter-in-law in Poughkeepsie, NY, and has been there for the past month. No connection that we can find with the victim."

"Did she work for the college?"

"Nope," he said. "Music teacher for the high school, recently retired. And before you ask, our victim went to high school in San Anselmo, California."

"So it was just a convenient site?" Shanna propped her elbow up on the table and put her chin in her hand.

"Apparently. According to Quinn, she'd hired a clean-up service to come and do some spring cleaning before she came home. The maintenance guy said he'd gathered up all the clippings and set them to burn last night before he left." Justin shrugged. "The fire should have burned out in an hour or so."

"Those were some pretty heavy duty coals we found," Shanna said, then straightened up. "The altar. They burned him on the altar board. But why?"

Justin shrugged again. "Trying to destroy the evidence?"

"Maybe." She sat back, pulling a reddish curl forward and running her fingers along the length of it idly. "Still doesn't tell us who the Mage is. Or why he did it."

"Yeah, Quinn didn't like hearing that." Justin picked up the nearest book and glanced at it. "Any luck on this end?"

"Quinn's not going to like this either," Shanna admitted. "I think this is only the beginning."

Justin stared at her. "Please tell me you're kidding."

She shook her head. "I finally realized what I was looking at— the sigil on his forehead. Look." She tossed over Mal's drawing. "Look at his forehead. It's clearly the Opening sigil. Whoever our Mage is, he's trying to bring something through. I just don't know what yet. But any Blood Magic ritual that starts with the Opening is a minimum three-day ritual."

"Timing the final ritual to coincide with the end of Beltane." Justin shook his head. "That's insane."

"Tell me about it," Shanna said. "If we'd found this guy in August, I'd be a hell of a lot less confused."

"What, you think it's a Corn God sacrifice gone wrong?"

"I don't know what to think anymore," Shanna admitted, frustration lacing through her voice. "It's not the Corn God webbing, though. And even if it were, the Corn God isn't a three-day sacrifice—it's a one-day celebration. I thought the pattern looked a bit familiar, but I'm not finding it here. Which is odd, considering how big a library of Blood Magic grimoires we have."

"Considering neither of us practice all that consistently, yeah," Justin said, tossing the book and drawing back on the pile in front of her. "So what's our next move, fearless leader?"

She scowled at him. "Don't call me that. Do you have any plans that can't be cancelled?"

"The night before Beltane?" Justin snorted. "Please. What would I be doing tonight?"

"The same thing you were doing this morning when Quinn called?" Shanna suggested, and grinned when he blushed. "I thought so. Can you bear to do magic with me instead of gracing her bed?"

"I'll suffer. It's going to be soupy out there, you know," he warned. "Want me to go spring Rick?"

"Yes. We'll need him to get through the morass." Shanna stood up and stretched, working out the kinks in her spine. "Go pry him out of Maddy's clutches and meet me in the president's garden."

Justin's grin was evil. "Harry hates it when we do magic there."

"Harry owes me his soul," Shanna retorted, grabbing a messenger bag and starting to stuff various things into it. "Besides, our fearless president is in California at some meeting, and what he doesn't know won't hurt him. I'll meet the two of your in the listening hollow there at midnight. Let's see if we can catch these bastards in the act."

April 30, 1995

The chill of early spring got her blood moving again as Shanna hurried across the largely quiet campus. Quiet in the normal noise sense: on the magical plane, it felt as if she were moving through a concert hall in which Nine Inch Nails, Poison and REM were all performing. At the same time.

And that was just one aspect of the cacophony.

Magic crawled along her skin like a lover's touch, exploring her with warm, feathery fingers that set her blood to racing for an entirely different reason. It was distracting, but once they started casting, Shanna knew exactly what she was going to do with all the energy she could sense.

–And that's the good thing about Beltane,– she thought smugly, unhooking the latch on the fence surrounding the president's garden. –Al this energy just swirling around waiting to be used. And most of our little witchlets have no idea what to do with it. God thing I do.–

–Then again, I'll bet our unknown knows how to use it too.– That thought brought her back down to earth. –I have to trust that Rick can find him. I have to. Otherwise, I'm out of ideas. and we're going to have more bodies.–

The center of the garden that graced the back of the academic building was set up like an upside-down pyramid: stone terraces stepped down into a small grove that circled a crystal-clear pool. The Earth Mage who had designed it had created a perfect magical listening post, and Shanna intended to use it. Luckily, it was still empty.

The charm that hid the grove from view when in use sprang to life as she stepped down the final terrace and passed the first row of trees, cutting off the magical discord. Shanna knelt down in the center of the grove and pulled out the four white candles she'd brought with her, fitting them into the bronze sconces set at the four cardinal points around the scrying pool. Then she simply sat cross-legged on the soft new grass, composing herself and waiting for the boys, knowing Justin would call out when they got close.

–It's just so tempting to stay here for the next two days,– she thought wryly, knowing it would have been impossible under the best of circumstances. –Honestly, I don't how the Sensitives deal with this time of year. I'm surprised even Rick isn't clawing his brains out trying to keep some of this stuff at bay.–

–Then again, he's got some damn thick shields. And maybe Maddy's finally doing something useful with her gifts and augmenting his shields.–

–At least he's talking to us again. I was afraid he'd be non-vocal forever there.–

She pulled herself back from that line of thinking sharply, reminding herself what was past was just that. Past.

–Dammit, what is taking them so long?–

The answer to that question popped into her mind as soon as the question did, and Shanna's lip curled. Maddy was probably pitching a fit. –Spoiled brat. What does he see in her?–

Noise from outside the garden pulled her back from her thoughts; the gate latch lifted, and then she heard an inane giggle. –Thank all the gods I got here first. Welcome to Beltane.–

"Can you really do magic here?" a breathy female voice asked, as footsteps echoed down the stairs. Shanna grinned and waited, knowing what would come next.

"Yeah, right here in the center." The young man's voice wasn't familiar, but she knew the type: they hung around the edges of the Pagan Student Association on campus and seduced young witchlets of both sexes with their 'special magic spells.' They were mostly harmless.

And amusing. Especially when they didn't know they were being watched.

She could see them through the trees, even though they couldn't see her. He was tall, dark-haired, with a bit of Power, probably just enough to work the enchantments on the grove. –Not tonight, my friend,– Shanna thought smugly as he groaned.

"What's wrong?" the little freshman on his arm asked anxiously, her buzz obviously fading a bit. "Isn't it here?"

"Yeah, but someone's in it." He pulled her back up the steps. "Don't worry, we'll find another space and make it sacred. Just the two of us…"

Shanna wished them good luck and went back to waiting. Rick and Justin showed up about ten minutes later; she was still chuckling as she opened the wards for them.

"How many would-be worshippers did you chase away?" Justin asked.

"Only one, surprisingly." She gave Rick a searching look. "How did Maddy react?"

His grimace told her all she needed to know. "Let's just say she's less than thrilled that I'm running off to help you again, rather than spending the night before Beltane working through her new sex spells set with her."

"Which one did she buy this time?" Shanna asked, half-dreading the answer.

"Anton."

The name sent both Greystones into howls of laughter. "Good Lord, Rick, what was she thinking?" Shanna asked when she could breathe again, wiping tears from her eyes. "What were YOU thinking?"

"That sex spells from a charlatan are a hell of a lot safer than some of the other things she's been in to." His tone sobered her up quickly; she just nodded, but made a mental note to go back and make sure Maddy wasn't attracting any undue notice with her screwing around. –That girl is too irresponsible to be as Talented as she is,– she thought privately, and felt Justin's agreement.

"Anyways," she said out loud, letting the subject drop for the moment. "I figured out that the markings were the Opening sigil on our victim's forehead. So our Blood Mage is going to be doing another ritual tonight and at least one more tomorrow. It's nearly midnight—let's see what we can find, before we end up with another body on our hands."

Rick settled himself on the grass in front of her, and she moved her legs to let him get closer. "What do you want me to do?"

"I want you to start looking for Blood Magic," she said, as Justin sat down on the other side of him. "Any dark magic, really."

"You don't think he'll be shielded?" Justin asked.

"Probably, but with me as a battery, Rick should be able to See a lot more than normal." She laid her hands on his shoulders and pulled him back against her gently. "Jus, ground us?"

"Of course," her younger brother said, calling up soft tendrils of green Earth Magic to twine around the two. "Be careful."

"Always," Shanna said.

Rick drew in a deep breath, and Shanna could feel him centering himself. She slowed her breathing down to match his rhythm, slipping easily into a light trance. The three of them had done this many times over the past two years, but never with such an important goal. She only hoped they were in time.

–Please, Mother Goddess, don't let us be too late.–

The link between the two of them allowed her to See what he was Sensing: magical energies, giving a whole new look to the familiar area around them. Rick, buoyed by the Power at Shanna's disposal, pushed his senses out past the emerald green of the garden into the brilliantly flaring magical atmosphere of the campus.

Gold and green energies dominated the atmosphere swirling around them, laced with crimson flashes, sex and fertility magics fueled by the lust and fervor of thousands of enthusiastic college students. Shanna reached out and pulled in the Power around her, channeling it to Rick, who pushed his search out to the very edges of Morrisville. There were dark holes in the magical landscape, and it was these holes he sought.

By the end of two hours, they had discovered several unsavory groups that Shanna made mental notes to keep an eye on in the future, including one "den of domination" that left her feeling like she needed a shower, and some odd echoes that had dissipated as soon as Rick had noticed them. But no Blood Magic.

"Dammit, he must be shielded up the wazoo," Justin said disgustedly as they broke down the circle. "How could we not have found him? With this much Power?"

"Power doesn't mean squat if we can't break his shields. You know that." Shanna chewed her lower lip thoughtfully for a few minutes. "I need to look at my books again."

"And what do we tell Quinn?" Rick asked somberly as they exited the garden.

"We tell him to expect another body," Justin said. "And hope it's not someone we know."

———•———

The second candle burned brightly as he knelt in front of it, the sacrifice's still-beating heart in a crystal dish in his hand. Behind him, he heard a faint rustling as the body vanished from the sacrificial altar; she was good at cleaning up after him, a true partner. He smiled, then picked up the small paintbrush from its velvet case and began the final preparations.

He worked slowly, a true artist, dipping the tiny bristles into the pulsating heart, then transferring the living blood to the final candle. The runes glowed wetly, red lacquer on the flat black wax. Once all the symbols were painted on, he dropped the paintbrush into his back pocket and placed the silver cover on the crystal container.

The heart would continue to beat until consumed. The sacrificial spells ensured it.

And the StarChild still didn't know. He'd had a brief moment of terror when he'd seen the girl outside the classroom, when she'd destroyed his tag, but that had passed. It had been a momentary lapse in judgment, nothing more. They were still safe. She was still safe. That was all that mattered.

Only one more day. She could wait that long.

Barely.

———•———

"Oh gross."

Shanna covered her mouth as her breakfast threatened to climb back up out of her stomach and run away. Quinn had called them as soon as the body had been found.

It wasn't that the girl was naked and lying on her back on the main altar of the Catholic Church, her blood creating an intricate pattern on the fine carpeting. Nor was it that her entire torso was ripped open in a single long, ragged gash, with strips of skin hanging down on either side of her body, fluttering in the early morning breeze that came through the open chapel doors. It wasn't even the fact that anyone could have brought her in during the night: after all, the Church's doors were open to anyone, at any time. No, that was all bad enough, but nothing she hadn't seen before.

No, the true horror was that the girl seemed to still be alive, despite the fact that her heart wasn't anywhere to be seen.

Shanna winced as the girl keened, a long, low, undulating sound that echoed in the church's rafters and scraped across nerves wrung raw by the remains of sex and pain that coated the area. The lawn outside swarmed with police, but inside it was only herself, Quinn and the pastor, who was praying at one of the side altars. Justin had hitched a ride in with her, but he'd stayed outside to help with crowd control. Rick hadn't been home when the call came – she'd left a message at Maddy's, figuring he'd catch up with them later. Now she was glad he'd missed it.

"Is it related?" Quinn asked, and she nodded. Even from here, the Blood Magic web around the girl glowed harsh white against the dark wood of the back wall. The large crucifix hanging above her on the wall only deepened the eerie atmosphere.

–He's getting more confident,– she thought, swallowing hard. Her feet refused to move. –Walk over, coward, and do your damn job. It's a sacrifice, nothing more. She can't even move on her own without her heart; she's a meat puppet, nothing more. Stop cringing and just go.– But the girl was still moaning, still breathing, even though there was no blood circulating… it was a mockery of life, a body going through the motions.

"I need Mal," she heard herself say in a high, strained voice, and then her feet were moving forward, bringing her closer to see every horrid detail.

No effort had been made to disguise what had happened to her. The cuts and slashes in her skin mimicked the Power web perfectly; Shanna shivered as the first victim's memory surged up again out of the closet in her mind where she'd shoved it before. She pushed it back down again and wondered if she dared try the same trick on this one.

The girl looked barely 18, probably a freshman—if she hadn't come from the nearby high school. Shanna memorized her face, then looked up as a set of footsteps announced a new arrival.

Mal's face was white but set; it probably matched her own, she reflected, as she motioned him forward. There was no need to feed Power to this web; he sketched quickly, finishing the drawing in a few minutes.

"You do excellent work, Mal," she said, taking the drawing.

"Thanks." He paused, looking from the girl to Shanna. "Can I ask you a question?"

"As long as it's not for my number, sure," she said, still studying the drawing.

He chuckled, a strained sound. "I have better timing than that." Then he turned serious. "What will you do when you find him?"

Shanna looked up and met his blue eyes. "Will I kill him, you mean?"

Mal nodded, and she sensed Quinn listening intently behind her.

"Only if I have to," she said finally. "Only if he forces me to."

Mal looked as if he wanted to say something else, then he turned and left quickly. She watched him go, wondering what he'd decided not to say.

"Flirt on your own time," Quinn rumbled behind her, and she shook herself. "What does that tell you?"

"It tells me that this is a three-day ritual," she said, turning around. "This is a classic pattern—the Innocent Sacrifice. That's why her heart is gone. Our unknown Mage needs it for the third part of the spell." She winced as the girl on the altar shrieked. "Is there a body bag I can use?"

"But she's still alive!" Quinn objected, clearly horrified. "We need to get her to a hospital!"

"No, she's not." Shanna shook her head. "The only thing keeping her animate is the link to her heart. She died as soon as they ripped her open. No hospital can help her now."

"But you could repair it, regrow it…"

Shanna was still shaking her head. "I'm a Mage, not a god, Chief. Miracles are a bit out of my league."

"What about a Healer?" Quinn insisted.

"It would take a god, Chief." The girl laughed again and Shanna shuddered. "And He's obviously not willing to interfere right now. I need that body bag."

"Then what?"

–Good question.– "Then we find Rick and figure out if we can track her heart down. Can I use one of the smaller autopsy rooms?"

"Sure." Quinn looked up at the altar. "We can't put her in a bag like that, though."

Shanna raised her hands, weaving a small golden web from the brilliant, uncaring sunlight pouring in through the stained glass windows. Once the web was complete, she laid it over the girl's face, whispering, "Sleep, little one, and suffer no more."

It was the least she could do.

Less than an hour later, Justin knocked on the autopsy room door and came in carrying several cups of coffee. "No Rick yet?"

"No," Shanna said from the desk in the corner, where she'd been assembling a small scrying bowl. "I left him another message at Maddy's. He'll be here when he gets here."

"Great." Justin handed her one cup. "What's the plan?"

Shanna sipped slowly, letting the hot liquid chase the chill of the room away. "Well, I want to make sure there's nothing else missing. Then I want to see if we can do a sympathetic ritual."

"Use the body to track the heart?" Justin said, and she nodded.

"The only one who should have the heart is our Mage. He's not going to let something that important out of his grasp." She sighed. "Not that he won't have it shielded either, but I don't know what else to do. I'm reaching for any straw I can find."

The door opened again, and Rick slipped inside. "Sorry, guys," he said, coming over to join them. "I just got your messages. Maddy's freaking out – Ashley didn't come home last night."

"Ashley?" Justin asked.

"Her little sister," Rick said. "Maddy's convinced she's shacked up with some jock or other, and has been dragging me all over campus looking for her."

"Fun." Shanna took one more drink of coffee and set the cup down carefully. "Well, here's the short version. Our killer struck again, and this time, the body isn't exactly dead."

Rick cocked his head at her, puzzled. "What do you mean?"

Justin and Shanna exchanged glances. "Do you know what an Innocent Sacrifice is?"

He shook his head.

Justin took a deep breath. "Oh. Well, the Innocent Sacrifice is the second sacrifice in most major summoning rituals. The Mage harvests the heart, still beating, after wrapping the victim in a special web designed to keep the blood moving. The body is technically dead, but the spirit is trapped inside, keeping the heart alive."

"The Mage keeps the heart in a special container," Shanna said, moving over to the body bag and pulling on a pair of latex gloves. "It's consumed at the third ritual, either by the Mage or by whatever he's pulling through."

"Charming." Rick shuddered. "So he just took the heart?"

"That's what we're about to find out." Shanna unzipped the bag, checking first to make sure the golden web was still firmly in place, keeping her still. It was, and she steeled herself, then stuck her hand inside the girl's chest cavity, feeling around for any other missing organs. "Nope, nothing else missing. Looks like the classic Innocent…what's wrong, Rick?"

Rick was staring at the body, his face ashen. "Take the web off," he whispered.

"If I do that, she'll start screaming again," Shanna said, stripping off the gloves and tossing them off. "And I doubt any of us want that. What's wrong?"

"I know her." Before she could stop him, he laid his hand on the girl's shoulder and closed his eyes. A shudder raced through him, and he swallowed. "Oh, Ashley, what have they done to you?"

Shanna and Justin both gaped at him. "You're kidding," Shanna said finally. "This is Maddy's sister?"

Rick nodded, and turned towards the door. "I have to tell her," he said, and bolted.

"Oh hell," Shanna said. "This is the last thing we needed."

———•———

"Are we ready?"

Her warm voice washed over his skin, caressing him with the barest breath of her Power, and he shivered. "Very nearly," he replied, running his hand over the crystal box that held the Innocent's slowly-beating heart. "Shouldn't you be resting? The sacrifice is in less than eight hours."

"I am rested." He could very nearly feel her standing beside him, even though he knew she was across the campus. *"You've done well, my love."*

"Thank you." He turned, even though he knew he'd see nothing more than a red mist hovering in the air next to him. "Soon, my love, it will all be over. Soon you'll be whole again."

"I know."

———·———

"It's nearly 4 pm," Quinn's voice boomed from somewhere above her, reaching into the dark pit of sleep she'd tumbled into and yanking her back to consciousness. "What do you have for me?"

"Coffee." Her head was spinning; between the magic building in the air and the lack of sleep over the past two days, combined with her own frustration at not finding the Blood Mage yet, had pushed her into taking one of Justin's herbal concoctions in an effort to powernap her way to a resolution to the problem. Unfortunately, her subconscious had been less than helpful, and the only thing she could remember was that there had been coffee involved somewhere. Coffee, and a red mist that hung over everything like lace dyed in blood.

"What?" Quinn was staring at her like she had two heads.

"Leave her alone for a moment, Chief," Justin advised, coming in with two steaming cups. "She doesn't wake up very well."

Shanna blinked at her younger brother as the remains of her dreams fled her slowly-reviving mind. "I wake up fine," she said. "I just need..."

"Coffee?" Justin offered her a cup.

Shanna frowned but sipped from the cup anyways. It wasn't quite right; there was a metallic aftertaste in her mouth, a coppery finish that the first mouthful of coffee washed away in a haze of sugar and mocha. The last shards of sleep fell away, wash from her mind by the warm caffeine. A tap-tap-tap made her look up; Quinn was glaring at her, obviously waiting for an answer. "Sorry, Chief, you've been running me ragged and I couldn't think. I had to sleep. What was the question again?"

"Cry me a river." Quinn looked like he'd been running on coffee for the last few days, which he probably had been. Eviscerated bodies weren't something he dealt with on a daily basis. "Well? What do you have for me?"

"Two bodies." Shanna shrugged. "One more coming tonight, at the very least. And who knows what coming through the World Walls, also possibly tonight." She turned to Justin. "That's something I didn't think of. What if our unknown is trying to make a permanent hole in the Walls?"

Justin paled, his hazel eyes suddenly bright against his ashen skin. "That's a horrible thought."

"I know." Just the possibility made her shudder. "But still, if that were the case, then we're going to see a lot more bodies."

"If that's the case," Justin said slowly, "then we'll have to…"

She cut him off with a sharp look. "I know."

"Have to what?" Quinn demanded. "I need to know what you're planning."

"At the moment, nothing." No need to tell Quinn what she'd need to do if that turned out to be the case. She and the Council of 9, the Lords who ruled the Elemental Planes, would have to begin the Cleansing. The Four Horsemen would be summoned. It wouldn't be pretty.

There was very little chance that Shanna would survive the experience. In most of the Cleansings she'd read about, the StarChild who facilitated it rarely did. But that was neither here nor there. If it needed to be done, she'd do it.

–Don't worry about it until then,– Shanna thought, sipping again on the coffee. Out loud, she said, "Justin, where's Rick?"

"He's with Maddy. Her parents are flying in tomorrow – they couldn't get a plane tonight." Justin set his own coffee cup aside. "Both he and Maddy are pretty upset right now."

"I can only imagine." –Poor Rick.– "You left them at the Home?"

"Yeah. They're surrounded by people there – less chance of either of them sneaking off to try and get some retribution."

"Good thought." Shanna leaned back on the couch and closed her eyes, trying to think of what to do next.

"I did find out something interesting, though," Justin said, and she opened her eyes again.

"Oh?"

"Yeah. I have a friend in the registrar's office. She managed to get me a copy of all the class lists for Anthony Brooks for this year and last year."

"Who?" Shanna asked.

"Our first victim," Justin said. "And guess who took a class with him last year?"

"Half the campus?" she said, shrugging.

"Madeline Peterson."

"So?" Shanna said.

"So both our victims have a connection to Maddy," Justin said. "What if this is aimed at her?"

"To what purpose?" Shanna asked frankly. "To bug Rick? Or are you insinuating that they're trying to get to us?"

Quinn's head went back and forth as he followed their comments. "It's not unthinkable," Justin said. "And it's at least as possible as your theory."

"It was an idea, not a theory," she said.

"Whatever. You're the most powerful force on this campus right now, and everyone knows that Rick's under your protection."

"Rick is. Maddy can go to hell as far as I'm concerned."

"Liar." Justin's lips twisted into a sly smile. "You know as well as I do that if she were in trouble, you'd be there just as fast as I would."

"Only to shake the hand of the person who killed her," Shanna said, but the comment lacked truth and she knew it. "Hell. Do you really think someone's trying to call me out?"

Justin shrugged. "Who knows. But you've got as much connection to our two victims as Maddy does—you're in the same department as the first victim, and the second is the younger sister of your best friend's girlfriend. There's also the very real fact that Maddy's pissed a lot of people off. This could be aimed at her."

"Good point. But why go through all this trouble just to get to Maddy? I mean, you can summon a low-level Blood Spirit in one night. This seems a bit extreme to deal with one pain in the ass."

"Which brings us back to you," Justin said.

"Damn you." Shanna sighed. "I hate it when you're right."

"Why would they go through all this to get to you?" Quinn interrupted. "Why not challenge you outright?"

"Because I'm the StarChild," she reminded him, and he shrugged. "So?"

"So I have access to a lot more Power than most Mages. Each of these sacrifices netted our Blood Mage a lot of Power. If they are preparing to challenge me, they're going to want a lot of Power stockpiled." She scowled at Justin. "And Justin's right, damn him. If Maddy's in trouble, I'll know it, and I'll go and rescue her ass. Again."

"Again?" Quinn's eyebrows rose. "Does she need rescuing a lot?"

"All the damn time," Shanna muttered, and Justin sighed.

"Maddy's a royal pain, and her mouth gets her in trouble a lot," he explained. "But Rick's devoted to her, and well, he's a friend of ours."

"If she's their final target, they'll have to get through us to get her," Shanna said firmly. "I won't…" A thought hit her, and she paled. "Sweet Lady of Light, Justin, you don't think Rick is the final sacrifice, do you?"

Justin was already reaching for the phone on the desk. "I'll make sure he and Maddy plan on staying home tonight." He cradled the phone against his ear. "Hey, Ty, is Rick there?"

Shanna watched his face fall as their roommate spoke.

"Shit. Where did they go?" Justin swore under his breath. "Okay, thanks. No, it's okay. You didn't know. If they call in, tell them to sit tight, call me and tell me where they are." He paused. "Yes, sitting on them is good if you can find them." He hung up and sighed. "Well, that sucks. Now what?"

"Now we see where they are." Shanna tossed her empty coffee cup into the trash can, then conjured a blue-green ball of witchfire. It hung in the air before her, and Shanna concentrated, feeding Power into the tag she'd put on Maddy long ago. –Okay, so I'm a hypocrite,– she thought, amused. –But I need to know where she is at all times. And at least my tags don't itch. Then again, I spent some time creating this one and hiding it on her, so she couldn't find it and get rid of it.–

–Besides, it makes my heart happy to know that she itches all the time. Of course, she probably doesn't even notice it.–

Blue-green light filled her mind, erasing the room around her for the moment. The tag she'd activated flared, a beacon in the dense magical atmosphere of the college; after a few seconds, she saw where they were.

"They're at the Student Union," she said, relief lacing through her voice. "With Carla and some of the others in Maddy's circle. They should be okay for the moment."

"Probably discussing the Beltane ritual tonight," Justin said. "I know both Maddy and Rick were planning on going to it tonight."

"And the odds our Blood Mage won't crash a Beltane ritual?" Shanna said, and Justin snorted. "My thoughts exactly. Guess we're doing this the old-fashioned way."

"By doing what?" Quinn asked, as she stood up and stretched.

Shanna grinned, and Justin laughed. "By going to an orgy, of course. What else does one do on Beltane?"

———•———

He paced in front of the altar, the large white candles already lit and the air faintly perfumed with the scent of smoke and incense. The Beltane fires had been lit—even here, in their secluded grove, a fire burned, ready to be jumped at the end of the ritual. And tonight, for the first time in years, he would have someone to jump it with.

As long as everything went right. As long as the StarChild stayed away.

The sacrifice was ready. The heart beat steadily in its container, ready to be consumed. All they needed was the final tolling of the bells, marking the death of the day.

His knife lay on the altar, beside the crystal dish and a matching crystal goblet. And in the center of the candles, the final black pillar waited, hidden by a small glamour. Once the heart was consumed and the sacrifice given, the runes would light it, and the final spells would be triggered.

And then, finally, everything would be right again.

———•———

"Are we ready?"

Shanna looked over at Justin, who nodded. "I've got the first aid kit here," he said. "Not to mention the portable wards and the shield spells. Anything else?"

"How many bombs do you have?" she asked pointedly, and he looked pained.

"Do we really have to bring those?"

"Yes." Shanna glared at him. "If we're fighting a major Blood Spirit or, God forbid, a Chaos Lord, I want as much firepower as I can get my hands on."

"But they're so…messy."

"Be neat on your own time," she told him bluntly. "That's why we have shield spells. Get the damn bombs."

He muttered something under his breath, but pulled out the small wooden box and stowed it in his messenger bag. "Anything else?"

"No, that should be it." She tossed him two cans of Mountain Dew, which he also stowed. "Did you find out where the ritual was?"

He shook his head. "Nope. No one wanted to confess they knew where it was – they all mumbled something about not having anything to do with Maddy if I was asking for you."

"It's a fucking Beltane ritual." Shanna rolled her eyes. "What, do they think I have nothing better to do than harass her? And you wonder why I want to strangle her on a regular basis. I'm trying to protect her – I don't give a rat's ass who she screws in a Circle. If it doesn't bother Rick, why should it bother me?"

Justin chuckled. "Good question. Remember, though, you've been…less than charitable to her and her friends. They're scared of you." He glanced at his watch. "It's 11:30. Now what?"

–Stupid children.– Shanna bit down hard on another comment and summoned her witchfire. "Then we do this the hard way." The ball floated, but no image came through. "Damn them, they've pulled up the shields already."

"Damn." He looked at her. "So how…"

The witchlight flared, and Shanna stumbled back as an explosion of fear/pain/horror/anger rocketed through her; Maddy screamed somewhere in her head, and she caught the briefest glimpse of Rick standing with something dripping blood in his hands. For a single moment, the shields around the Circle Maddy was a part of shattered as she reacted to whatever had frightened her. It was just enough to give Shanna a direction – and then the shields were pulled back, blocking her again.

"Shanna!"

"Blood." She could taste copper in her mouth and pushed herself away from the wall she'd stumbled against. "Let's go. This is going to get ugly."

May 1, 1995

The direction Maddy's scream had echoed from was, of course, the most heavily-wooded part of the campus. Shanna surveyed the thick wall of trees in front of her distastefully. –One of the disadvantages of a rural college setting,– she thought. –Too many damn places to hide in.– "Well, we have two choices," she said out loud. "We can either go in blindly and hope we stumble over them…"

"Or?" Justin said when she paused.

"Or I can make a whole lot of new enemies and blow every Circle within a three-mile radius to hell," she said finally. "And if I do that, you'd better be ready to buy me a few minutes. I'll be a little out of it when I come back."

"Are you insane?" Justin choked out. "How the hell are you going to get enough Power to blow all those Circles?"

Shanna smiled grimly, taking off her shoes and socks and digging her bare toes into the still-chill ground. "Leave that to me," she said. "I'm not the StarChild for nothing, you know. And if they are trying for a permanent Gate into Chaos, well, it's up to a creature of the Balance to make sure that doesn't happen. And the Balance helps those who do Her work."

"You're going to channel the Balance." It wasn't even a question. "You'll burn out."

"Do you have a better idea?" she snapped. "I don't. So stand back and get ready."

"You really are insane," Justin grumbled, stepping away from her and dropping his bag. "Go ahead. I'll give you a good burial."

"Thanks for the vote of confidence." Shanna drew in a deep breath. "Are you ready?"

"Are you?"

–Am I?– She didn't dare answer. Raising her hands high above her head, Shanna looked up into the star-filled sky, with the barest sliver of a moon floating in it, and opened her innermost shields. Her aura flared into all the colors of the rainbow, sending out a beacon in every direction, and she felt Justin ground himself, reaching for his own Power in case they drew any unwelcome visitors. Shanna reached out for the sex and lust magic swirling in the air, building a fire deep within her soul, an inferno that roared up around her, consuming her, as she sought the one thing that set her apart from all the other Mages in the world – the direct connection to the Spirit of the Balance that infused her soul.

Hotter and hotter she burned, destroying all traces of her humanity as she fed the conflagration, seeking the purifying heart of the fire, the source of magic, pure and clean, beckoning in the distance. Shanna reached for it eagerly as it flickered and the mundane world fell away from her.

–Why do you seek me, my child?– The voice of the Spirit of the Balance echoed through her, a shimmering glissando of a question.

–I need your help, Mother,– she replied. –I need to borrow your Power. There are Circles I must break.–

–Breaking Circles is not something I condone, child.– The faintest hint of reproach cut her. –Why do you ask me to help you do this?–

–Because those who created the Circle are doing so to help one of the Chaos-born through,– Shanna replied, as she bled flames in the starry landscape she stood in. –They will harm your children if I cannot stop them, but I cannot find them behind their Circle.–

–This is an odd way to do a Cleansing.– The Spirit floated in front of her, a phoenix of flame and starlight.

–I do not want it to come to that,– Shanna admitted. –I cannot prove they are doing this maliciously yet. But without your help, I will not find them until it is too late.–

–It may already be too late for you.–

–What?– Shanna asked, confused.

–This will be a test of you, my child.– Wings of flame surrounded her and a cold supernova of Power roared through her, burning away doubt, fear and questions. –Break the Circles. Preserve my Balance. And if you survive, perhaps we shall meet again.–

Shanna was spun abruptly back down to herself, shedding Power like a whirligig of fireworks as she released the gifts of the Spirit. In her heightened state, just before she touched down, she felt the Circles around her crumple like Styrofoam walls, exploding in a kaleidoscope of shattered spells. Howls of fear and fury erupted from the woods as rituals were destroyed, but she only cared about one thing – finding Maddy.

And then the Power left her in a rush that sent her crashing to the ground. As she clung to consciousness with her fingernails, Shanna felt Justin hone in on Maddy's location before raising his own shields. The ground she lay on pulsed with the heartbeat of the planet; she concentrated on that primal rhythm, drawing strength from it, reaching for the reserves she knew she had, somewhere. –I have to come back,– she thought grimly. –I have to find her and stop what they're doing.–

"Shanna?"

Justin pulled her upright, propping her against him and holding an open bottle of Mountain Dew to her mouth. The first sweet drops spilled from her numb lips, but gradually, enough of the liquid made it down her throat for the caffeine and sugar to jumpstart her system again. How Mages did a speedy recovery before soda appeared, she'd never know. After a few moments, she coughed and pushed the bottle away.

"Are you sure?" he asked her, and she nodded.

"Do you have a tag on her now?" Shanna asked him, and he nodded.

"There's a Spirit there too," he said and her heart sank. "I couldn't tell what kind—I didn't want it to find us."

"Shit." She pulled on her socks and shoes and then they set off deeper into the woods.

She felt it as they got closer: an angry throbbing, like a toothache or headache that pulsed with a malignant energy. "I think…" she started, and then stumbled backwards as a shower of sparks exploded around them, catching her off-guard. Without realizing it, they'd nearly walked right into the clearing they'd been looking for.

"Welcome to my Circle, StarChild," a mocking voice, hardly recognizable but faintly familiar. "I'm so thankful you helped me through. That final push was a bitch, you know."

Justin yanked her behind a tree as another shower of sparks erupted around her. "Pay attention!" he hissed, and she shook her head.

–Damn, I'm more out of it than I realized.– She peeked around the tree, and then pulled back. Bodies were scattered in the clearing in heaps; the altar in the center of the grove was split in two, and a lanky blond figure slumped near it. Standing in the midst of the carnage, laughing, was Yvaine Boxer.

–No, it's what used to be Yvaine Boxer,– Shanna realized, her heart sinking. –Oh shit. Where's the Blood Mage?–

"Okay, this is a problem," she breathed to Justin, who nodded. "I hope to hell that she wasn't the Mage, because if she was, I'll have to kill her, and I don't want to."

"I know." Justin opened the messenger bag and tossed her a few spell balls. "Take these. Maybe we'll get lucky and the Mage is the guy on the ground over there."

"Hopefully he's still alive too." She peeked out again. "Okay, here's the plan. I don't see Rick or Maddy, so you find them first. Get them under a shield spell. I'll take care of the Professor."

"Right." He peeked out. "How are you going to do that?"

–Good question.– "I'll think of something. Once you get them safe, find out if that guy is the Mage. If he is, we're okay. I think I can send it back without killing her."

"You know, it might be better if you did." Justin held up a hand to stop her protest. "You said it yourself, Shanna – she's dying of cancer. Send her out cleanly."

"I'm not a murderer," Shanna said firmly. "I won't do that unless I have to."

"Shanna…"

"Just go, Justin." She fingered the shield spell in her pocket and then took a deep breath. "Now!"

She rolled out from behind the tree, bringing up a dark green translucent shield of Power in front of her. Through the shield, she could see Yvaine stalking towards, not her, but the altar, and the body lying beside it. "Hey, what about me, Professor?" she called, tossing a ball of Power at her former teacher. "Let's dance for a while."

"I don't dance," Yvaine spat, batting the ball away contemptuously. "But I suppose I could drain you. That would give me enough Power to fully cement myself here. Then I can get busy doing what I need to."

"And what would that be?" Shanna asked, ducking as another bolt of energy shattered against her shield. "Taking over the world? Or is that too overdone?"

"And what would I need an entire world for?" Yvaine laughed. "I'm incarnated now. I'll be happy with a small part to call my own. This campus would do nicely."

"You're incarnated in a dying body," Shanna pointed out. "You'll go back soon enough."

"It was a dying body," Yvaine corrected her maliciously. "That was part of the bargain. She invited me in, and I Healed her."

Shanna's stomach flipped. "She thought she could resist you. And you let her believe that Healing her was all you were going to do."

"Of course." Fire snaked from Yvaine's fingertips, reaching around Shanna's shield with hungry mouths. She dropped the shield and conjured a rainfall, drowning them. "She was so desperate, she'd've believed anything."

"I'll bet. And Maddy?"

"Who?" Yvaine looked puzzled. "Oh, the silly girl who broke the Circle? What about her?"

"You didn't choose her for the final sacrifice?" Shanna flipped another ball of fire at Yvaine, who batted it away.

"I didn't choose anyone. They gave so freely…"

–Found them!– Justin shouted in her head suddenly, throwing her off-balance. Yvaine took advantage and whipped a long chain of thorns at her; Shanna ducked, but the whip gouged a strip of flesh from her back and she swore.

–Wonderful,– she thought back. –Now leave me alone.–

"It won't matter, you know," Yvaine called to her, swinging the whip around again. "You can't send me back."

"That's debatable," Shanna replied. "See, I can't let you stay here."

"How do you intend to send me back?"

"How about I start like this?" Shanna spread her fingers and lightning flared from each fingertip, arcing towards Yvaine. She ducked, but the lightning changed as it passed her, forming vines that tied her down.

"Is this the best you can do, StarChild?" Yvaine laughed. "I don't need to be moving to kill you. I'll let them do it."

"What?" Shanna stalked over to her. "You having delusions of grandeur already? I knew you Blood spirits were unstable, but this is ridicule…" The world spun for a moment, and she fell as something hit her across the back of her head. Rolling aside, she saw one of the coven members standing above her, a rock in her hand.

"Will you kill them all, StarChild?" Yvaine mocked her. "They're all a part of me. All tied to me. How will you defeat me when I'm in each of them?"

Shanna stared up at the girl; her eyes were dead, the white iris red as blood. "What did you do?"

"Blood," Yvaine purred. "It's always come back to the Blood."

–How fucking stupid can you get?– The pieces fell into place with a loud thump and she gaped at the girl, amazed at the sheer audacity. The final sacrifice had been their own free wills – blood, given freely to the woman they thought they were curing.

"So what will you do, StarChild?" Yvaine taunted her. "How will you save them and send me back?"

The girl loomed over her, raising the rock again, and Shanna ducked. "Justin!"

"I'm a bit busy!" he hollered, and she saw him struggling with another coven member.

"Did you put dragon's blood in the bags?"

"What?"

"Did you use dragon's blood in the shield spells?" she shouted, tripping up the girl in front of her with a kick of her legs. The girl fell over and Shanna scrambled to her feet, feeling for the bag in her pocket.

"Of course!"

"Good!" She ripped the bag open and dug for the irregularly shaped piece of resin. "Then most of them might survive this."

There was a knife on the ground near her; Shanna grabbed it as she ran by and then knelt next to Yvaine. "I'm sorry," she said honestly, as the woman snarled at her. "I really am."

Sparks rained down as Yvaine lashed out at her, but Shanna ignored the pain as she stabbed the knife into her former professor's side, ripping a long gash. Blood poured out; she then drew the knife across her own hand and then tossed the blade away. The dragon's blood began to glow with an unearthly silver light as she bathed it in her own blood; with a deep breath to center herself, Shanna shoved the resin and her own bloody fist into Yvaine's side, shouting, "Blood of the Balance, purify this body!"

It was ugly spellcasting, but it worked. The Spirit howled, trying to twist away from Shanna's hand, but she set her jaw and continued to dig. The silver Power in the dragon's blood traveled up her arms, cool tendrils that tied her to Yvaine, letting her see the ties that bound the coven to her. One snaked behind her; Shanna set her jaw, knowing there was nothing she could do to stop the blow that was coming and hoping she could finish the spell before the knife hit.

"No!" The girl behind her drove her ritual blade into Shanna's back, looking for a vital spot. "You're killing her! Leave her alone!"

Shanna ignored her, bending over Yvaine, forcing the dragon's blood deeper into the body. White starlight, cool and still, erupted from Yvaine's eyes, the Power of the Balance driving the Blood Spirit back behind the walls. As the Spirit retreated, Shanna called out, "Justin, Heal them!"

"What?"

"Heal them!" she shouted. "Cleanse the infection! Otherwise we'll lose them all!"

"I don't have enough Power here!"

"Then make some!" It was getting hard to concentrate. Between the dragon's blood and the knife in her back, Shanna was beginning to waver. "Use the bombs!"

"Oh, right!"

It was a cooling rain that he conjured, a rain that carried the Power of the Balance with it, washing away the traces of the Blood Spirit from the others. Yvaine screamed and frothed beneath it, and Shanna continued to shove the Blood Spirit within her back behind the World Walls. The howls grew deeper, blocking out every other sound from Shanna's ears, but she continued, knowing that even as she forced the Spirit back that Yvaine was dying beneath her.

–She chose this,– Shanna reminded herself. –I had no choice.–

Finally, the Walls closed back around the Spirit, and Yvaine's body stilled. The coven stood around in the pouring rain, blinking at one another. Justin shoved the girl at Shanna's back away and knelt down beside his sister. "Stop, Shanna," he said quietly. "It's done."

"I killed her." Shanna looked up at him, her arm still buried to the elbow in Yvaine's side. "I couldn't save her, Jus."

"You can't save them all, Shanna."

"Why not?"

"Because not everyone is worth saving." He pulled the knife out of her back and threw it away. "But you saved the innocents. That's what we're here to do. Now let me help you."

"You saved the innocents," she whispered, her eyes closing. "I just kill people."

THE WORLD THROUGH PATRICK

Stuart Jaffe

The first time Patrick changed the world he had been sitting by his bedroom window. Trapped in his wheelchair, he watched the children run and swing on the playground. More than that, though, he watched the world from there. Every day passed him through this glass. He knew the best angles for the widest view. He knew when and where the sun would hit, which side of the frame to look from depending on what he wished to see, and whether to raise or lower his head to counter glare. He had become a window-watching master, and on this particular day, he had been watching a little girl at the playground who appeared to be unpopular.

The other children refused her a turn on the swings or a place in line for the slide. The girls pointed at her and giggled to each other. They wore belly-shirts exposing their midriffs more than a decade too early. The sun glinted on their sunglasses as they attempted an "adult-cool" and only looked ridiculous and perverse. The one parent on-duty spent her time reading a trashy romance novel.

The little girl took the verbal abuse without comment. Her blue, corduroy dress had been patched with a paisley butterfly fueling the murmured insults, but she wore it with confidence, not shame. She meandered around the playground's edges, looking for an opportunity to participate even though nobody wanted her.

Patrick wished he could help this girl. He wished he could walk outside and set things right. He wanted her to see his wheelchair, his immobile legs, and to know that the teasing by a few snotty brats meant nothing. He became so engrossed in her actions that he lost all sense of the world around him.

He never noticed when his mother walked in to place his lunch tray on the bed. He never acknowledged her when she kissed his forehead and let out a tear. He never spoke when she drifted out of the room as silent as a ghost. Patrick only saw that little girl on the playground.

She had decided to climb on the jungle gym, and despite the nasty glares she received from two other girls, she climbed. Patrick's chest swelled as if watching his own daughter face down a bully. With each step upward, his heart quickened its pace. She could do it. He knew it. She could show them that no matter what they said or did, she would survive. When she reached the top, she sat with her legs swinging free and smiled. Patrick slapped his wheelchair's arm and shared the smile. The triumph lasted the length of a breath. Then one of the brats snuck up behind his little victor and shoved her off.

Things became strange. He saw her fall forward, her surprised expression disappearing as she toppled over and cracked her head on the metal bars, blood flying from the gash. Her body tumbled to the mulch. Strands of her hair clung to the bars with blood. She did not move. But Patrick also saw a golden hand grow out of the ground, reaching her before she fell, steadying her, giving her the chance to flash her own glare back at the girl who attempted to hurt her. Both moments existed at the same time. They layered on top of one another as if superimposed. It was difficult to see everything, but Patrick focused on that golden hand. He wanted that to be the truth.

And it happened.

As the girl, safe and happy, climbed down and walked away, a smile greater than any Patrick had ever experienced crossed his lips. He did not believe at that moment that he had caused anything nor did he notice the numb feeling in his thumb. For Patrick, it had been an odd sensation, one to be dismissed like deja vu, one that washed away with the relief of the girl's safety.

For awhile, his life returned to routine. He delved deeper into the art of watching others live their lives. Still, he failed to notice when his mother arrived with a meal or left with half-full plates. When she washed him or drained his catheter bag, he kept his eyes on the window. He barely blinked when she sat on his bed, bawling as she explained that his father, unable to deal with the stigma of a crippled son, had left them.

At night, when he could not keep his eyes open, he dreamed of running, standing, walking. He dreamed of his mother smiling and laughing. He had true dreams—images of things he believed would never become reality.

One Wednesday afternoon while all the children were at school and most of the adults were at work, Patrick changed the world again. He had been taking particular note of the affair spawning between Mrs. Parkson, the corner neighbor's wife, and a young man who stopped by once a week. She had taken care of Patrick when he was younger, and for a few years back then, he had had a crush on her. Mrs. Parkson's young man often left the window shades open, and though Patrick could feel nothing from the waist down, his body still reacted at the sexual sight. Just seeing Mrs. Parkson disrobe and smile toward a stranger brought back the old dreams. On warm days, Patrick would crack open his window and listen to Mrs. Parkson moan. Each pleasured cry forced him to wonder if, had his legs worked, he could have been that young man. He tortured himself in watching them, lusting and hating with every visit.

This particular time, however, a fire started in the Parkson basement and in seconds the whole house was ablaze. Flames snaked up the walls as black and gray smoke billowed from the windows. Like before, Patrick saw two images, one layered over the other. In the first, the house went up with such ferocity that he could feel waves of heat hitting him in the face. Lost in their love-making, Mrs. Parkson and her beau died from carbon monoxide poisoning. In the second, the house raged as before, but a golden arm reached through the walls startling Mrs. Parkson. She screamed, unsure of what she had seen, but it woke her to the fire, and the two managed to escape through the bedroom window—naked and embarrassed, but alive. Patrick wanted her to live, and so the second vision took hold.

This time, however, his right forearm went numb. When the fire department had put out the fire, he had lost all feeling in his arm. When morning came, he could not move it.

With controlled fear, Patrick watched the street as his mother dressed him for the hospital. The doctors took their tests and murmured to each other down the hall, and in the end, they could agree that he had some degenerative disease. Beyond that, they knew nothing. As they drove home, he stared out the car window and listened to his mother sniffle tears.

Weeks passed, and life existed through his window. Winter hit hard that year, and the snow blanket glittered in the sun. He thought over those two moments in which he knew he had altered the world around him and attempted to recreate each minute in his mind, hoping to catch a glimmer of what he had done before. He pictured the little girl and Mrs. Parkson, the jungle gym and the fire. He thought of how his hands felt or his chest or his head.

Nothing stood out. No single way of knowing how it had happened, and more importantly, how to avoid it. The idea of such a power might have seemed cool earlier in his life, but Patrick could not accept the sacrifice now.

That was the missing ingredient, after all. He felt sure of it, even as he denied it. If he had some degenerative disease, he would have weakened or lost more body functions, but nothing had changed since his doctors' visit. The blatant truth was in Patrick's still body—his changing the world and his physical losses were interconnected.

Two days later, he watched his mother shovel her way toward the mailbox. He saw the slow way she moved, the patience in her shoveling, the determination in her steady progress. Every stroke cut into the snow with a sharp crunch, and each time she lifted the cold mass, she grunted. About halfway across, she stopped to take a breath—the bottom edges of her purple long coat as damp and weathered as her eyes. After twenty minutes, she reached the mailbox. Patrick saw her face as she peered inside. Her mouth remained a grim line, and her shoulders slumped. She walked back empty-handed, dragging the shovel.

As she left the window frame with the shovel clanging on the concrete walk, he wished he could reach out to her, put an arm on her shoulder, and let her know that he had seen her. He noticed a small patch of grass near the walkway that had been shoveled clear. His chest tightened as he poured all his attention on this scrap of dirt. Before he could think, before he could stop himself, he saw two images. The first—merely the frozen grass with nothing different. The second—a single tulip poking through in full bloom, the edges shimmering golden light. And as he made it real, his left hand grew numb.

A few hours later, he watched his mother check the mail again. She noticed the tulip right away, stopping and staring for several minutes. Patrick could not see her facial reaction, but he believed it made her a little happier. He hoped so—even as he cried in silence for his own loss.

The last time Patrick changed the world occurred in the middle of the spring. Twice during the winter, his chest tightened and double-images began to form in his mind, but he had been quick to shake off the sensation, to break his focus. He buried the images with his unwillingness to give any more of himself and with his fear. Every day since then had felt like constant guard duty—one slip and he might lose all feeling from the neck down . . . or worse. But even good soldiers must rest, and Patrick had no one to offer relief.

Time drifted. He ate when he noticed food. He slept whenever it snuck upon him. His mother kept him going like a benevolent ghost.

The final day arrived with a painful howl from downstairs. The sound hacked into Patrick's head, startling him awake. He looked at his bedroom door, his eyes wide, his lips trembling. The howl turned into heaving sobs, and he noticed his mother had not arrived to clear away the breakfast tray.

Five minutes later, the cries died down. Patrick never took his eyes from the door. He thought he should roll over to it, but he had lost usage of his one good hand during the last few days. Then he heard the front door open. His head darted to the window.

He saw his mother walk outside, cradling a dead cat. Mascara tears lined her face and mucous dribbled from her nose. The cat had a dusty, black coat and a red collar with a bell that kept jingling as Patrick's mother shook with silent sobs.

She stopped at the tulip Patrick had created for her and laid the cat next to it. On her knees, she rocked as if locked in a strange ritual.

Patrick could not look away from the cat. He never knew it had existed before. When had his mother bought a pet? He looked at its lifeless eyes and wondered why his mother had never cried like that for him or for his father. Why this cat?

He pictured the cat and its secret life downstairs—a whole world existing just out of reach. He saw how the cat had started with a rich coat that paled with age, and how it had curled in its favorite spot that morning to die in peace. He saw how his mother had found the cat and how the loss twisted her face. He saw the mounting pressure of all her losses finally geyser from her with those deep howls.

And as he imagined this, a second image came to life. He saw the cat take a shocked breath of cold air. He saw its green eyes widen and its small mouth yawn. He saw the surprise in his mother's face and the sudden joy that overwhelmed her. His heart tingled a little, and he saw his mother continue to take care of him for several days even though he had died. He saw her shed her tears for him but still have something to love in that cat.

With a hesitant breath, he opened his mouth to say goodbye, but he had no voice. It had died long ago. But he could still smile.

Triceratops Summer

Michael Swanwick

The dinosaurs looked all wobbly in the summer heat shimmering up from the pavement. There were about thirty of them, a small herd of what appeared to be *Triceratops*. They were crossing the road—don't ask me why—so I downshifted and brought the truck to a halt, and waited.

Waited and watched.

They were interesting creatures, and surprisingly graceful for all their bulk. They picked their way delicately across the road, looking neither to the right nor the left. I was pretty sure I'd correctly identified them by now – they had those three horns on their faces. I used to be a kid. I'd owned the plastic models.

My next-door neighbor, Gretta, who was sitting in the cab next to me with her eyes closed, said, "Why aren't we moving?"

"Dinosaurs in the road," I said.

She opened her eyes.

"Son of a bitch," she said.

Then, before I could stop her, she leaned over and honked the horn, three times. Loud.

As one, every *Triceratops* in the herd froze in its tracks, and swung its head around to face the truck.

I practically fell over laughing.

"What's so goddamn funny?" Gretta wanted to know. But I could only point and shake my head helplessly, tears of laughter rolling down my cheeks.

It was the frills. They were beyond garish. They were as bright as any circus poster, with red whorls and yellow slashes and electric orange diamonds—too many shapes and colors to catalog, and each one different. They looked like Chinese kites! Like butterflies with six-foot winspans! Like Las Vegas on acid! And then, under those carnival-bright displays, the most stupid faces imaginable, blinking and gaping like brain-damaged cows. Oh, they were funny, all right, but if you couldn't see that at a glance, you never were going to.

Gretta was getting fairly steamed. She climbed down out of the cab and slammed the door behind her. At the sound, a couple of the *Triceratops* pissed themselves with excitement, and the lot shied away a step or two. Then they began huddling a little closer, to see what would happen next.

Gretta hastily climbed back into the cab. "What are those bastards up to now?" she demanded irritably. She seemed to blame me for their behavior. Not that she could say so, considering she was in my truck and her BMW was still in the garage in South Burlington.

"They're curious," I said. "Just stand still. Don't move or make any noise, and after a bit they'll lose interest and wander off."

"How do you know? You ever see anything like them before?"

"No," I admitted. "But I worked on a dairy farm when I was a young fella, thirty-forty years ago, and the behavior seems similar."

In fact, the *Triceratops* were already getting bored and starting to wander off again when a battered old Hyundai pulled wildly up beside us, and a skinny young man with the worst-combed hair I'd seen in a long time jumped out. They decided to stay and watch.

The young man came running over to us, arms waving. I leaned out the window. "What's the problem, son?"

He was pretty bad upset. "There's been an accident—an *incident*, I mean. At the Institute." He was talking about the Institute for Advanced Physics, which was not all that far from here. It was government-funded and affiliated in some way I'd never been able to get straight with the University of Vermont. "The verge stabilizers failed and the meson-field inverted and vectorized. The congruence factors went to infinity and . . ." He seized control of himself. "You're not supposed to see *any* of this."

"These things are yours, then?" I said. "So you'd know. They're *Triceratops*, right?"

"*Triceratops horridus*," he said distractedly. I felt unreasonably pleased with myself. "For the most part. There might be a couple other species of *Triceratops* mixed in there as well. They're like ducks in that regard. They're not fussy about what company they keep."

Gretta shot out her wrist and glanced meaningfully at her watch. Like everything else she owned, it was expensive. She worked for a firm in Essex Junction that did systems analysis for companies that were considering downsizing. Her job was to find out exactly what everybody did and then tell the CEO who could be safely cut. "I'm losing money," she grumbled.

I ignored her.

"Listen," the kid said. "You've got to keep quiet about this. We can't afford to have it get out. It has to be kept a secret."

"A secret?" On the far side of the herd, three cars had drawn up and stopped. Their passengers were standing in the road, gawking. A Ford Taurus pulled up behind us, and its driver rolled down his window for a better look. "You're planning to keep a herd of dinosaurs secret? There must be dozens of these things."

"Hundreds," he said despairingly. "They were migrating. The herd broke up after it came through. This is only a fragment of it."

"Then I don't see how you're going to keep this a secret. I mean, just look at them. They're practically the size of tanks. People are bound to notice."

"My God, my God."

Somebody on the other side had a camera out and was taking pictures. I didn't point this out to the young man.

Gretta had been getting more and more impatient as the conversation proceeded. Now she climbed down out of the truck and said, "I can't afford to waste any more time here. I've got work to do."

"Well, so do I, Gretta."

She snorted derisively. "Ripping out toilets, and nailing up sheet rock! Already, I've lost more money than you earn in a week."

She stuck out her hand at the young man. "Give me your car keys."

Dazed, the kid obeyed. Gretta climbed down, got in the Hyundai, and wheeled it around. "I'll have somebody return this to the Institute later today."

Then she was gone, off to find another route around the herd.

She should have waited, because a minute later the beasts decided to leave, and in no time at all were nowhere to be seen. They'd be easy enough to find, though. They pretty much trampled everything flat in their wake.

The kid shook himself, as if coming out of a trance. "Hey," he said. "She took my *car*."

"Climb into the cab," I said. "There's a bar a ways up the road. I think you need a drink."

He said his name was Everett McCoughlan, and he clutched his glass like he would fall off the face of the Earth if he were to let go. It took a couple of whiskeys to get the full story out of him. Then I sat silent for a long time. I don't mind admitting that what he'd said made me feel a little funny. "How long?" I asked at last.

"Ten weeks, maybe three months, tops. No more."

I took a long swig of my soda water. (I've never been much of a drinker. Also, it was pretty early in the morning.) Then I told Everett that I'd be right back.

I went out to the truck, and dug the cell phone out of the glove compartment.

First I called home. Delia had already left for the bridal shop, and they didn't like her getting personal calls at work, so I left a message saying that I loved her. Then I called Green Mountain Books. It wasn't open yet, but Randy likes to come in early and he picked up the phone when he heard my voice on the machine. I asked him if he had anything on *Triceratops*. He said to hold on a minute, and then said yes, he had one copy of *The Horned Dinosaurs* by Peter Dodson. I told him I'd pick it up next time I was in town.

Then I went back in the bar. Everett had just ordered a third whiskey, but I pried it out of his hand. "You've had enough of that," I said. "Go home, take a nap. Maybe putter around in the garden."

"I don't have my car," he pointed out.

"Where do you live? I'll take you home."

"Anyway, I'm supposed to be at work. I didn't log out. And technically I'm still on probation."

"What difference does that make," I asked, "now?"

Everett had an apartment in Winooski at the Woolen Mill, so I guess the Institute paid him good money. Either that or he wasn't very smart how he spent it. After I dropped him off, I called a couple contractors I knew and arranged for them to take over what jobs I was already committed to. Then I called the *Free Press* to cancel my regular ad, and all my customers to explain I was having scheduling problems and had to subcontract their jobs. Only old Mrs. Bremmer gave me any trouble over that, and even she came around after I said that in any case I wouldn't be able to get around to her Jacuzzi until sometime late July.

Finally, I went to the bank and arranged for a second mortgage on my house.

It took me a while to convince Art Letourneau I was serious. I'd been doing business with him for a long while, and he knew how I felt about debt. Also, I was pretty evasive about what I wanted the money for. He was half-suspicious I was having some kind of late onset mid-life crisis. But the deed was in my name and property values were booming locally, so in the end the deal went through.

On the way home, I stopped at a jewelry store and at the florist's.

Delia's eyes widened when she saw the flowers, and then narrowed at the size of the stone on the ring. She didn't look at all the way I'd thought she would. "This better be good," she said.

So I sat down at the kitchen table and told her the whole story. When I was done, Delia was silent for a long while, just as I'd been. Then she said, "How much time do we have?"

"Three months if we're lucky. Ten weeks in any case," Everett said.

"You believe him?"

"He seemed pretty sure of himself."

If there's one thing I am, it's a good judge of character, and Delia knew it. When Gretta moved into the rehabbed barn next door, I'd said right from the start she was going to be a difficult neighbor. And that was before she'd smothered the grass on her property under three different colors of mulch, and then complained about me keeping my pickup parked in the driveway, out in plain sight.

Delia thought seriously for a few minutes, frowning in that way she has when she's concentrating, and then she smiled. It was a wan little thing, but a smile nonetheless. "Well, I've always wished we could afford a real first-class vacation."

I was glad to hear her say so, because that was exactly the direction my own thought had been trending in. And happier than that when she flung out her arms and whooped, "I'm going to *Disney*world!"

"Hell," I said. "We've got enough money to go to Disneyworld, Disneyland, *and* Eurodisney, one after the other. I think there's one in Japan too."

We were both laughing at this point, and then she dragged me up out of the chair, and the two of us were dancing around and round the kitchen, still a little spooked under it all, but mostly being as giddy and happy as kids.

We were going to sleep in the next morning, but old habits die hard and anyway, Delia felt she owed it to the bridal shop to give them a week's notice. So, after she'd left, I went out to see if I could find where the *Triceratops* had gone.

Only to discover Everett standing by the side of the road with his thumb out.

I pulled over. "Couldn't get somebody at the Institute to drive your car home?" I asked when we were underway again.

"It never got there," he said gloomily. "That woman who was with you the other day drove it into a ditch. Stripped the clutch and bent the frame out of shape. She said she wouldn't have had the accident if my dinosaurs hadn't gotten her upset. Then she hung up on me. I just started at this job. I don't have the savings to buy a new car."

"Lease one instead," I said. "Put it on your credit card and pay the minimum for the next two or three months."

"I hadn't thought of that."

We drove on for a while and then I asked, "How'd she manage to get in touch with you?" She'd driven off before he mentioned his name.

"She called the Institute and asked for the guy with the bad hair. They gave her my home phone number."

The parking lot for the Institute for Advanced Physics had a card system, so I let Everett off by the side of the road. "Thanks for not telling anybody," he said as he climbed out. "About . . . you know."

"It seemed wisest not to."

He started away and then turned back suddenly and asked, "Is my hair really that bad?"

"Nothing that a barber couldn't fix," I said.

I'd driven to the Institute by the main highway. Returning, I went by back ways, through farmland. When I came to where I'd seen the *Triceratops*, I thought for an instant there'd been an accident, there were so many vehicles by the side of the road. But it turned out they were mostly gawkers and television crews. So apparently the herd hadn't gone far. There were cameras up and down the road and lots of good looking young women standing in front of them with wireless microphones.

I pulled over to take a look. One *Triceratops* had come right up to the fence and was browsing on some tall weeds there. It didn't seem to have any fear of human beings, possibly because in its day mammals never got much bigger than badgers. I walked up and stroked its back, which was hard and pebbly and warm. It was the warmth that got to me. It made the experience real.

A newswoman came over with her cameraman in tow. "You certainly look happy," she said.

"Well, I always wanted to meet a real live dinosaur." I turned to face her, but I kept one hand on the critter's frill. "They're something to see, I'll tell you. Dumb as mud but lots more fun to look at."

She asked me a few questions, and I answered them as best I could. Then, after she did her wrap, she got out a notebook and took down my name and asked me what I did. I told her I was a contractor but that I used to work on a dairy farm. She seemed to like that.

I watched for a while more, and then drove over to Burlington to pick up my book. The store wasn't open yet, but Randy let me in when I knocked. "You bastard," he said after he'd locked the door behind me. "Do you have any idea how much I could have sold this for? I had a foreigner," by which I understood him to mean somebody from New York State or possibly New Hampshire, "offer me two hundred dollars for it. And I could have got more if I'd had something to dicker with!"

"I'm obliged," I said, and paid him in paper bills. He waved off the tax but kept the nickel. "Have you gone out to see 'em yet?"

"Are you nuts? There's thousands of people coming into the state to look at those things. It's going to be a madhouse out there."

"I thought the roads seemed crowded. But it wasn't as bad as all of that."

"It's early still. You just wait."

Randy was right. By evening the roads were so congested that Delia was an hour late getting home. I had a casserole in the oven and the book open on the kitchen table when she staggered in. "The males have longer, more elevated horns, where the females have shorter, more forward-directed horns," I told her. "Also, the males are bigger than the females, but the females outnumber the males by a ratio of two to one."

I leaned back in my chair with a smile. "Two to one. Imagine that."

Delia hit me. "Let me see that thing."

I handed her the book. It kind of reminded me of when we were new-married, and used to go out bird-watching. Before things got so busy. Then Delia's friend Martha called and said to turn on Channel 3 quick. We did, and there I was saying, "dumb as mud."

"So you're a cattle farmer now?" Delia said, when the spot was over.

"That's not what I told her. She got it mixed up. Hey, look what I got." I'd been to three separate travel agents that afternoon. Now I spread out the brochures: Paris, Dubai, Rome, Australia, Rio de Janeiro, Marrakech. Even Disneyworld. I'd grabbed everything that looked interesting. "Take your pick, we can be there tomorrow."

Delia looked embarrassed.

"What?" I said.

"You know that June is our busy season. All those young brides. Francesca begged me to stay on through the end of the month."

"But—"

"It's not that long," she said.

For a couple of days it was like Woodstock, the Super Bowl, and the World Series all rolled into one – the Interstates came to a standstill, and it was worth your life to actually have to go somewhere. Then the governor called in the National Guard, and they cordoned off Chittenden County so you had to show your ID to get in or out. The *Triceratops* had scattered into little groups by then. Then a dozen or two were captured and shipped out of state to zoos where they could be more easily seen. So things returned to normal, almost.

I was painting the trim on the house that next Saturday when Everett drove up in a beat-up old clunker. "I like your new haircut," I said. "Looks good. You here to see the trikes?"

"Trikes?"

"That's what they're calling your dinos. *Triceratops* is too long for common use. We got a colony of eight or nine hanging around the neighborhood." There were woods out back of the house and beyond them a little marsh. They liked to browse the margins of the wood and wallow in the mud.

"No, uh . . . I came to find out the name of that woman you were with. The one who took my car."

"Gretta Houck, you mean?"

"I guess. I've been thinking it over, and I think she really ought to pay for the repairs. I mean, right's right."

"I noticed you decided against leasing."

"It felt dishonest. This car's cheap. But it's not very good. One door is wired shut with a coat hanger."

Delia came out of the house with the picnic basket then and I introduced them. "Ev's looking for Gretta," I said.

"Well, your timing couldn't be better," Delia said. "We were just about to go out trike-watching with her. You can join us."

"Oh, I can't—"

"Don't give it a second thought. There's plenty of food." Then, to me, "I'll go fetch Gretta while you clean up."

So that's how we found ourselves following the little trail through the woods and out to the meadow on the bluff above the Tylers' farm. The trikes slept in the field there. They'd torn up the crops pretty bad. But the state was covering damages, so the Tylers didn't seem to mind. It made me wonder if the governor knew what we know. If he'd been talking with the folks at the Institute.

I spread out the blanket, and Delia got out cold cuts, deviled eggs, lemonade, all the usual stuff. I'd brought along two pairs of binoculars, which I handed out to our guests. Gretta had been pretty surly so far, which made me wonder how Delia'd browbeat her into coming along. But now she said, "Oh, look! They've got babies!"

There were three little ones, only a few feet long. Two of them were mock-fighting, head-butting and tumbling over and over each other. The third just sat in the sun, blinking. They were all as cute as the dickens, with their tiny little nubs of horns and their great big eyes.

The other trikes were wandering around, pulling up bushes and such and eating them. Except for one that stood near the babies, looking big and grumpy and protective. "Is that the mother?" Gretta asked.

"That one's male," Everett said. "You can tell by the horns." He launched into an explanation, which I didn't listen to, having read the book.

On the way back to the house, Gretta grumbled, "I suppose you want the number for my insurance company."

"I guess," Everett said.

They disappeared into her house for maybe twenty minutes and then Everett got into his clunker and drove away. Afterwards, I said to Delia, "I thought the whole point of the picnic was you and I were going to finally work out where we were going on vacation." She hadn't even brought along the travel books I'd bought her.

"I think they like each other."

"Is that what this was about? You know, you've done some damn fool things in your time—"

"Like what?" Delia said indignantly. "When have I ever done anything that was less than wisdom incarnate?"

"Well . . . you married me."

"Oh, that." She put her arms around me. "That was just the exception that proves the rule."

So, what with one thing and the other, the summer drifted by. Delia took to luring the *Triceratops* closer and closer to the house with cabbages and bunches of celery and such. Cabbages were their favorite. It got so that we were feeding the trikes off the back porch in the evenings. They'd come clomping up around sunset, hoping for cabbages but willing to settle for pretty much anything.

It ruined the yard, but so what? Delia was a little upset when they got into her garden, but I spent a day putting up a good strong fence around it, and she replanted. She made manure tea by mixing their dung with water, and its effect on the plants was bracing. The roses blossomed like never before, and in August the tomatoes came up spectacular.

I mentioned this to Dave Jenkins down at the home-and-garden and he looked thoughtful. "I believe there's a market for that," he said. "I'll buy as much of their manure as you can haul over here."

"Sorry," I told him, "I'm on vacation."

Still, I couldn't get Delia to commit to a destination. Not that I quit trying. I was telling her about the Atlantis Hotel on Paradise Island one evening when suddenly she said, "Well, look at this."

I stopped reading about swimming with dolphins and the fake undersea ruined city, and joined her at the door. There was Everett's car—the new one that Gretta's insurance had paid for—parked out front of her house. There was only one light on, in the kitchen. Then that one went out too.

We figured those two had worked through their differences.

An hour later, though, we heard doors slamming, and the screech of Everett's car pulling out too fast. Then somebody was banging on our screen door. It was Gretta. When Delia let her in, she burst out into tears. Which surprised me. I wouldn't have pegged Everett as that kind of guy.

I made some coffee while Delia guided her into a kitchen chair, and got her some tissues, and soothed her down enough that she could tell us why she'd thrown Everett out of her house. It wasn't anything he'd done apparently, but something he'd said.

"Do you know what he *told* me?" she sobbed.

"I think I do," Delia said.

"About timelike—"

"—loops. Yes, dear."

Gretta looked stricken. "You too? Why didn't you tell me? Why didn't you tell everybody?"

"I considered it," I said. "Only then I thought, what would folks do if they knew their actions no longer mattered? Most would behave decently enough. But a few would do some pretty bad things, I'd think. I didn't want to be responsible for that."

She was silent for a while.

"Explain to me again about time like loops," she said at last. "Ev tried, but by then I was too upset to listen."

"Well, I'm not so sure myself. But the way he explained it to me, they're going to fix the problem by going back to the moment before the rupture occurred and preventing it from ever happening in the first place. When that happens, everything from the moment of rupture to the moment when they go back to apply the patch separates from the trunk timeline. It just sort of drifts away, and dissolves into nothingness—never was, never will be."

"And what becomes of us?"

"We just go back to whatever we were doing when the accident happened. None the worse for wear."

"But without memories."

"How can you remember something that never happened?"

"So Ev and I —"

"No, dear," Delia said gently.

"How much time do we have?"

"With a little luck, we have the rest of the summer," Delia said. "The question is, how do you want to spend it?"

"What does it matter," Gretta said bitterly. "If it's all going to end?"

"Everything ends eventually. But after all is said and done, it's what we do in the meantime that matters, isn't it?"

The conversation went on for a while more. But that was the gist of it.

Eventually, Gretta got out her cell and called Everett. She had him on speed dial, I noticed. In her most corporate voice, she said, "Get your ass over here," and snapped the phone shut without waiting for a response.

She didn't say another word until Everett's car pulled up in front of her place. Then she went out and confronted him. He put his hands on his hips. She grabbed him and kissed him. Then she took him by the hand and led him back into the house.

They didn't bother to turn on the lights.

I stared at the silent house for a little bit. Then I realized that Delia wasn't with me anymore, so I went looking for her.

She was out on the back porch. "Look," she whispered.

There was a full moon and by its light we could see the *Triceratops* settling down to sleep in our backyard. Delia had managed to lure them all the way in at last. Their skin was all silvery in the moonlight; you couldn't make out the patterns on their frills. The big trikes formed a kind of circle around the little ones. One by one, they closed their eyes and fell asleep.

Believe it or not, the big bull male snored.

It came to me then that we didn't have much time left. One morning soon we'd wake up and it would be the end of spring and everything would be exactly as it was before the dinosaurs came.

"We ever did get to Paris or London or Rome or Marrakesh," I said sadly. "Or even Disneyworld."

Without taking her eyes off the sleeping trikes, Delia put an arm around my waist. "Why are you so fixated on going places?" she asked. "We had a nice time here, didn't we?"

"I just wanted to make you happy."

"Oh, you idiot. You did that decades ago."

So there we stood, in the late summer of our lives. Out of nowhere, we'd been given a vacation from our ordinary lives, and now it was almost over. A pessimist would have said that we were just waiting for oblivion. But Delia and I didn't see it that way. Life is strange. Sometimes it's hard, and other times it's painful enough to break your heart. But sometimes it's grotesque and beautiful. Sometimes it fills you with wonder, like a *Triceratops* sleeping in the moonlight.

Last Respects

D.K. Thompson

I pulled the sharpened dentures from my mouth and dropped them in the cup of water. Crimson strings threaded from the incisors through the liquid. The bed creaked as I lay back, the taste of blood still lingering on my tongue. It had been a long night and even vampires get tired, especially ones my age.

I looked at the picture of Jesus nailed to the wall. He stared down at me with a sad smile and I felt my wife's cold impression on the bed. Moments like these were the hardest, forcing the realization she was dead. Even with her funeral coming the next day, I couldn't believe she was gone.

Downstairs, my grandchildren stomped and crashed about, giggling and ignoring their parents' admonishments. They had arrived earlier that night for Catherine's funeral. Children are great but grandchildren are better. I don't have to get up in the middle of the night and their parents pick up after them. It's a joy to see them grow, learn to walk, speak, and eat. There's a pleasure in their faces at meal time that most of us older folk have forgotten.

Us older folk.

It's humorous to hear the stories our ancestors told about our adversaries before the war: *we* are immortal and will never die. But you, *you* will not last and will leave no trace of your existence. You will be forgotten because your lives are not only unmemorable, but insignificant. These are the fears of every people and culture so what could be more terrifying than an enemy who cannot be destroyed, as we claimed to be. But they were only stories. No one lived forever, certainly not us.

I've read stories about the sorrows immortals suffered because of how much they had seen over their long lives. What rubbish. I would trade my mortality for their immortality in a heartbeat if it meant another day with Catherine.

A scream rang out from downstairs. I smiled when I heard applause, my grandchildren now being praised by their mother as the scream faded to a whimper and the giggles were replaced by slurping sounds.

———•———

"You spoil them too much," my daughter Molly told me the next evening, less than an hour after dusk. She stood over the stove, frying up the leftovers from the last night. There was a large pail next to her, filled with body parts, waiting to be tossed onto the griddle. The aroma of garlic filled the room and I felt my mouth watering.

"I just wanted them to have a good time and get some exercise, Molly," I told her. "Get their natural instincts flowing. Kelly especially looks a little pale. She could use a bit more blood in her veins. But I didn't clean up after them."

Molly grunted, flipping the meat with her spatula. Thankfully, she'd inherited her mother's cooking skills. "They're too young to move the bodies themselves. I had to drag the carcasses in here before I went to bed so I could cook them up first thing this evening."

"What?" I asked, over-doing my incredulousness enough to cause Molly to crack a smile. "Did my parents ever pick up after me when I made a mess eating? I think not. I had to both catch my dinner and clean up after myself. That's the problem with kids today: not enough independence."

"It's just we try to keep the children in a routine. We want them to be strong and fend for themselves. And Patrick and I never give them seconds."

I bent down and kissed Molly's forehead. "How can I refuse my grandchildren's wishes? Permit an old man some pleasure, my dear. Where is Patrick, anyway?"

Molly sighed. "Kel and Jamie started bouncing on our bed before sunset. Patrick took them out for a walk around the farm while I slept a little more."

"That was very kind of him."

"Yes. He's very kind," she said. "Sometimes I think maybe too kind. Papa, I need to ask you something. Did you ever wonder if you made a mistake? If you shouldn't have married Mama?"

"Is something wrong between you and Patrick?"

"No, not exactly. We're fine, I guess. But he feels so far away from me sometimes, like he's isolating himself."

"He's not isolating himself right now," I said.

"Not from the kids, at least," Molly replied. "Sometimes, he talks to me about things I don't understand, wants things I don't know how to give him, and doesn't want what I can."

I crossed my arms. "Do I really want to hear about this kind of problem from my daughter?"

Molly laughed. "No, not that kind of thing, Papa. I don't know, maybe it's nothing."

"Maybe. Have you talked to him about it?"

"Better. I fight with him about it."

"Ah."

"Did you and Mama ever fight?"

"No, not really. Not for a very long time, at least. We were very happy, your mother and I." I remembered how hard it'd been on Catherine to move out to the farm but eventually she got used to it. And after being married for forty-seven years, it hadn't seemed like there was anything new or worthwhile to fight about. "So what is it Patrick does or doesn't want?"

She poked the meat in the frying pan and let out a sigh. "All of this," she said, gesturing around the house. "Anything about me, about us."

I shook my head. "Molly, what are you talking about?"

Just then the door opened, and Kelly and Jamie rushed inside, hugging my legs. "Grandpa, Grandpa," Kelly shouted. She was dressed in overalls and her hair had been braided into pigtails, much like her mother's had been at that age. "We saw all the animals out in the barn. Can we have another? Please?"

Patrick walked in after them, pulling off his mittens, his thin face white from the cold. He shook his head and I could see his cheeks flushing red.

"You already asked your father, didn't you?" I asked.

Jamie's freckled face went red when our eyes met and he thrust his hands in his pockets, and looked at the floor. Kelly watched me, waiting.

"What did he say?"

"That we had to wait until tonight," said Kelly. She stuck out her bottom lip, hoping I'd spoil her still.

"Well, then you'll have to wait until tonight, my sweethearts. I'm sure there will be plenty for us all."

Patrick smiled and mouthed, Thank you.

Molly scooped some of the leftovers from the frying pan onto a plate. Kelly grabbed one of the leg bones and started gnawing on it, but Jamie just shook his head. "I told you it wouldn't work," he hissed at Kelly as they marched up the stairs.

"Why did you give them those?" Patrick asked Molly. "It'll spoil their appetites."

"It's only a snack," Molly replied. "Dinner's a long way off. They'll be fine."

Patrick muttered something and walked out of the room. Molly never stopped to look at him, just kept poking the meat with her spatula.

Feeling awkward, I walked to the door and put on my old hat, the one with the ear muffs my grandfather had worn during the war. "I better go see to the livestock and make sure your little monsters didn't scare them too badly."

"I'll come with you," Molly said.

I remembered how much fun she had helping me when she was a little girl, how Catherine had tied up her thick blonde hair into pigtails. The top of her head couldn't touch my waist. Now she was only a head shorter than me and her pigtails were gone, her hair cut at her shoulders in a very contemporary fashion. Was it really that long ago? Did time move by so fast?

"How can I say no to my little girl?" I asked and a smile lit up her face. "Just make sure you bundle up. It's cold out tonight."

———·—·———

Howls from the livestock filled the night air. The snow had started to fall, covering the grass with a thin blanket. Our boots crunched through the snow, echoing across the field. The pale light of the full moon lit up the field as we walked back to the old barn, the red paint peeling off its wooden planks. Our breath floated before us in the chilled air, lingering like apparitions reluctant to disperse. Part of me was thankful for the cold. It helped bury the stench of human waste that usually permeated the farm.

The animals whimpered and cowered away from the door as I opened up the pen.

I have a movie in my head of Molly helping me in the barn as a little girl, dressed in overalls and just a little older than her own children. She would carry a pail that splashed water with every step she took and put it in the livestock's troughs. She always had such a calming effect on the animals out in the barn.

For parents, such memories are sometimes only figments of the imagination. The way they want to remember their children often replaces the reality.

Such was not the case with Molly. If anything, her movements were more graceful, attaining even more trust with the animals.

All those years ago, I had always worried she would spook one of them, that they'd strike out at her. I am not ashamed to say that even that night I tensed at the thought – so many of them towered over my Molly when they stood up straight (though they rarely did that anymore). What could be more terrifying than something horrible happening to your child? It's in the nature of parents to protect. And I had already lost so much in the last week.

"Be careful, dear," I told her when one of them growled and backed away. "They're not used to you."

"It's okay, Papa. I'm fine."

Molly didn't seem to notice my fear and her confidence actually seemed to relax the animals. They backed away from her at first but she talked to them, holding out her hands so they could sniff and touch her with their own, and realize she meant them no harm. Eventually, they let her close enough to ruffle their hair and beards or massage their backs (they always loved that) or even hug them as she had when she was a little girl. She had never been squeamish about the livestock's fate, even back then. It was a fact of life to her. A benefit of growing up on the farm, I suppose.

"I forgot how peaceful it is out here," Molly said. "How quiet it can get."

"You always did like the country," I said. "Your mother and I didn't think you'd take to the city like you have."

"How are you doing, Papa?"

"Tired. I am always so tired."

"But how are you *doing*?"

I realized then what she was asking, why she had come out to the barn with me. "I'm fine, Molly. It's sweet of you to worry but you don't need to. Really. I - " My throat ached and I had to swallow and take a deep breath before I continued. "Most of the time I don't even realize she's gone."

I tossed out some of the leftovers Molly had prepared, fried meat, some that still resembled arms and legs. The blood had all been drained, of course, because the livestock had no taste for it. They pushed and shoved and dove down in the straw and dirt to capture their food.

"Do we need to move some of them over to the church?" Molly asked.

"I already did last night, before you and Patrick and the kids arrived. I wanted to make the most of our time together."

She gave me a hug. "Are you sure you can afford it, Papa?"

"It's the least I can do for your mother's funeral," I told her.

———•———

The church was only just up the street. By the time we got there, the sanctuary was already half-full but the first row had been reserved for us. I sat down beside Molly, my grandchildren squirmed between her and Patrick, uncomfortable in their Sunday clothes.

Jesus hung on a crucifix at the front of the church. Strange that our adversaries used to shove the image of our God into our faces, thinking He would save them instead of us. They did not understand that the God they worshipped was ours, not theirs.

The preacher shook my hand and said how he was sorry for my loss. He was a handsome young man, always smiling. Even that night, he had a small smile on his face. I did not tell him Catherine never appreciated his sermons. Instead, I said, "Thank you."

After everyone sat down, the preacher handed me a dish filled with tiny strips of fried meat. Catherine had wanted her funeral begin with communion.

"The last night with his disciples, Christ feasted with his friends," said the preacher. "He passed food to them and said, 'This is my body which has been broken for you. Eat it in remembrance of me.'"

I put the piece of flesh inside my mouth. It was tough and difficult to swallow. The church bought from an overstock warehouse, not from my crop.

I tried to focus on the symbolism of the act instead of politics. Jesus had shed His blood for our sins and asked us to drink it so we would one day be resurrected, just as He was. But all I could think of was Catherine, how much I missed her and wondering why she had to leave so soon.

The preacher continued, "After the meal that same night, Christ passed a cup around to his disciples and said, 'This is my blood which has been shed for you. Drink it, in remembrance of me.'"

The blood tasted metallic on my tongue but went down much easier than the flesh had.

"'I am the resurrection and the life. No man comes to the father but through me.'" Was the road to heaven that narrow? Was there a heaven at all? I wondered. Was this just another myth our ancestors created? But looking at Catherine's casket and Christ hanging on the cross over her, I started to wonder if even Gods die. I didn't know, but I hoped that wasn't the case. I wanted to see Catherine again, filled with life. Not like the last time I'd seen her in the bathtub, wrinkled and spent, her tongue hanging out of her mouth, her eyes empty.

I didn't hear the rest of the preacher's sermon. Usually I found them enlightening but maybe Catherine had been right about him after all. Easier on the eyes than on the ears. She'd had a way of judging character, even though I'd often been blind to her observations.

After the preacher finished, friends and strangers approached to hug me or shake my hand, offering condolences after viewing the body.

Patrick and Molly kept a tight grip on the children, telling them not to look, worried what it might do them psychologically, but most of all wanting them to remember their grandmother as she'd been when she was alive, not the artificial way she'd been displayed in the casket. It had been my idea to leave the casket open during the service. Old-fashioned, I guess. Catherine had always said I was a traditionalist. But when they finally closed the lid, I was thankful.

Patrick helped carry the casket out into the fading night before dawn arrived. They put it down in the fresh white snow, re-opened the lid, and trudged back toward the church.

A funeral is an all day affair, starting very late in the night. The departed is prayed for and set outside, awaiting the sun to lay it to rest. Instead of sleeping, we stay up to commiserate, mourn, and stare out of the tinted windows into the beautiful, forbidden light. Then the body is gone, the casket left almost as empty as Christ's tomb.

But dawn did not come, at least not right away. Dark clouds had rolled over the plains, blocking the daylight. A storm was on its way. A part of me felt relieved. I wasn't ready to let go of her. I felt something nagging at me, something I needed to understand first.

Snow started to fall. The animals I'd brought over the previous night began to bray and cry out, their moans echoing throughout the sanctuary. At least today that custom would be satisfied.

Then, for a few seconds, the clouds broke and the sun cut through the sky. In the empty field, Catherine's body caught fire inside the casket.

I cried out, realizing I would never see her again. Not in this life, at least. She was gone. There was so much I still wanted to tell her, so much I wanted to share. I just wanted her to hear me say "I love you" one more time.

The clouds soon returned, hiding the ground from the sun but the flames continued to flicker above the casket, their warm orange tongues licking at the gray sky. Plumes of smoke curled above the field. The surrounding snow began to melt from the heat and the casket sank a little into the newly created mud.

Jamie started to sob, burying his head in his mother's knee, but Kelly just stared out into the field, her eyes wide and her mouth opened. Molly clutched them both to her and I felt her body sink against mine. Patrick watched, standing apart from his family, his face strained.

After the flames died down, the preacher spoke up. "The family has provided a meal downstairs in the basement and requests that you join them. It's important that in this hour, we be with the family of our dear sister and show them our love and support."

The animals were shivering in their chains downstairs, waiting. We selected our dinners and the animals were moved to the tables and forced to lie down. They writhed in their chains and whimpered as we took our seats beside them, stroking them gently to calm them and then lifting their limbs to our lips. Some of the livestock screamed when bitten. Others soon got over the initial shock and became, not less excited, but seemed to take some pleasure from it, as if they understood the price their sacrifice paid for us and were at peace with it.

Molly and the children had already started eating, blood staining their faces. Patrick sat with his head bowed, probably still blessing the food.

Poor bastards, I thought as I looked into the eyes of the female strapped to our table. I wonder if they feel as we do?

Then I chuckled to myself, appreciating the ridiculous questions we find ourselves grappling with in grief. I tore into her flesh and her warm blood filled my mouth.

—— • ——

The food did not comfort me. I don't even remember hearing the woman as I drank from her veins, whether or not she screamed and kicked or moaned.

The day finally ended. The guests had eaten most of the livestock but not all. Patrick agreed to take the leftovers back with him when he and Molly and the kids returned to the farm. The children had fallen asleep before dusk and I knew he and Molly must have been tired. But I wasn't ready to go home yet.

"Are you going to be okay?" Molly asked me. "It's so cold outside."

"I just need some time alone," I told her. "I'll walk home." I pulled her aside, away from Patrick and her children. "You didn't get to tell me last night. What is it that Patrick wants?"

"Oh, it's nothing, Papa. I shouldn't have said anything to you about it. It was selfish and horrible timing."

"Please."

She stared at me, a confused look on her face. "You know how thin he is, how pale he looks? When we first started dating he never ate a lot. I didn't think much about it then." Her voice trailed off and she shrugged. "He doesn't like eating the livestock, Papa. He doesn't think it's right. He says that they aren't really animals and he should eat other things instead."

I shook my head, remembering how I thought Patrick had been praying before dinner. "Other things? What other things?"

Molly sighed. "Other kinds of livestock. Cows. Pigs. Anything else."

"Pig blood?" The idea disgusted me. "He wants my daughter and grandchildren to drink pigs' blood?"

"No, not all of us. Just him."

"Just him?" I repeated. My thoughts drifted to Catherine, everything she'd wanted that I hadn't given her, that I had refused to give her. Her misery when she'd first moved to the farm. All the things I hadn't understood, that had gone unsaid. I thought she'd change but she was stubborn and I thought she wanted to change me. But I couldn't change anymore than she could.

I'd never understood, I realized. Why is that only now, when she's gone, I finally understand?

"Papa?" Molly asked. "What's wrong?"

"I'm sorry, Molly. I don't know what to tell you."

Molly kissed me on the cheek. "I didn't expect you to."

"I love you, my Molly," I said, hugging her to me.

"I love you, Papa. Come home soon."

I watched them go before I walked out to the field, saw Patrick open the door for Molly and lift the kids into the backseat of the pick-up truck without waking them. I waved as they pulled away, and then walked into the field.

The casket would be gone before the night ended but nobody would have moved it yet. I'm not sure what I wanted to see or do when I got out there. Certainly not fall down in the snow and cry like a child, but that's exactly what I did as I looked inside the casket, empty but for the ashes.

"There's so much I didn't tell you," I sobbed. "So much I didn't understand."

The moon hung above me where the sun had been hours before. I spent the next few hours sobbing and praying, trying to make up for past mistakes and regrets. I talked and talked and talked, hoping for some kind of answer or sign from God that my prayers weren't in vain, that there would be a resurrection, that I would see Catherine again. But all I heard was the howl of animals from my farm, their cries surrounding me, filling the field, empty except for me.

I stayed out there beside her empty casket, waiting.

MISTER ADVENTURE AND

THE EMERALD TURTLE

Davey Beauchamp

All was at it should be at the Sapphire City Museum of Antiquities. Or so it seemed. At this late hour, only security guards walked the halls of this hallowed institution of knowledge and history. The strange thing was, however, that tonight, the guards' usually echoing footsteps could not to be heard. As a lone form moved methodically through the museum, she ensured that no one would sound an alarm that could alert Sapphire City's ever-vigilant hero, Mister Adventure.

Jewel Monroe, the Platinum Fox, was well aware of Adventure's reputation of appearing any and every time a vile or villainous act was being committed. It made her wonder if there was actually more than one Mister Adventure, because Jewel couldn't believe that someone had the sort of uncanny luck that would always land him in the right place at the right time. But she was not willing to put her theory of multiple Mister Adventures to the test; at least not this night. And she also wasn't ready to make her presence known to the general populace of Sapphire City or to its heroes and villains.

One by one Jewel had taken out the guards. They would live, though she did not envy them the headaches they would have when they awoke. Jewel may have been many things, but she was not a killer. She was, however, a very skilled thief, and took great pride in that fact.

She had run across just one tiny problem with her plan thus far. It appeared that the museum had moved the exhibits around after she had received her information. This was causing her to spend more time in the museum then she would have liked. Jewel planned to have a conversation with her informant about that. She thought about it as she searched through each of the darkened exhibition rooms.

Finally, after all of Jewel's searching, the glint of emerald caught her sapphire-colored eyes. A smile crossed her face. She had finally discovered what she was looking for.

Quickly, she made her way over to the glass case containing her prize: the *Emerald Turtle of the Chinchatta*. A plaque next to the pedestal noted that the turtle had been discovered by Dr. Solomon Stone while on an expedition in the Andes Mountains of South America during the late 1930s.

Jewel pulled her long blonde hair, highlighted with strands of platinum, away from her face and tied it in a ponytail. She didn't want it interfering with this job, as it almost had during the Tsarskoye Selo job in Russia. And if the Nazis ever realized the fast one she had pulled on them, there would be no more trips to Europe for the foreseeable future.

Jewel looked over the glass case and pedestal, searching for any alarms that might be triggered if the turtle was removed, or for any other *surprises* that her informant may have neglected to mention. Amazingly, just as he had told her, the alarms were already disabled, and there didn't appear to be any other traps lying in wait for her.

She gripped the glass case, lifted it off of the pedestal, and placed it quietly on the floor. The emerald turtle looked at her, and she looked back at it. Getting her hands on this turtle had taken her quite a long time. It was worth far more than any other item she had ever stolen.

Jewel grasped the emerald turtle and gently wrapped it in the protective padding she had brought, then placed it in her side bag. All the work of stealing the turtle would go down the drain if it ended up damaged.

———•———

The car sped down the streets of Sapphire City. The driver, Jimmy "The Tommy Gun" Milanese had only one destination in mind: the Sapphire City Museum of Antiquities. He had gotten a tip that tonight, someone was planning to steal some emerald turtle they had on exhibit there, and Tommy Gun was always one to steal what had already been stolen. He figured it was easier that way, because then he never had to do any of the work or careful planning that went into stealing from places like secured vaults and alarm-ridden museums. Instead, he let others do all of that for him, then stole from them. He had found his Tommy gun was usually quite an effective negotiating tool when dealing with his fellow crooks.

What Jimmy didn't factor into his plan was that his erratic driving had caught the attention of Sapphire City's champion of justice, Mister Adventure.

Mister Adventure knew this city like the back of his hand. As he leapt from rooftop to rooftop following the car, he kept track of each turn it made. Thanks to his friends at the Rainbow Room, he had heard Tommy Gun was planning to stage a heist. Adventure hadn't had any idea at the start of this shadowy midnight chase where Jimmy was heading, but by now he had a pretty good idea, and no longer needed to follow the car. Mister Adventure would just beat Jimmy to his destination, where Adventure could wait at his leisure until Jimmy showed up, then catch him in the act. Adventure turned and set off on a diagonal route across the rooftops.

Several minutes later, Jimmy's car pulled up to the back of the museum and screeched to a halt in front of a door which had been left wide open.

And above, looking down, was Mister Adventure; a silent silhouette waiting for his moment to strike.

Tommy Gun got out of his car equipped with his favorite negotiator, which was locked and ready to go. And right on cue, out stepped the Platinum Fox, unaware of the greeting she was about to receive. Glancing around the parking lot, she saw Tommy Gun and froze.

For Jewel, things began to move in slow motion as Tommy Gun screamed words that appeared to possess no meaning. He waved his gun about with reckless abandon. From Mister Adventure's vantage point on the roof, all he could see was Tommy Gun getting ready to shoot a shadowy figure exiting through the door. Assessing the situation in an instant, he knew he would have to act in the only way that he could.

Mister Adventure leapt from the rooftop to land in front of the doorway and take the impact of the bullets himself, and he did so with a smile on his face.

The Platinum Fox moved through the apparent slow motion unhampered. It was something she could always do. When danger was about to occur everything slowed for her, allowing her to move faster than those around her.

Jewel knew that the bullets leaving the Thompson Machine Gun would never touch her, but now this crazy man, whom she could only assume was Mister Adventure, was landing in front of her as if to protect her from the hail of bullets. Jewel had to wonder if this man saw all women as damsels in distress who had to be saved. But it looked like this time, Mister Adventure was a gentleman in distress, and she would have to save him. The irony brought yet another huge smile to her face.

The Fox leapt into the air and grabbed Mister Adventure by the shoulders, thrusting him downwards. Using the momentum from the thrust, she vaulted up over the volley of incoming bullets. Jewel shot forward and landed with her knees squarely in Tommy Gun's chest, sending him crashing to the ground and causing his weapon to fly from his hands.

Alex could not believe what had just happened. He had never seen anyone move that fast, except for maybe Dr. Phantom, but that was for a whole other reason. Alex was truly at a loss for words.

The Platinum Fox and Mister Adventure both rose to their feet. Jewel spun around, not wanting to give Mister Adventure the advantage. They both stood there in silence trying to size each other up.

This woman was a new one for Alex. He had never seen her before, in the city or in any of the files. He knew he had never met her, because he would have remembered someone dressed like that. Women in black thigh high boots, a black mini trench coat, and a domino mask tended to stand out. And then there was her perfect smile. It radiated forth, complementing her glowing blue eyes.

Alex sometimes wondered why the villains always came to Sapphire City. The answer was an obvious one, but at least he could say that this woman wasn't, so far at least, trying to blow up his city of tomorrow, today. He could see, though, that she appeared to be taking a souvenir from the museum with her as she left.

"I can't let you leave with that," he said, looking at the bag.

"What are you going to do stop me?" she said. A devilish smile crept across her face, and she hoped on some level that he would actually try.

The confidence in her voice could give Vicky Stone a run for her money, Alex thought, but he could tell there was something more going on here, and he was going to find out what. "I will do what it takes," Adventure said. "What you have in that bag belongs to the museum."

The Fox began to laugh at the stupidity of what Mister Adventure had just said. "Is that what you think?" she said, looking Adventure squarely in the eye. "Do you think what I have here just magically appeared in the museum? Let me tell you, it was stolen before the museum received it, and all I am doing is returning it to its rightful owners."

She looked sincere, but Alex had a hard time believing it. He knew Solomon would never commit such an act of theft. They had been friends for years, and the only time he had taken anything was from dead and normally long forgotten civilizations. The unknown and the forgotten were Solomon's specialty. "Sorry, I can't let you leave with it," he said. "At least not until I talk to Dr. Stone."

The Fox shook her head. "You really are as trusting as they say, even though you wear that mask."

Alex just grinned; she had no idea just how wrong she was. "Well," he said, "I guess we are going to have to do this the hard way."

"You really think you can keep up with me?" the Platinum Fox said with a slow smile.

Adventure smirked and cocked an eyebrow. "I am up for the challenge."

"Well, I am afraid I just do not have the time to fight you today. But not to worry," the Fox said, shrugging flirtatiously. "I'll be back; I like your smile." And with that, Jewel was gone. Mister Adventure didn't even have a chance to react.

Great; now he was going to have to deal with Solomon and let him know something from his museum had been stolen. Alex was not looking forward to that meeting. But it was a consolation that at least he now had Tommy Gun in custody.

———•———

A week later, deep in the mountains of South America, Jewel Monroe finally made it to her destination, the emerald turtle tucked safely in her bag. It had been quite some time since she had last visited this long forgotten village, nestled away from the outside world and only spoken of in folklore and legend.

The village looked as though it was a part of the landscape, hiding itself from a passing glance. The homes looked like large rocks and boulders. The doors only appeared to be half the height of a full grown man.

As she neared the first homes, Jewel began to speak in a language consisting of clicks, chirps, and what sounded like the whine of a sad puppy. Slowly, shadowed forms appeared in the crudely made doorways and windows of the village. Anthropomorphic creatures that looked as though they were a cross between chinchillas and men began to emerge from their homes. Then a man, who had to crawl out of one of the larger homes on hands and knees, appeared and stood up.

The village leader came forward, wiggled his nose, and spoke with Jewel in an almost inaudible dialect. Jewel was the only human who fully understood the language, though Dr. Solomon Stone, now brushing dirt from the knees of his pants, was trying to learn it as quickly as possible.

Jewel took out the emerald turtle and handed it to the chief of the Chinchatta. They exchanged a few more sounds and Solomon understood at least one of them, *father*.

Jewel walked over to Solomon. There was an awkward silence when she arrived.

"So, are you finally going to explain to me why you needed me to steal the turtle instead of just returning it yourself?"

Solomon had been expecting this question, and he had been mulling the answer over in his head. He only had a single word answer for her now: "Politics."

"Don't make me laugh," Jewel said. "You are going to have to give me a better answer than that."

"Sorry, I know," Solomon said with a sigh. "There was no other way to return the turtle without it being stolen again. The Board of Directors at the museum would not be willing to let go of something this precious, even if it was wrongfully taken in the first place. I still feel guilty about that; if I had known who the turtle belonged to when I first discovered it, I never would have given it to the museum. Because as much as I believe these items of antiquity belong in a museum for all to see, they should never be taken if the rightful owners still exist, and never should they be given, bought or sought by private collectors."

"I see. So, what is next, Doctor Solomon?" Jewel asked, wondering if he would be hiring her again to correct other mistakes he had made while making a name for himself in the archeologists' community.

"I need to return to Sapphire City," Solomon said, "and deal with the fallout of the robbery. And then I will be off again to find something to replace the turtle in the collection. And what is next for you, my fair lady?"

"I am not sure," Jewel said with a smile, but she thought to herself that she wouldn't mind crossing paths with Mister Adventure again.

www.ingramcontent.com/pod-product-compliance
Lightning Source LLC
Chambersburg PA
CBHW071855020726
47502CB00003B/756